Mind Trap

Alan Baulch

About the Author:

Alan Baulch is a multiple genre Author as demonstrated by his latest novel 'Finding Bridie' and previous works 'Mind Trap' and 'The Tracer' together with his first volume of short stories entitled 'Love, Life, Fantasies & Poetry'.

A British, London born retired former Businessman, IT professional and Foster Carer. At an early age heavily influenced by Dennis Wheatley, Aldous Huxley and further by the French writer Guy de Maupassant. His modern day favourites include Dick Francis, Patricia Cornwall and John Grisham particularly in style. He belongs to a Prose & Poetry group with the U3A (University of the Third Age) where he collaborates with other like-minded authors and writes both short stories and poetry.

He is currently writing the sequel to Mind Trap and lives in Woodhall Spa, Lincolnshire.

By the same author:

The Tracer

Finding Bridie

•

Love, Life, Fantasies & Poetry

(Volume One – Short Stories)

MIND TRAP

Copyright © 2015 by Alan Baulch
All rights reserved.

Printed by Amazon.
Available on Kindle

No part of this book may be reproduced in any form or by any electronic or mechanical means including information storage and retrieval systems, without permission in writing from the author. The only exception is by a reviewer, who may quote short excerpts in a review.

This book is a work of fiction. Names, characters, places, and incidents either are products of the author's imagination or are used fictitiously. Any resemblance to actual persons, living or dead, events, or locales is entirely coincidental.

To Janet

Chapter 1

Wearing the light blue hospital gown, the split down the centre of his back showing his nakedness, avoiding a cover up as the clinics staff had supplied him with some underwear.

"What the hell am I doing here?" He cried out as a bewildered soul, feeling threatened because no one heard him or could hear to his cries.

A hunched frame, the man stood facing out of the drawing room's centre window twice as high as he is overlooking the grounds of Ditton Manor.

Despite his thirty year's he forced himself to move shuffling as an old man carefully around the room, concentrating on the floor and proximity of the walls in case he should fall. Noting the white line two feet from the walls stretching around the room creating its own square. Like a drunk in a Police test attempting to walk the straight line around the perimeter. How far had he moved since being at his window and was it his window? There is three in the room, he had just passed a corner after the young girl at her window, she looked sad not sure why he had not stopped at her window?

Needing order he moved on, focusing on the white line, his own feet overlapped its edges stepping one foot in front of the other, he missed the line and swayed an arm his left automatically outstretched pushing at the wall allowing him to be still. Standing as tall as his height would allow looking up to the ceiling taking in the full weight of the room pressing down on his very soul.

Watching scenes within this vast drawing room. Tables five he counted, people were talking their mouths were moving. The door opened people came in people went out. His head began to spin.

The walls bore down upon him demanding attention, shifting his body clockwise, a gap again to steady himself between two gold ornate framed pictures allowed him a moment to catch his breath.

Raising his bony frame, one particular picture portrayed a grey haired portly, well-dressed man, not of this century he surmised judging by his ringlet styled hair and clothing. Looking closely at the words on the plaque on the wall under the gold painted ornate frame, forcing space for thought hoping the words in front of him would bring back a piece of his own sanity.

"Ditton Manor was originally mentioned in the Doomsday Book (1066). In 1331 Sir John de Molyns married Egidia de Pages. By 1325, he rose to great eminence as the treasurer to King Edward III. Molyns obtained royal licence to develop the building into the style of a castle to fortify the manor house and build the original park within its 38 acres."

Almost passing with the effort of the read he swayed reaching for the centre rail underneath the plaque and steadying himself gripping onto it as if his life depended on the hold, edging slowly, studying his surroundings, high ceiling, lavish coving, the bell shaped original crystal chandeliers, a presence all their own. A rare survivor of 19th century styles with unchanged decoration, displaying lavish textiles, gold and silk adorned the four walls, the curtains elaborate swags of crimson and silk, enveloped the three twelve paned white wooded windows.

Another portrait, this time of a Scottish architect, the plaque again highlighted the Manor's records commissioning the creation of one of the most striking and instructive interiors of a period that loved its rich and colourful effects.

'Ditton Manor and the park is now owned by Connectiqua, the multi-corporate IT software house and with land purchase has expanded the site until the Manor centred grounds of around 200 acres. An attempt by the current owner to recreate the previous ambience of the interior of the manor has been met with considerable success.' He noted an award by the British Heritage Society.

Making the decision to cross the centre of the room by sheer will frustrated by the adulation meted out under every picture deciding to cross back over to 'his' window which looked out of one of the 11th century Manor windows to rest his mind, once the home for Anne Boleyn and Mary I.

Out of breath, Samuel Thornton stared at the grey haired gardener in green wellingtons and waxed jacket sitting astride his red Hayter Heritage garden tractor mowing carefully, purposefully lining the already manicured lawns. Drawing closer to the view of the gardens, the comforting smell of freshly mown grass made him relax.

The voice inside his head tapped at him at first becoming louder, he screamed without sound mouthing his horror, inside laughter in the distance at first, gradually building to an unbearable level filling his head space, hands pressing hard at his temples, physical shaking.

He began to rock from side to side, spinning 360 degrees, eyes like radar scanning all instead of 220. Attempting to rationalise, he could see above, ahead, below and behind, he gripped the window frame, a round bell clapper touching all sides of inside space at will, but not his.

Locked in a cage of spirit, he became aware of them watching, did they hear his screams? Seeing inside himself yet seeing them, head ached, his arms wrapping it protectively.

"Alive or dead?" he could not decide, unsure if he cared, white coated observers scribbled constantly.

Two others each with their own window appeared as confused. On Sam's left, a man slightly older, shorter and stockier stood flat in tartan bedroom slippers, also staring across the gardens through one of the panes of glass. Also dressed in a hospital gown, the same light coloured shade of blue, too big for him. A hospital wristband hung loosely on his right wrist. Too far for Sam to make out the name written on it.

The troubled man, aware of his surroundings, running his hand repeatedly through his brown thinning hair like a nervous twitch. He kept mumbling loudly. Sam was unaware he and the nearby girl were the only ones who could hear him scream. Watching him intently, as his own nightmare the laughter subsiding, realised by the nervy swaying and hands constantly grabbing then releasing his head, same problem, his mind gripped in fear, the man looked at him and mouthed the words "help me" his large rounded frame shuddered in terror.

At the third window, he had passed the young girl on his way around the room wore a wraparound cloth like a sarong, too large for her slight figure draped to the floor with huge pockets adorning the front containing her twitching petite hands. Pink socks offered comfort against the cold polished wooden floor. Her dark hair matted with sweat from the ordeal.

Sam realised they were all staring out of their own window but looking at each other. He shivered. There was no mirror, but he could see himself watching them watching him.

He could see a wooden chair with red leather seat upholstery, a small diamond patterned emblem on the material. Conscious of looking at it through himself, but also behind, there is only one chair, yet he is seeing it twice. Becoming giddy, still looking out of the window and looking at the other two, he began to shake violently.

The man at the next window breathed harder, still mumbling, the girl began to cry, "help me too, help me too" tears were running down her cheeks, brown eyes burrowing deep into Sam's.

Both men stared at the girl, they heard her cry, powerless to respond, rigid in their positions, tired, unable to move exhaustion overwhelming them. Both expected someone to help little realising only they could hear her cries. Their gaze fixated toward her trying to summon their depleted strength to comfort her. She too had a wristband causing Sam to look down at his own wrists, a name and date of birth is on his.

In one corner of the room, the white heavy panelled door creaked as it opened, all three flinched together, watching two men in white jacket length coats walk into the room. Something strange had happened, Sam could not think properly. He heard the noise of the door they had all heard, it creaked, since his arrival he had not heard sounds before.

Until two minutes ago, his had been a silent world, now he had heard the man groan, the girl cry out, as well as the creaking door. What did this mean? He still could not speak out to ask the others.

Sam looked at the men coming toward him, their purpose evident. Despite his stoop, he towered over both men but knew they were stronger. He heard and felt their breathing close to him as they began to exert themselves.

They began to pull him gently, he tried to struggle only to realise the futility he had so little strength. The commands did not reach his body, he watched them hold his arms above the elbows, unable to resist and he wanted to. They had name badges pinned to their jackets Bradley and Terrence he tried to call by name to let him walk without pressure and could only mouth their names without sound.

The window two were watching him knowing their turn will come. They avoided his eyes and watched his back as he approached the door.

Being dragged his fear overwhelming, sweating although the men were quietly talking, comforting, but still pulling.

Panic! Sam heard them again it startled him and shouted at them to let him go only for them to ignore him to them he made no noise. Begging the other two for help knowing they would hear him, cowering they both shied away.

With the men continuing to pull, he passively walked with them. Samuel Thornton had not spoken during the last four weeks while in their care and they did not expect him to now. They had tried to communicate with him, but as one of the men liked to point out jokingly, no one was home.

Sam could hear them and they not him, except now he had heard them twice what did it mean? Puzzled, confused, his fear increased heart pumping with each step.

Once through the door the corridor beyond stretched 20 metres as the two men negotiated with the frightened struggling patient down the red-carpeted walkway. High ceiling and mahogany panelled walls served only to close in on him. The men began kindly, gently talking to him as he, zombie like, walked with them trying to quell his apparent fear they could not hear the screaming developing inside his head.

The men recognised a terror in Sam's eyes kindly they continued to speak softly to him not appreciating, his world once again closing down into a silent one. No longer could he hear them stress had the effect of closing his senses down.

The room they placed him in, cold, white and clinical, a striped mattress lay on the floor, a grey painted plain brick wall to the left side of the room. To the right, plasterboard hastily erected as a partition with a mirror at its centre providing a watch point for his keepers, the grey fixing nails forming the only pattern on the walls.

The two men were still holding his arms, darkness becoming a relief, he was falling, struggling to understand, a needle, its welcome release, peace. He shook to the sound of the lock as the door to his prison closed.

"It's good of you to come with me Tisha I really appreciate it I am going out of my mind with worry." Ross Mansell had been visiting his best and oldest friend Samuel Thornton in the Psychiatric unit for the past few weeks. The medical clinic is a benefit for employees of Connectiqua and for any organisations who rent space at the Manor. The unit within the clinic set up to deal with business stress.

A month had passed since his best friend Sam had arrived back into the UK from China and immediately placed into the clinic suffering from extreme mental anguish, so far without a solution to his problem. The stress beginning to tell on Ross frustrated at not being able to help his friend whatever is going on with his mind. Ross realising he needed help, Sam a strong-minded individual had become a quivering wreck so he turned to their mutual friend Tisha Pascoe.

Ross had met Tisha through Samuel some years before. Sam spent his life chasing mysteries of one sort or another. He had explored the occult through Ouija boards and séances from an early age, starting to delve into the paranormal via various religious cults designed to take over the world. He had been fortunate to meet Tisha, who recognising his naivety and vulnerability set him on the right spiritual path. Fortunately, Sam quickly moved on to the next fad, safe and well. In the meantime, Tisha and Ross had become firm friends and she became a firm part of both Sam's and Ross's lives.

He hoped being a friend and a writer of psychological and spiritual drama, she could help guide him through the minefield he was going to face when dealing with Sam's doctors.

Tisha suspected Ross of being under some strain for quite a while and assumed it was a work thing. Given his job in the city connected to the financial stock markets worldwide and half expected him to implode later in life if he continued, but right now, he is a young man and strong in mind. Once he tried to explain to her how the pressures of making or losing money can cause severe stress, she took little notice, believing him to be invincible.

"You mean this isn't our long awaited first date where you're going to sweep me off my feet?" She saw the pained expression on Ross's face as he drove his Panhard through the leafy winding lanes of the Berkshire countryside. Grimacing, she observed the strain etched deep across his face, his right eyebrow raised itself involuntarily. A thirty something handsome intelligent man, his dark close cut hair accentuating the chiselled features of his jaw. She had never seen him as concerned almost panicky it was time for her to be serious.

She changed the conversation and spoke of the comfort found in his car, and how it always impressed her. He had lovingly restored his 1965 Panhard 24. The body, blue in colour, free from adornments of any kind apart from a corvair style strip of chrome beading emphasising its curves. Headlights mounted behind a transparent housing giving it a modern feel with the back resembling the early BMW two thousand series. Its 800cc air-cooled engine ideal for these country lanes. The sporty look and feel belied its lack of any real power, but it was gloriously comfortable and rich feeling with its vegetable tanned leather interior. With a terrific restoration, she never tired of explanations about what use he had made of Japanese tissue or polyester fabric.

"I have been coming to see Sam for nearly a month, watching and hoping to see any sign of improvement. I will do and pay anything to get him well again." Ross responded, with only Sam on his mind.

"You finance people think that all you need do is to spend money and it will fix everything and it won't." Tisha gently scolded him. "It is time you told me what's happened to him before we get there. I'm there for him, but you cannot pay to fix his mind."

"I know, I know, he was my best friend."

"Past tense?"

"Is my best friend, although I think I have lost him for good, Ferral the guy who runs the clinic is doing everything he can."

"Then Samuel is getting the best care possible, they must eventually come to a conclusion," Tisha hated to abbreviate names, especially those of her friends. "What the hell happened to him?"

"As far as I can make out Sam has been acting strange for a while, having delusions, hallucinations, he progressively became incapable of holding a lucid conversation."

"He became paranoid, thinking people were trying to get him," he spoke of his friend gravely. "When attending meetings, Sam kept speaking, convinced someone was with him listening to the thoughts inside his own head. Apparently he would openly have arguments with the fictitious person next to him."

"What finally made the people he worked with do something?"

"Sam started to hide in corners, afraid of moving, not hearing them. By this time his colleagues had seen enough and decided he needed proper help."

"Surely the Doctor's did tests to get to the bottom of what was wrong?"

"They have done all the tests physical and mentally and nothing identified why his system appeared to be shutting itself down and he had stopped speaking completely by then." Ross automatically adopted a paternal tone. "Fact is, the Chinese didn't want to be responsible for Sam's treatment and discussed his condition with Connectiqua as they are his employing agent and supplying his services as a contractor and in turn spoke with me, as I had introduced him to them!"

"Do Charles and Jennifer know yet?" Tisha wanted to be sure Samuels parents knew.

Ross nodded.

"They asked me to get him home whatever the cost so I arranged he came back to Connectiqua's well-being clinic." With a friendship going back to their childhood, Sam had helped Ross through the loss of his parents, his mother had died after a long debilitating illness and sadly, crushed by his loss, Ross's father died of what was termed a "broken heart" some six months later. For him Sam is the brother he never had, and now it was his duty to help him, they had a special bond.

He had pushed his brilliantly minded friend into working for Connectiqua some years earlier knowing the fit would work well for both parties.

"Who are Connectiqua?"

"They're an organisation offering people and financial computer solutions worldwide. High profile contracts, governments, oil companies and international consortiums," Ross offered. "They own Ditton Manor and are responsible for setting up the clinic within."

"Has the clinic been set up just for Samuel?"

"No, it is a corporate clinic but it has not dealt with anything quite like Sam's case," he believed. "More like an occupational health check clinic for organisations to provide a perk for their staff to use."

"How do you know them?"

"My finance partnership got involved with them during a messy takeover bid quite a while ago and they offered a role to me. I declined offering my services to find good people to work for them," he was proud of the relationship created with them. "I've built a rapport with them over the years and Sam was one of many introductions to them. For me it has been quite lucrative."

Following the loss of his own family, he had gotten close to Samuels. They trusted his judgement where their son's welfare was concerned.

"So what was their diagnosis on Samuel? They must have some idea?"

"It will upset you," he said shaking his head in dismay.

"Tell me Ross, I'm a big girl I can take it."

"Schizophrenia!"

"Rubbish, never!"

"Exactly, I don't believe it either, never a sign or indication," he agreed.

"Wasn't he working in China?" A sadness starting to develop within her, she looked to him for confirmation.

"Yes, he worked in Pudong a suburb of Shanghai," he continued. "The tests were inconclusive which is why I needed to bring him home."

They turned into Ditton Park. Ross drove the Panhard through the black three-metre high wrought iron entrance gates into the immense landscape of the Manor" grounds, which physically seemed to miniaturise them.

Tisha gasped at the sight before her.

The breath-taking landscape spread out before them as they drove for several minutes watching two small herds of red and fallow deer, walking calmly within the grounds, regal in their pursuit of food.

Their approach with the Manor majestically playing with them, they watched its towers and turrets appear and disappear amongst the trees, driving in awe of this two hundred-acre blaze of green rolling parkland.

The gravel sound as he slowed the car to the front of the eleventh century terracotta manor impressed Ross, as did the close up rising size of the Manor itself. He had been here several times since Sam's arrival and continued to be in awe by the stature of this double winged, double fronted two-tier building in this outstanding setting. Businesses flocked to Connectiqua to get space for their own operations in the Manor providing prestige they could not buy.

Once home for a wealthy family, now housing a variety of companies with signs of gold nameplates held at the entrance door. The conference halls and welcome signs on the lawn and, ghastly though he felt it was, a large satellite dish and telephone mast neatly hidden behind and strategically arranged within planted trees and foliage.

At reception, they were expected and immediately given guidance for the Medical Directors office on the second floor.

"The Director will be with you shortly Sir, Madam, but has asked if you would kindly wait in his office." The young receptionist breathed a sigh of relief pleased she had delivered her message flicking her brown hair sideways and returned to something more riveting on her computer screen.

They stopped many times to look at the portraits hung on the walls of the corridors at the end of one where they found the lift taking them to the second floor and another familiar corridor the portraits painting a history long gone.

An oak leather topped desk backed onto the single floor to ceiling twelve paned white painted windows. The large high-ceilinged room overlooked an integral open-air courtyard standing proud at the centre of the manor.

An original granite fireplace standing higher than the tallest dominated the room majestically.

"Who are we meeting Ross?"

Tisha made herself comfortable on one of the two red tanned leather couches facing one another across a thick glass-topped coffee table. Ross was interrupted, as he was about to answer. The door of the office opened framing the two people entering.

"Welcome to you both," The flushed red faced man reminded Tisha of Christmas, his clean shaven face crying out for white whiskers, a dimpled chin beamed at her as he shook Ross's hand while looking appraisingly at her. Ross introduced Dr Ferral Goldlay, the Medical Director to her.

Ferral had been looking forward to meeting Tisha ever since suggesting to Ross he needed support to deal with Sam's illness, especially when he began, as they hoped, to get better, knowing Ross is struggling to cope.

She noted the character shine from Ferral's red complexion, his round rimmed spectacles held up magnificent clumps of eyebrow red hair, keeping a tight hold of the twinkle shining from the deep grey eyes.

Tisha observed the two men and noted they had obviously become close friends during the past month.

Behind the doctor, putting down a tray of refreshments, a raven-haired woman of slight build in her early forties offered the group their choice of drinks.

"I am sorry Susan," quickly Ferral apologised.

"Ross, Tisha meet Susan Brackden, she is here to help us with Sam."

"His name is Samuel," Tisha prickled, aware of Ross's stifled intake of breath as he soaked up Susan's beauty. Tisha had never seen Ross blush this could be interesting she mused.

Susan smiled appraisingly at Ross and bowed to Tisha.

"Ross mentioned that Samuel had been diagnosed as having Schizophrenia. I cannot believe it of him, how on earth do you come to that conclusion?" Tisha queried bluntly looking at both Susan and Ferral.

"Let me tell you how we do make the assumption and I stress that is just what it is, an assumption. We believe another element or factor may be involved. Let me explain to you what we've done so far," Ferral looked toward Susan for support.

"The diagnostic evaluation includes a complete physical examination and also covers a history of the symptoms. For example when they started, how long each has lasted so far as we can tell, how severe these are, whether they've occurred before and whether the symptoms had been treated and in particular what type of treatment was given," he pressed on. "We also check for alcohol, drug use and abuse, if there is any history of thoughts of death or suicide. Our checks include details of his family members and whether they have had a mental illness, and if treated how? Which medication, if any given, were effective. Finally, a mental status examination is carried out to determine if the speech, thought patterns or memory has also been affected." Looking at Tisha, he continued.

"Ross has been a great help liaising with Sam's family. We fully understood his background and you're right," Ferral acknowledged. "His history does not match the diagnosis. However, many professionals in the field of mental health agree a psychiatrist is best qualified to conduct a diagnostic evaluation and as a psychiatrist and a physician I confess I have been at a loss with Sam case, which is why I decided to bring in Susan who is a Psychologist," he bowed deferring to her.

"Psychiatrists often work in hospital settings, though many practice privately and are called upon to treat severe mental illnesses, such as, Schizophrenia, manic-depression, and paranoia. Psychologists are trained to look at emotional interactions, behaviours, cognition's, and environmental factors, work, home, interpersonal relationships, is this helping you?" Susan looked at them.

They both nodded.

"Many patients with problems such as eating disorders, mild depression alcohol or drug addiction are often referred to Psychologists for therapy sessions, but also see Psychiatrists for their drug treatments which is why Ferral and I are working together," she added.

"Susan you're not talking about Schizophrenia but behavioural problems? How come you've put the label on him," Ross said accusingly.

"I need to give you an idea what Schizophrenia really is and at the same time show where it logically matches with Sam," Ferral suggested.

"Schizophrenia is a disease of the brain, and most people accept this, however it is also one of the most disabling and emotionally devastating illnesses known to man. The illness, which has been misunderstood for far too long, has received relatively little attention and its victims have been undeservingly stigmatised," he stressed. "Like cancer and diabetes, Schizophrenia has a biological basis and is not caused by bad parenting or personal weaknesses, but unlike these because of the imbalance it causes within the brain we associate it with violent attacks, certainly with the destruction that can be caused. The fact are this is a relatively common disease with an estimated one to two percent of the U.S. population diagnosed over the course of their lives.

"But there's a cure, or help for it right?"

"No Ross definitely treatment, but no cure just a management regime of the symptoms and not the cause." Susan looked to Ferral for explanation.

"There's no known cure for Schizophrenia but it's very treatable. Most of those afflicted respond to drug therapy very well and many sufferers are able to lead productive and fulfilling lives."

"So what are its symptoms?" Ferral continued, as if questioning Ross and Tisha. "They include thought disorder, delusions and hallucinations. These are Sam's issues," Ferral looked at them not expecting a response. "A constant inner struggle, two parts vying for control in the main. Thought disorder is the diminished ability to think clearly and logically. Often it is manifested by disconnected and nonsensical language that renders the person with Schizophrenia incapable of participating in conversation, contributing to his or her alienation from family, friends, and society," he discussed. "Delusions, on the other hand, are common among individuals with Schizophrenia. An affected person may believe that they are being conspired against, paranoid delusion," Ferral went on. "Another is broadcasting and this describes a type of delusion in which the individual with this illness believes that others can hear his or her thoughts."

Ross spoke solemnly. "It is clear to me, this is how Sam has been behaving and you say it can be treated with drugs?"

"Not so fast, there is more to this. The point is when a patient believes he's being conspired against, these hallucinations can be heard, seen, or even felt, most often they take the form of voices heard only by the afflicted person," Susan reddened realising Ross looked at her directly, appraising. "Such voices may describe the person's actions, warn him of danger or tell him what to do. The individual may hear several voices carrying on a conversation where the patient in not participating.

These problems manifest themselves in Sam, lack of emotional expression, apathy, and social withdrawal. It all points to Schizophrenia, except for one solitary point."

Ross and Tisha clinging on to anything which would give them hope, sensed the significance of what they were about to learn, both listened intently.

Susan looked to Ferral for confirmation he took over from her.

"The point is Sam is not vocal."

"Meaning?" Both chorused.

"Schizophrenia takes many forms, but generally there is some dialogue that goes on within the individual feeding the paranoid delusion. Arguments with us, within themselves rage constantly inside their heads the point being it is sickness that demonstrates itself by being just that, vocal, with Sam he doesn't speak. It may have begun the way it normally manifests itself, but his mind appears strangely controlled." Ferral was disheartened at his own failings to find a solution for his patient.

"I don't understand Ferral," said Tisha distressed and confused. "Are you telling me Samuel doesn't speak at all?"

"He hasn't spoken a word since he' arrived here," informed a saddened Ross. "I should've told you."

Ferral raised his eyebrows at Susan and noted the mood had changed to one of sadness amongst them.

Despite his misgivings he decided to tell them what he and Susan suspected was going on.

"Look, what we're going to say now is confidential about the patient and mind numbing as a consideration, but we offer it as a theory. You need to be aware that Sam's case is not unique. There are others also from China."

"You're telling us more people are acting like Sam?"

"Yes I am Tisha, two others so far and they are here in this clinic." Ferral raised his hand to stop them asking more questions until he had finished.

Becoming agitated Tisha ignored his gesture.

"What you're saying, there are external forces affecting them, which is specifically linked to China?"

"Tisha that is a giant leap, however there are influences involved which we do not yet understand, we both believe Sam and the others are already in grave danger," Susan offered solemnly.

"They're going to die aren't they?" Tisha started to cry. "Oh my God!"

"Surely something can be done we just can't let this happen." Ross was comforting Tisha.

"We hope it doesn't come to that."

"What are the odds all three have come from China with the same symptoms as Schizophrenia?"

"That's just it Ross there are none." Ferral declared.

"So it's not Schizophrenia?"

"No Tisha we don't believe so."

"More to the point, someone somehow, is messing with their minds," Susan said gravely. "We need to find out who and why!"

Chapter 2

The following morning Ross and Tisha sat quietly eating the splendidly presented breakfast the luxurious Marriot Hotel had provided, set in the centre of four mature tree lined gardens surrounded by ten acres of parkland. Built in the 19th century and renovated in the classical style of an impressive old English country grade II listed house full of character and elegance offering the best of facilities set within an acre of woodland.

Ross had spent most of the previous evening in the hotel's extensive gym and sauna, although refreshed after a good night's sleep he struggled to understand how he could help Sam. He felt guilty too as Susan was not too far away from his mind either. He hoped Tisha had answers because he was struggling to the point of despair not knowing what to do.

Tisha meanwhile spent her early evening in the swimming pool, followed by an indulgent session enjoying the pampering of the beauty treatment salon.

She did not have such a good rest as Ross preferring to work through what they had learnt, trying to come up with a positive way forward, but like Ross, she too struggled to find a solution for Samuel.

The waitress busy serving the silent pair with cereal, toast and coffee placed on their white clothed circular table without ceremony took their hot plate order, before finally leaving them alone to talk.

"I've been coming here for a month now and it's the first time Ferral has opened up to me, Susan worried me about the messing with their mind comment. I'm not sure what she meant by it."

Tisha noted the depressive tone of Ross's voice.

"Come on Ross, we have to stay positive and come up with things to help," she scolded. "You need to speak to Connectiqua to get a list of all of their contractors working in China. Find out how these people are, where they are and which organisations they're working with."

"I could find out what had happened to the other two to see if the behaviour has been the same," Ross brightened and spoke more positively she had given him something he could do he would asked Ferral about the other two patients. "We need to find a better link between them instead of just China and Connectiqua which are weak. The only other links are the hospitals or clinics they attended."

"Yes," agreed Tisha. "What were they working on, what about their colleagues and friends and what were their interests?"

"Their connected illness is a factor!"

"We need to see them and Samuel today and plan with Susan and Ferral what more we can do," Tisha considered. "We also need to know just how long we have got before Samuel is seriously and permanently harmed by this."

"Tisha, this mind thing, you're into psychological and spiritual stuff, do you take it seriously?"

"Oh yes, very much so," she shifted uncomfortably, finishing the last piece of toast in the rack. "There are forces and elements," she left the words hanging over them, like a curse.

Ross finishing his breakfast stood up. "We'd better get off to the manor."

Driving to the manor the Panhard glided through the country lanes with its occupants silently reflecting on their friend's plight. They hoped there might be some change or a sign of improvement in Samuel. They would be disappointed.

Tisha looked forward to seeing him for the first time in several months worrying how he would look to her.

Susan greeted them both and Tisha noted the bumbling and stuttering effect she had already gained over Ross she smiled inwardly. Susan walked them to the main drawing room where Sam would be.

Entering the imposing room, it pulled them into the history of the manor with the room highlighting the pictorial march through the centuries of change. It's what Sam would have silently appreciated and on cue they immediately spotted him staring out through a large window onto the grounds of Ditton's Parkland.

"It is his normal position I am afraid," Ferral stated arriving behind them in the room. "Spends his days at the window, my guess he's attempting to make his own sense of his surroundings."

"But he has been here before."

"Yes Ross, but unfortunately he's not the one in control."

Sam dressed in a patient's gown, seemed agitated. At the other windows stood two other patients, they also appeared distressed and noticed by everyone.

"They seem to have a level of communication between them," Tisha observed. She felt chemistry existed between the three, she suspected it might be keeping them alive.

"Can we talk to him?" she asked.

"You can try, he is unlikely to acknowledge you," replied Ferral. "It doesn't help him because he becomes more agitated and frightened at any outside contact. However, you're right about the communication between them, observe him and the other two closely, they're locked in their own world together which suggests Susan's theory of some mind control going on is more likely."

As Ferral spoke, he ushered them both to sit on red leather sofas positioned by the large granite fireplace. It replicated his office where they met yesterday.

"If you look very closely, although they are not speaking, sometimes certain sounds can be heard by them. They each acknowledge the noise. This is highlighted by a sharp sound like the door being opened or closed causing them to react," Ferral suggested.

As if to confirm what he was saying Susan Brackden, Sam's psychologist entered the room and they watched as two of the three people at their own window, turned to look at her. Susan understood what Ferral had been saying and commented. "Unfortunately that's about as good as it gets at the moment, more importantly, if you continue to observe, they're communicating with each other more feelings and thought, rather than actual speech."

Tisha confirmed. "I feel it, but how can you treat this. It's a collective problem, not an individual one?"

Both Ferral and Susan agreed.

"How do you see that?" asked Ross. He found himself studying this raven-haired obviously intelligent, woman. Realising much of his thoughts were resting on her. He gauged she was in her early forties, noting she was wearing a simple white collared patterned blouse and black straight knee length skirt.

He was surprised at the reaction she caused within him, vowing to get closer to her.

"Study them and their body language. There's awareness of each other," Susan suggested. "The nodding between them the mouthing of words, the struggling, the difficulty of thought and understanding together with the physical frustration of lacking movement."

Each one of the patients heads were gently rocking from side to side arms dropped limp with hands tapping their own legs nervously, eyes blinking at one another almost speaking in silent gestures.

Tisha noted that Ross was fast becoming besotted with Susan. Although happy for this to develop, she wanted to concentrate on Samuel and his new friends.

"What about the other two, Susan?" Tisha asked, breaking the perceived spell between Susan and Ross.

Susan's face coloured as she realised she had only been talking directly to Ross.

"Starting with Matt Shanahan," she stammered, pointing towards the right window Ross and Tisha looked at the middle-aged man who appeared agitated, uncomfortable in the wearing of a light blue gown with tartan flat bedroom slippers. With a close fitting white towelled robe across his rounded shoulders, too small for his substantial robust frame. Being just five feet tall helped pronounce his stomach. When wearing a shirt he would be the man with buttons breached with his trousers underpinning the overhanging beer belly.

"Late fifties a tough high earning financier, he's spent 30 years in Montreal building up the Premier National Merchant Bank, a shrewd operator by all accounts who managed to turn a small family business into a multi-billion international enterprise," Susan informed them, reading her patients notes, she showed them newspaper cuttings of his exploits.

"Wait a moment, I've heard of him, an Irishman made good." Ross offered. "As I understand it he has had a hand in most of the mega financial deals during the past decade."

"You're right," said Susan, picking up the thread from Ross. "He left the Premier to become a troubleshooting deal maker and has forged several ground breaking mergers, cut massive loan deals and buyouts worldwide."

Ross was surprised a power broker such as Matt Shanahan, should not be in this state.

"What happened to him?" asked Tisha impatiently.

Ferral raised his hand in answer. "It's frustrating as it has followed a similar pattern to Sam's." His voice went quiet. "This has been a closely guarded secret he was leading a consortium of North American businesses, who are looking to develop a chain of hotels across China's coastline stretching fourteen and a half thousand kilometres, facing the South and East China Seas as well as the Yellow Sea. He was seeking billions in investment from several of the top ten major companies there and I might add looked on target to get it until this happened to him."

"Are you suggesting there's a connection?"

"I'm not ruling out anything at this stage."

"China again," observed Ross. "Any connection with Connectiqua itself?"

Ferral shook his head. "Not that we can tell from what we know so far."

"I have always believed China has quite a cold arctic climate certainly too cold for a chain of hotels to be successful," Ross was uncomfortable questioning another person's motives especially a man rated as highly as Matt Shanahan is.

"It's a myth Ross," responded Susan. "In the north, Urumqi close to the Russian border can be 'artic' temperatures for parts of the year however, the south coastline stretching from Guangzhou onto Shanghai and ending at Tianjin near Beijing has more of a Mediterranean climate, generally about 10 degrees above the British Isles throughout her best times of the year, ideal for hotels wouldn't you say?"

"Tell us about the girl, Susan," Tisha felt they were straying from the point it caused everyone to look at the left multi-paned window of the drawing room, where a girl stood rocking from side to side staring straight ahead out toward the manor gardens. "Does she have the same Chinese connection?" still putting her questions directly at Susan.

Susan's face flushed a crimson colour wondering if Tisha had noticed her looking at Ross a little too intently. She tried to put some control in her voice. "Unlike Matt or Sam, we do not have any idea what she was doing in China. We do know she is the daughter of the much respected John B. Kefford Jr, M.D. 'Jack' as he was known to his colleagues and friends."

"Was?" queried Tisha.

"Sadly he died recently and Kefford's scientific career was in its prime," continued Susan. "He was Professor of Neurology at the Harvard Medical School and Director of the NIH-sponsored Parkinson's disease Centre of Excellence at Massachusetts General Hospital." Susan paused for thought standing up to stretch her legs by drawing water from the nearby dispenser. Ross's eyes followed her every line.

"At the age of 51, Jack Kefford died unexpectedly from a myocardial infarction in a hospital in China. I have yet to meet his widow, Lecia. Ellen their daughter, we know has her own career as a psychologist, but why it took her to China is anyone's guess. The most likely reason she was searching for answers about his death."

Ross looked closer at Ellen. She seemed familiar. Strange, he felt he knew her, odd, unlikely, but something! He dismissed his thoughts.

"What's NIH?" queried Tisha sipping her now cold coffee.

"The National Institutes of Health which is the steward of medical and behavioural research in the US, an agency under the U.S. Department of Health and Human Services. There's particular emphasis on behavioural patterns and Ellen works for the governing body."

"Jack Kefford was quite young to have had a heart attack. Were there any suspicious circumstances?"

"None we know of, Tisha," responded Ferral. "We've managed to piece together Ellen's movements and what we do know is, immediately following his death she caught the next Lufthansa flight from Boston's Logan International, made an Air China connection flight at Frankfurt International in Germany to Beijing Capital airport. Her trauma following the same behavioural patterns as Sam's at the Shanghai Bell Company on her visit to the same company she created quite a nuisance of herself."

"How come she was at this particular company?" questioned Ross. It was not lost on him that Samuel had been working for the same company.

Ferral answered. "Unfortunately, it's another thing we need to investigate. At the moment we don't have enough answers to tell you."

"Why bring her here?" inquired Ross. "She's American and if I think about it, what brings Matt here, he's Irish?"

"Fair points, we were lucky, if it can be described as such. Matt was working closely with a company called Alcatel," Ferral looked at both Ross and Tisha and realised the company name was unfamiliar to them. "Alcatel is a multi-billion dollar organisation operating across 130 countries, it's enterprises include Satellite operations, Transport, Oil and Gas sectors, Government institutions and much, much more. This is where Matt would have expected the majority of the funding for his hotel project to come from."

"I still don't see the connection with Sam or Ellen or even Connectiqua," observed Ross.

"Please have patience," interjected Susan. "Matt was taken to the local Huadong hospital in Pudong by the personnel from the Shanghai Bell Company."

"Isn't this the same company Sam was working on contract with Connectiqua for?" queried Tisha.

"Quite right," Ferral said picking up the thread. "It also happens to be the same hospital that Ellen was found in her state and the same one her father died in. The staff realised that Sam, Matt and Ellen had all been showing similar symptoms, although Ellen was initially diagnosed as having bipolar."

"I still don't see what Matt was doing in Shanghai or why they are all here together," Tisha was confused.

"Alcatel, the company whom Matt was dealing, owns 51% of the Shanghai Bell organisation, which suggests he was there to get local funding for his project and sanctioned by the parent company. Ellen could have been at the hospital either searching for some word concerning her father or in her role working for the US Health Department, we need to check this. More likely for her father's death and using the influence of her position as health inspector," Susan mused.

"Because Sam was in the Huadong hospital, arrangements were made by Connectiqua for him to come here as I mentioned yesterday, it was natural for the people at the Shanghai Bell and the hospital to contact them first to determine where he had gone. Connectiqua asked us to get involved with the other two."

"Given all three of them were western people, in the same region, similar symptoms and in the same hospital, it was more than a coincidence," Susan followed on. "And, as you can see for yourself, having observed all three together, there is a definite link of acknowledgement between them."

"You mentioned a bipolar disorder for Ellen, a different diagnosis for her than the others?" Ross raised his eyebrows at Tisha for directing her question to Susan again.

Susan felt herself colouring again as she checked her growing feelings for Ross. More and more she warmed to this rugged blonde man. She found her thoughts turning to his age putting Ross in his early thirties and began to doubt any attraction between them as fanciful on her part.

"This has more to do with a Consultant's view of the condition rather than the problem being diagnosed as Schizophrenia. Bipolar disorder is one of a series of recurrent mood swings with the key being the patient showing periods of normality, which is exactly how Ellen behaved in the beginning until her condition deepened into a more paranoid state, which is a constant in Schizophrenia. The earlier diagnosis could have appeared correct at the time. In fact, all the judgements would have seemed right."

Both Ross and Tisha looked at each other intensely. Reading each other's mind Ross spoke for them both. "Are you saying they're all not suffering from either Schizophrenia or bipolar disorder?"

It was the turn of Ferral and Susan to look at each other as if confirming their diagnosis. "What we're saying is their minds are being affected by outside influences, outside of our control, it's not either of these two medical definitions, at least as we currently know them to be," qualified Ferral.

"I mentioned yesterday that I felt someone was interfering with their minds, I still believe this to be the case." Susan offered. "We need to investigate further and for that we need your help."

"Of course, we would be glad of the opportunity to help, I still have another question," said Tisha.

"What is this doing to Samuel and the others for that matter?"

Susan answered gravely. "While it's possible they could all snap out of their condition and recover fully, it's more than likely they will continue to plunge deeper into the recesses of their minds locked into worlds unknown. Gradually we will begin to see their physical functionality deteriorate and then their minds will start to vegetate finally leaving us with empty shells."

"Good God, Are you serious? What about the communication between them? Surely it counts for something, their minds must be working on some level," Ross exclaimed.

"Absolutely! Its keeping them from deteriorating further, unfortunately in time this will diminish as they each get weaker and have to let go. It means if we don't do something soon, it's the most likely outcome," Ferral conceded.

Tisha asked. "When you say soon, what does that mean?"

"I guess no more than four weeks. It could be more but probably by this time the decline will have begun and be irreversible," Ferral stated.

"There is something strange, no correction, something evil going on," Susan looked at Tisha and Ross. "Quite frankly we're out of our depth."

The words hung in the air as each appreciated the full impact. Tisha looked at the three poor souls facing out through the windows to the parkland beyond and wondered if they could hear the discussions going on. Fighting back a tear knowing if she was to help, she needed to be strong for them.

Susan spoke softly as if becoming aware they were speaking in front of the patients. "Sam is the weakest of the three at the moment. He has been under the most pressure and been displaying the symptoms for far longer. While his systems helped to spot the pattern in the others, he is beginning to show signs of deterioration. Look at the way he holds himself, the pronounced stoop, when walking he is starting to drag his feet, suggesting the brain's messages aren't through to the rest of his body. Couple this with his despairing look he may soon decide to give up his personal fight."

"What about the others Susan?"

"Matt being older than the other two, is the most at risk. He is physically unfit, although reported to be extremely strong mentally and emotionally. Ellen, on the other hand, is herself physically strong but emotionally weak. Sam falls somewhere between the two." Susan paused to look at the three still peering out of their respective windows. "Given all three are at various stages of degradation both of physical and mental strength, Ferral's estimate of a month overall is a fair one."

"I think it's time we adjourned to my office." Ferral suggested. "You've seen them all now and as Susan said earlier we need your help, so we need to plan the way forward."

As they got up and moved away from the fireside, Tisha walked slowly towards Samuel standing by one of the windows, its shadow had begun to envelop him as midday passed. Touching him, she pulled herself up to his face and kissed him gently on his cheek. He was warm, yet unresponsive. Quietly she whispered. "We're trying to help you my love. Soon we will take away your pain trust us." Unconvinced in what she was saying to him but hoped somehow he could gauge her strength of feeling.

The group watched as she pulled Samuel towards her, he bending towards her as if allowing the kiss. She hugged him and walked back to join the group, following them out through the doorway of the drawing room, the tears running down her cheeks, there was very little response. The other two patients watched without any expression or emotion.

The group settled into Ferral's office and Ross found himself sitting with Susan on one of the two red leather sofas. Never had he been able to gauge body language in a woman but he felt drawn to Susan. He became aware of her subtle fragrance, feeling her presence with each movement made sitting beside him. He felt guilty realising he should be thinking of Sam, Matt and Ellen. He wondered whether someone as sophisticated would be interested in him, thinking he was too immature for her realising it is exactly what he is now demonstrating, he hoped not, but he couldn't stop thinking about her unable to switch his thoughts off.

Deep in thought, Tisha looked out of Ferral's only office window looking out onto the manor's central courtyard. Daydreaming, she watched tearfully as a sparrow found a feast resting on the gravel near one of the wooden benches used by staff in break times.

Completely lost, watching the pretty-winged creature constantly fishing amongst the gravel for an ounce of crumb. Pecking incessantly watching for signs of danger or a challenge for the food in its grasp. Something startled the bird it decided to fly. Not too far, just out of reach to watch looking for the next opportunity.

As a Psychic Medium Tisha would regularly attend and arrange festivals to celebrate the phenomenon and at one many years ago Samuel shown an interest, taking him under her wing she immediately felt drawn to him and they had become instant pals. People attending the festivals have many divergent reasons for being there, some are anticipating enjoying the rhythmic drumming, come to see friends, to listen to key speakers, and others just want to be around those with a like mind. All are bound to have different agendas, needs, goals, and visions. Samuel just displayed a genuine interest in learning and understanding all things spiritual, their friendship had grown over time, neither asking much of the other.

She helped Samuel protect his own personal energy sensing he did not look after himself properly, physically or mentally. He continually charmed her with his boyish good looks and turn of phrases. She felt protective of him as an older sister would.

"Come and join us Tisha," Ferral spoke calmly behind her breaking into her thoughts noting the bird had flown a second time on hearing Ferral's voice.

"Have some more coffee," he could see Tisha was feeling the strain, but had to press on.

"How well do you really know Sam?" Ferral asked posing the question at both Ross and Tisha. "I'm looking for levels of strength in mind and body, resistance levels that type of thing."

Tisha responded noticing that Ross seemed to be wrestling with inner thoughts of his own.

"Samuel is not good at controlling his personal energy," Tisha offered.

"An unusual comment to make about someone," expressed Susan. "What do you mean?"

"The last time I saw Samuel, I noticed he had a lot of tension and had difficulty dealing with stress or so it appeared. He said it was the thought of working in China, although surprisingly, he was looking forward to going. I offered to help him," Tisha responded.

"How would you do that Tisha?" asked Susan genuinely interested.

"Have you heard of Chakras?" she asked.

Each shook their heads.

"These represent centres within everyone's body. Without the right balancing a person can rarely be at one with their spirit," she discussed. "It is learning how to breathe properly, understanding colours, sounds and levels of consciousness. It is also creating energy forces throughout the body and protecting with self-reflection and meditation. "Self-awareness, limitations and belief in your own possibilities all play a part. I needed to make sure he considered his spiritual well-being. Unfortunately, as expected he would not believe he was at risk and could help himself, I wish I had insisted on him taking my help now," Tisha went on. "He did say he was going to take a week's break before he went to China."

"And go where? Asked Ferral, Tisha shrugged unsure.

"Tisha is a medium," offered a smiling Ross. "You would think she might know."

"Well I didn't know, he never mentioned it," scowled Tisha, looking sharply at Ross, not amused.

"You mean you're into hereafter stuff?" asked Susan, she too smiling at his humour.

"No, it is mainly about healing, spiritual readings, clairvoyance plays a part of course with plenty of discussion on the hereafter," Tisha explained. "but it's about how to protect each other from psychological and psychic dramas, or at least keep them to a minimum."

"Do you believe Samuel was going through some sort of drama at the time?"

"Yes Ferral I do." Tisha replied. "There's no knowing what form this was taking or how deep this was festering inside him, but he never took very good care of himself, I don't just mean spiritually. For example, you mustn't get overheated, always drink water, rest and eat right, basics for every human being. I cannot tell you how many people forget these simple things and Sam did. Spiritually, each of us need to take time out every day for some quiet moments where you can centre, internalise and manage our own personal energy. Personal time for reflection is the key to each of our ongoing well-being. Silence around you, silence within stopping your mind from the constant chattering to yourself strengthens wisdom as well as peace in thoughts," she suggested. "Unfortunately Samuel ran rapidly in mind, soul and body all the time."

"You're saying he was a prime candidate for a breakdown anyway," Susan offered. "As doctors we can at least try to treat that."

"What you need to do from what Tisha is saying is to save his mind," insisted Ross. "Except I sense we're losing a battle here."

"Exactly why we needed you both here to help us. Our medical world sometimes leaves us blinkered, unable to cope with the outside world, with business. We are too weighed down by ordinary medical practice without appreciating the wider picture," Ferral paused. "Most certainly with consideration of spiritual and psychic phenomenon for example."

Ross, ever the planner, took the lead.

"Tisha and I have discussed this already. I'll look into the Chinese angle as I have some contacts through Connectiqua, They must have a list of contractors who have gone to China as well as knowing the organisations they are working for," Ross offered.

"You're assuming Connectiqua is the link?" queried Susan.

"No, but we have to start somewhere. There must be something connecting all three of them. I will start with the Shanghai Bell Company and do the trawl around the other main companies. I'll also approach the Huadong Hospital," Ross continued. "The problem is we cannot even be sure that China is one of the keys."

"My task has got to be to focus on the well-being of the patients here, but I will contact the World Health Organisation in Geneva. Unfortunately, unless there is an epidemic, they are unlikely to have any register of patients with similar symptoms," Ferral considered. "It may be worth contacting the foreign office for Chinese Embassies as there must be an overall list of foreign nationals, surely it wouldn't be linked to one organisation here or in China."

"I'll get some people onto this, the size of the list may be too large for us to deal with alone, but we should be able to establish how many of those that had fallen ill while working there," Ross said frowning, clearly working out who he was going to get to do this.

"I'm concerned for you Ross. Whatever has happened to these three whilst in China could also happen to you if you're not careful, especially as you are searching for answers someone may not want to be investigated," a worried Tisha said. "I think you and Susan should both go."

Tisha looked across at Susan. "How does this fit in with your plans?"

Susan tried hard to hide her elation at the possibility of spending time with Ross and determined to suppress it for the patient's sake.

"I'm available to work on this right now," looking at Ferral for confirmation, "If this is what is required?"

"More valuable to the patient's well-being than if you stayed here Susan," agreed Ferral.

Ross reddened and started to object. Tisha held up her hand to him and went on.

"Ross, you cannot do this all on your own, you have no medical background for a start, Susan can speak with the hospital and if your people find more names, more hospitals, she could determine whether the symptoms were the same. If you need a Chinese interpreter just hire one!"

"What do you think Susan?" Ferral asked. "We can cover while you are away and Tisha's right there is safety in numbers."

Susan felt a well of excitement building inside, trying unsuccessfully to curb. She wanted to do this, but felt she should put up a reasoned argument for not going. Time with Ross alone, her thoughts racing with barely controlled excitement.

"Are you sure I'm not needed more here, with you Ferral?" she had no wish to give this up. "I could help with these three as well as any others if they came in."

"No, it is vital you go as a pair. Ross needs your medical knowledge and we need to get to the bottom of this fast," suggested Ferral, himself oblivious to the growing feelings between the two.

Tisha watched Ross and Susan closely and both were struggling to hide their feelings, she could see how they were delighted with this unexpected outcome and realised she was pleased for them both.

The door opened to the office and a white uniformed male nurse entered moving straight toward Ferral leant down and whispered in his ear.

As the nurse left, Ferral looked glumly at the others. "Bad news I'm afraid, Matt has collapsed into sporadic fits. I fear his deterioration has just begun."

"I now know what I'm going to do and it cannot wait," Tisha stressed, as they all looked quite bemused. "We need help, serious help, and it's not physical."

"What do you mean Tisha?" asked Ferral. "I can look after the patients while Ross and Susan fly to

China, it is surely all we can do for now, I had hoped you would co-ordinate our various findings."

"Of course I can do that, but I'm sorry Ferral, I cannot, will not, just sit around waiting for something to happen, for people to get worse or even die, I need to speak to a friend, an acquaintance of mine. I'm sure he will help us!" Tisha emphasised.

"We can certainly do with as much help as possible right now, for all their sakes," Susan emphasised.

Ross drove Tisha back to the Marriot to pack enabling her to take the next train to London where she intended to go on her own mission. He had asked Susan if he could return later to finalise the details for travel to China. Susan lived locally and suggested he might like to have dinner with her at her cottage.

Ross waved off Tisha telling her not to worry as he watched the train push out to London and wished her luck with Tisha telling him to be careful.

Leaving the station he went in search of the charming rented cottage nestled amongst a working farm and looked across fields where sheep and cows idled their days chewing constantly. The warmth he felt as he entered her private domain gave him an insight to the beautiful woman he had only just met. The rush of excitement and expectation within told him he was at the beginning of a special relationship, he would enjoy these precious moments that come once in a lifetime. Offering locally just purchased red wine, he smelt the fragrance of roasting meat as Susan ushered him into the lounge adjacent to her kitchen.

Their intimacy beginning immediately, their eyes acknowledging one another with the sensuality of touch in a greeting lingering longer than normal.

As the evening wore on they never stopped talking, learning of each other and inevitably, naturally found themselves entwined by the fireside enveloped in its romantic glaze, sheer bliss the memory would last forever.

Knowing they were about to embark on their own adventure, filled them with delight looking forward to more time together. Reluctantly in the morning, they would part to prepare for the Chinese journey to come.

Chapter 3

At his old university's solid oak desk, six feet in length and four feet in depth, his rare desk once adorned Cambridge, used for huge quill penned professorial symposium's bound theses in oversize leather binding. He fell in the love with the desk, at least a hundred years old and begged his tutors to sell it to him. They refused only to suggest if he should excel in his studies it would be his as a gift on condition, he return it when he finished with it. He doubted that day would ever come.

The desk was in character in the Victorian setting of his London apartment he had purchased with the desk in mind. The desktop sloped downwards flanked by two doors either side opening to thick wooden shelves. He loved the feel of the old worn brown leather top bronze studded around its edging, an inkwell and nib wooden pens completed the magnificence of the oak structure. Sitting in his fine soft brown leather chair, he believed this could have been how any head teacher had felt on a university campus, proud and austere all at the same time.

David Bareham studied his day's diary searching for his upcoming events, had begun to feel that each one was rapidly becoming the same as the last.

He had already started his day at prayer in the nearby Our Lady of La Salette and Saint Joseph Church. Each morning he enjoying the walk across London Bridge, recalling the story of the bridge as he walked toward his favourite church.

The bridge built in 1820 by John Rennie and badly in need of repair when news in 1967 came of the intended demolition of Rennie's bridge. There were protests from many quarters for it to be preserved. Some even suggested restoring it to its original form, including the surrounding buildings that were once part of the 19th century. In the end an American representing McCulloch Properties, put in a bid and purchased London Bridge with the aim to take it back to the USA.

The bridge, divided into sections, marked out by numbers, like a puzzle, dismantled and shipped across the Atlantic. It arrived in California on July 5th 1968. The first stone laid by the then Lord Mayor of London, Sir Gilbert Inglefield on September 23rd 1968, Lake Hatsu City, halfway between Phoenix and Las Vegas. It was rumoured that the Americans thought they had bought Tower

Bridge with its middle opening and high walkway long shut off to the public. He always chuckled to himself when crossing the newer London Bridge.

"Sad really," he said aloud grinning to himself.

The church in Melior Street, with its half dozen pew rows dominating like galleons marching towards a fine sacred altar, reinforced his memories of his long ago priesthood. The story of the church itself had lost none of its charm or beauty over time.

Hanging for all to see was a large wooden framed picture of two peasant children dressed in rags without footwear, a Shepherdess of fifteen together with a boy shepherd of eleven years of age staring in wonder at a woman seated on the mountainside. A weeping apparition of Mary, the Mother of God in 1846 captured in the picture preceded a revival of faith and devotion, leading to thousands coming in pilgrimage to La Salette Fallavaux in the Diocese of Grenoble in France.

Who would have thought that fifteen years later a church dedicated in her honour would be opened in Melior Street and her shrine set up at the time of poverty stricken Bermondsey part of the famous east end of London. Steeped in the history of how this had come to be built, the struggles and problems and the sacrifices past priest and parishioners alike had made, he always felt humbled by its magnificence every time he prayed here.

His priesthood had ended after some twenty years. Being a London boy, he'd been drawn to the Catholic Church by the teachings he received at school and although his father had been very disappointed, his mother with the rest of his family learnt to accept his decision and became proud of him.

He had loved his vocation. A priest touches people at all the memorable times of a human life, both joyful and sorrowful - in baptisms and weddings, funerals and hospital visits. He celebrated mass with his congregation and had brought comfort and meaning to modern day life in his sermons.

Whatever type of work he did now he always tried to include in his life enough study, prayer, physical exercise, leisure and recreation. This balanced life brought with it a high degree of personal satisfaction. Born with a rare gift of heightened psychic awareness David had been no ordinary child. From an early age, he could usually be found reading metaphysical books, but with such scepticism and dismissal of his gift. He hid his psychic abilities especially while in the priesthood.

A near-fatal car accident ten years previously, those skills suppressed for so long were suddenly released. He had become a different person overnight he almost died and could no longer suppress his gift. Since, David had become a renowned psychic medium, spending these past years investigating and developing his abilities as a skilled spirit messenger. Turning down numerous offers of television and theatrical work, he shied away from any hint of publicity. The Arthur Findlay, one of England's foremost spiritualist colleges, trained him properly he gained a Ph.D. in

Metaphysics complimenting his years of theological studies.

Specialising in trance spiritual workshops with the aid of his known Chinese spiritual guide, he'd come to prefer a quiet solitary life previously afforded to him by the church and had no wish for fame at any price. His spartan lifestyle funded mainly by the inheritance left to him by his parents now passed on and supplemented by his private readings. In his early fifties, learning as a human being he is frail as the next man. As a spirit however, he knew himself totally and is extremely strong. One of his past lives no longer a mystery and he was learning constantly from his spiritual travelling.

In 1856, he had become a Martyr of China. Born a Frenchman in 1814, he was ordained to the priesthood in the Paris Society of the Foreign Missions. Sent to China after a brief period of parish work, going to Kwang-si. There he was taken prisoner during the persecution of the Christian Church's teachings and was put to death, brutally. Francis Chapdelaine lived on in David. It explained his need for belonging to his religion, his spiritualist make up and his affinity with all things Chinese confirmed by his own spiritual guide.

At the time of Francis Chapdelaine's death, he met his spiritual guide who, as a fellow prisoner, disappeared executed, only to help him cross to the other side spiritually to live as naturally with esoteric beings just like humans. Liu Ying had been with him ever since acting as his guide and mentor. When he awoke spiritually from the crash he realised his mentor had been in his head and by his side all his life, Ying was there supporting his journey. A wise old Chinaman, many centuries old, a known supporter of many religions particularly Buddhism, many of his followers established Buddhism communities. He had been a member of the eastern Han dynasty, dating back to the common era of sixty-five, the Chinese version of beyond the birth of Christ. He would never again reincarnate to the physical world. David felt blessed to have him as a dear friend.

His diary of the one page a day, A4 daily sheet variety with timings down the left hand side, the black book had become his lifeline to his daily being. Today, he had three readings before lunch, a young couple starting out together and wanting assurance of a life yet unknown. A regular, a gracious old woman who had now become very a dear friend, she just needed comfort and a chat. Generally brightening his day with her anecdotes of the past and if given her time all over again what she would do differently. |Third appointment an Indian man, had called validating himself by suggesting a mutual acquaintance his reference, persuading him to see him at short notice.

He wanted a psychic spiritual life reading which generally takes the form of an in-depth evaluation of a person's soul including both past and present.

Surprised by the man's preciseness in his request as if he knew what the differing types of readings were, made more unusual as the Indian culture is a homeland for spiritualism. Why would he want to specifically see him surely, there are better more focused spiritualists within his own religious sect.

feeling uneasy about the session he had a sense of foreboding, for all his learning and teaching, he couldn't put his finger on what may be wrong, a shiver went through him.

Moving down the diary page, his lunchtime he would spend at a traditional psychic fair. Although he found them quaint and never participated as an expert himself, he enjoyed testing and trying out any new psychic medium he found at the fairs to see if they were or could be the real thing. Sadly, it proved there were many charlatans.

Today he had a free afternoon, which was unusual, but he had a cry for help call from a new acquaintance, Tisha Pascoe interested him, a nice pretty woman in her early thirties. He knew she had written a couple of psychic defence books which he actually read finding them fascinating and believable. He was intrigued to learn whether she had tested the theories she put forward in them. She sounded quite desperate for his help.

David owned the modernised apartment in the heart of London within an old Victorian style renovated building. At the centre of the double fronted five storey building, a high arched entrance way with push button panel access to the inhabitants led the way past the individual bronze mailboxes and onto the imposing staircase which centred the whole structure spiralling around the caged steel lift and rose majestically to each floor above.

The building itself had been radically modernised throughout and had retained its Victorian charm and character within each of the apartments. With the help of the renovators, David had restyled it into more of an open plan feel, giving him smaller, private areas surrounding a larger open area. It helped when his readings took in groups, couples or individuals. The high Victorian windows on this fifth floor apartment reached out across the Thames River claiming its London life. From here, he could listen to the ringing of his favourite church bells and gain comfort in their sounds.

Patterned carpets centred the main areas leaving borders of polished floorboards, curtained bay windows with rich dark colours of ruby reds and forest greens. He avoided the flock wallpapers of the Victorian period preferring more pastel shading. His overstuffed, canvas style, plump armchairs and sofa with button backs on their buff coloured fabric crowded the main living area. The fireplace, ornate, ostentatious and in pewter cast iron, gave presence to its central position. Sadly, not allowed an open fire, having to make do with a fake, coal effect, gas fire. It cheapened the character of the room in the interests of modern day safety. Pride of place in the bay of the main window stood his beloved desk.

The delightful young couple arrived for their reading full of life's expectations. At 24, the prematurely balding fair-haired man only had eyes for the dark-haired girl on his arm. They were clearly in love and hungry for any insight he could give them. He did what he always did with couples and spoke to them individually at first, which tended to help them open up privately to him about their personal fears, worries or concerns each had about their future time together, and excited about what they were to hear from him.

At such a short hourly session, he stressed to them both more readings would be necessary the more insight they wished for over time. When they joined each other, David explained the longer-term readings were for an in-depth evaluation of one's soul, both past and present. Telling them about a Psychic spiritual life reading for those who want a deeper insight about their soul's evolutionary journey.

Suggesting at this stage they have a reading covering more fundamentally karmic relationships, which helps to understand past histories of relationships so they can create a loving expression of support towards each other for their future and how to help family members, friends, why people are together and what they learn from each other.

The pair were totally besotted, dominating this relationship reading. They were 'real' soulmate's, he stressed they would have hard times as well as good, and they should make what they could of each experience they had together. He suggested that a year of marriage should pass then another, more realistic reading, could be done.

His hope filled words created for them a platform for their future together. The couple went off believing they will conquer the world. He prayed for them and was already looking forward to the time when he saw them again.

David realised on many occasions recently that he lacked a real circle of friends. Sessions like the one he just had brought home all too well the lack of companionships in his life. Unfortunately, because of his background, he had never gotten close to anyone except God. Once it would have been enough but progressively he was becoming lonelier, no one to just call and chat to, rarely would he pass the time of day with anyone. Once he had never minded but lately he could go days without saying a word to anyone.

Never been to those dinner parties where couples, who grew up or worked with each other, sharing life's ambitions or woe's. He felt sometimes that people found him difficult, unable to get close to him because of what he did and were afraid he would be constantly looking into their minds and souls, suspicious of his motives, he despaired at friendship not even lost, just never had.

A buzzer sounded at the apartment buildings entrance forcing David out of his melancholy. He had recognised his loneliness many times and while he helped many people and loved what he did, he was at a loss to know with all his skills how to form real and lasting friendships for himself.

"Hello Theresa, it is so lovely to see you again," as he opened his door to his next appointment. He felt warmth enveloping him pushing away his feelings of unease with her sheer presence looking forward as he always did to the moment they met once again lifting him as a tonic. Theresa stood in the doorway smiling at him lovingly. A grey haired bright sprightly woman in her late seventies had been coming to see him for a long, long time.

"Hi, my dear," she always greeted him as a long lost soul of hers. "You're looking thin, you know, I hope you're eating properly?" she admonished, pushing into his hands a freshly baked sponge cake, made especially for the occasion.

David nodding smiled at the dear, dear, beautiful sweet person who stood in front of him with her best grey worsted coat, with a well-worn imitation fox fur around its neck. This was her Sunday best.

David had over time, been through every kind of reading with Theresa and their relationship had progressed to him knowing that she had the most kindly, beautiful, loving soul. Her past lives had been only to serve gentry, he hoped they had felt some of the charm she gave him.

Together David and Theresa acted as if they were grandmother and grandson, he provided the tea she the cake, they chatted forever. It seemed both never tiring of each other's company. David loved her totally.

She had long since taken over their sessions and he had stopped charging her for his time. He looked forward to her incessant ranting and raving about the price of things, next-door neighbours, of her children and grand children's lives and general injustices of life, he loved every moment.

Plying her constantly with tea and her homemade sponge, he listened to her with an admiration that can only come out of respect for the hardship she had been through in her current life, yet still remaining optimistic for the future. She had become the nearest he had for a family, having lost his parents to age related illness several years ago.

Too soon, their time together was up. She visited as often as she could but lived with her daughter in the country, and was well looked after now although she had lately become quite unsteady on her feet she told him. So full of life yet frail in years, he savoured her hugs and kisses. When she had gone, he wondered whether this time he would see her again in this world. He felt sad and knew the answer already.

Checking his diary noting his next appointment would shortly arrive. He recalled the man had introduced himself over the telephone and recommended to him by a mutual acquaintance.

Shyam Rosha pressed the buzzer button against David Bareham's name. He was early for his appointment. Nervously looking at the stained glass in the main door to straighten his blue shiny tie, which matched in colour to his mohair jacket. He smoothed down his black creamed hair with sweat moistening his hands. He heard the man's voice directing him to a lift or stairs for one of the top floor apartments, he push open the main door on hearing the opening click of the lock.

Rising in the lift Shyam felt tired pulling open its gate on arrival. He approached the open door of the apartment and shook the proffered hand outstretched from the man he assumed to be David

Bareham noting him to be greying and taller in stature than himself. An aura about the man clearly noticeable to him, it unnerved him further.

"Welcome to you and to my home," said David. "We've not met before so please make yourself at home."

David offered Shyam a drink as he shook the man's hand. It was damp and limp without feeling or life. He wiped his own hand of sweat discreetly on his trousers and studied the young Indian man standing before him a shudder went through David as he did this. Suddenly he felt afraid, he was unused to fear, evil seemed to ooze from every pore of the man stood now by the fireplace. It shocked him.

He poured water for his visitor as requested and hoped the session would soon be over. Worried, he was becoming very uncomfortable.

"You mentioned over the phone you were pursuing soul growth and spiritual understanding by developing one's spiritual energy," bravely, David tried to appear calm as he spoke. "Unusually strange words from someone who has never been to a medium nor ever had a reading before."

"I've had readings before, but I am looking for the Christian path as the way forward," Shyam Rosha offered, gaining a strength of purpose as Bareham began to appear weaker. He believed he was feeding off the man.

"May I ask why?" David questioned noticing him brighten and becoming tired. "The path is the same but surely you would know this if you have been through this before," the man in front of him seemed to struggle with this.

When Shyam spoke to him, he felt the words were hollow, like breathing ice into the air around him. There were strange pauses as if he was being controlled and had to confer with something or someone else.

"I am interested in what you can teach me and how far along the path you have travelled, spiritually." Shyam's eyes were trance like, almost glazed, and staring without looking at him directly. His voice stuttering when he spoke, short and sharp. The man in front of him controlled by something or someone.

"Why are you interested in my spiritual attainments? David questioned.

His pallor grey as dust in colour, David looked directly into his eyes as he spoke, they were not moving but fixed directly ahead. David moved from side to side deliberately testing Shyam. He followed his movement with his whole body as one rather than only moving his head. David spoke to him of trivia without response and purposely moved in a circle slowly at first but began to quicken imperceptibly twice clockwise then twice anti-clockwise. This frustrated Shyam, so much movement caused beads of sweat to form on his face his speech started to slur, he must have been programmed, David had never seen this before, spiritually he knew it could be done with enough will exercised over an individual.

Dangerously David ventured. "Do you have a master, Shyam?"

"I am India's messenger and I arrive from China." Shyam Rosha shouted at him panicking he could not cope with the man continually circling him.

"Who sent you here Shyam?" David was facing a frightened man edging back toward the apartment door. He moved closer toward him cringing at the pungent smell his heavy rotting stench of breath seeping from his pores eroding the freshness of the apartment. David was ready to retch.

He is not getting through to this man. There was literary a blank wall behind the dark eyes. Trying to help this terrified man, David suspected the meeting had not gone to plan. He touched Shyam on the arm to comfort him and immediately felt the recoil as if stung. Spiritually he tried but could not read him.

"I, have to go, I have to go, now!" Shyam said stuttering, physically shuddering, still panicking, out of his depth.

"Please stay I'm sure we can contact your master."

"Very tired, have been travelling far." He backed toward the exit door looking for an escape route.

"Wait, wait, please don't go, we haven't done any work or readings yet," implored David. Although frightened he hoped to find more out about who is controlling him.

"No! No! I done, I go home," His face the pallor of death. He turned and grabbed at the door handle pulling the door open. He started to run and headed down the five flights of stairway not bothering with the lift, tripping and falling down the steps in his haste to get away.

In a moment, the man was gone, David noticed the oppressive atmosphere lift as quickly as it came, the smell will take a little longer. He had gotten close to whoever was in control he realised.

Within minutes of Shyam's hasty departure, he became aware of a raw, rotting smell of flesh. He searched his apartment and gauged it was coming from his full bookcases.

As he began removing his old collection of books from each of the shelves, the stench became unbearable.

Searching the apartment, he found what he was looking for. Shyam had obviously left the maggot ridden dead rat in the brief moment it had taken for him to get his water. A psychic symbol, a warning, a clear message destined to disgust or frighten the receiver suggesting there could be problems ahead. He was confused. It was the first time he felt there was something spiritually happening. Time will give him the answers. He knew he had to be patient but it did not stop him being nervous and very afraid. The message had fulfilled its task.

Chapter 4

Lunchtime saw David devouring the sights at another popular psychic fair. These took place in cities around the country. He tried attending as many as he could get t

Luckily, todays fair held in the Bermondsey Village hall at Leathermarket Gardens only a short walk from London Bridge. Typical of past fairs, people offering readings via tarot cards, palmistry, clairvoyance, pet psychics, aura cleansing, past life investigations, finding angels, spirit guides, mediums and full of channelling techniques.

It amused him to see the products on offer especially when he barely understood them. Chair massage, foot reflexology, incense, jewellery, soaps, oils, books, candles and even ear candling a method which places a candle in a person's ear and sets light to it, meant to cleanse and remove wax from the ears. David shuddered at the thought. What it had to do with a psychic fair was beyond him except for the selling of candles.

He enjoyed playing with those claiming to have special powers of the mind and calling themselves clairvoyants, masterminds and even "international" psychics.

Each promised to read minds, to help discover such powers of our own, to promote healing, to see the future, to bring out our "sixth sense", to read character, to meet our guardian angel, and more recently, to read the mind of our pet.

Unknown to David, Tisha was at the same fair. She had realised that one would be on nearby where she was going to keep her arranged appointment with him.

By coincidence, they kept missing each other as interest dictated the particular stall catching the eye. Tisha had met the man she was going to see a couple of times before and been extremely impressed with him as an individual, a person of stature, sure of himself and his spiritual level, unlike quite a few at the fair. She knew him to be, what was the current wording? "The real deal".

Convinced he would help and give the advice they needed to help Samuel and the others. Soon tiring of the fair she decided to make her way to David Bareham's home.

A good feeling came upon her as David welcomed her. His greeting warm and comforting genuinely pleased to see her as he ushered her into the apartment. Tisha dropped into one of David's plump canvas armchairs and instantly felt at home.

"Tisha, what can I help you with, you sounded extremely anxious on the telephone, I'm sure you don't want an urgent reading of any kind from me. I, at least, know you that well." He liked her, one of the few he valued as a friend.

"It's so good of you to see me so quickly David, you're truly the only person I could think of to turn to and who could help us," Tisha emphasised.

"Us?" queried David.

"Yes, I need to go over what I believe has happened so far, then I am sure you will realise why I came to you," she looked at him hopefully.

"Before you begin Tisha let me hold your hands to help us both settle our minds and reflect on any journey ahead of us, a few minutes closed eye silence will refresh us both," encouraged David.

Tisha nodded in agreement and trustingly shut her eyes holding her arms outstretched to David. Gently he took her hands she felt it natural and safe.

David, unknown to all, had the ability to venture into the mind, to pick up feelings, thoughts and search for stress patterns. He felt alarming shock waves coming from inside her. As they sat, her eyes closed, he explored each part of every area of her mind delving deeper and deeper into her subconscious, watching her thoughts so jumbled seemingly trying to place events in sequence for him recognising his presence within.

At the beginning of his mind search Tisha was automatically "shielding" herself from his intrusion, only to relax when he mentally comforted her.

Trawling through what he likened to an underground train packed full of minds trying to get his attention, key words were dominating her thoughts, Ditton, Samuel, India, Setna, Hospital,

Shanghai, Connection and Ford all of equal importance. Willingly she attempted to guide him through the minefield of her brain and intelligence of the thought process she possessed.

Realising he had skilfully extracted as much information as possible suggested to her they should wake and simultaneously they opened their eyes and both drew a deep breath.

"I felt you David, in here," Tisha pointed to her forehead laughing embarrassed. "I couldn't stop you and I did try. You were too strong spiritually for me I hope you never saw all my secrets."

"We can develop better protection for shielding your thoughts more some other time however, it does tend to put off most unwanted spirits."

"To business," he spoke firmly. "Before you tell me anything, I need to tell you what I have found in your mind and can work through these then what hasn't come to light we can discuss further, agreed?"

Tisha nodded as David continued.

"Tell me about Samuel," he queried. Tisha felt her jaw drop in astonishment as she openly burst into a flood of tears, it was the first time she truly thought of the implications of Samuel's predicament. Her dear, dear friend could die or worse spend the rest of his existence as a vegetable.

Her voice adopted a harsh gravelly sound as she fought back her sadness. "I have known Samuel for a number of years he is a young man who tends to live life at pace. Always looking for the next thing without fear."

"Ah! The rash of youth, do we not all know of this feeling?" David injected. "Especially when we have lost it?"

"No! No!" Tisha shook her head and wagged her finger at him. "He was not racing for the next buzz, everything tried he went into wholeheartedly, he is very intelligent and well-meaning young man who never considers the consequences because he has always won, never lost."

David considered this mental strength carefully. "It is important to know Tisha, tell me what you know has happened."

He quietly listened as Tisha unfolded the story and felt the same unease gradually sweeping through his soul the second time today. Tisha explained how Samuel had been working under contract for the software giant Connectiqua, who had recently won a number of resource provider contracts managed by a business consortium set up between the ten largest Chinese organisations in Shanghai. A friend of Samuel's for many years she knew of his excitement having the opportunity to work in China.

"I had received the occasional 'I'm doing great' cards so there was no need to worry until a month ago, Ross had been contacted by Connectiqua asking for his help with Samuel."

"Ross?" Queried David.

"He's Samuel's best friend and part of the reason why he worked for Connectiqua. Ross works as a Financial Consultant, shares and taxes, I think," she said dismissively. "He introduced Samuel to the organisation a long time ago and because of this they looked to Ross for his help, so he arranged for Samuel to be treated at the clinic within Ditton Manor set up for stress related conditions amongst executives, corporate health care they call it."

"Tisha I'm not a medical man, I'm not sure how I could help you."

"Both Ross and I felt Samuel was going through some sort of breakdown, stress at work and also being in a country where cultures are different as chalk and cheese to us. However this is what we found is this not the case."

"How so?"

"Because two others that we know of are suffering exactly the same symptoms."

"It is possible," although he was sceptical.

"Not if those symptoms are identical surely?"

Tisha continued by going over their meetings with Susan and Ferral and the diagnoses each had received at the Huadong Hospital in Shanghai.

"And there diagnoses were?"

"Schizophrenia."

"Reasonable I guess." Still sceptical.

"But that's the thing both the hospital and Ditton Manor Doctors say in all three it takes the form of being controlled."

"Pardon?" He didn't understand.

"Their mind is in some sort of grip which they all share."

"I see." Trying not to alarm Tisha this greatly concerned him, he started to realise he would have no choice but to help. "Tell me of the other two."

"Matt Shanahan is an Irish financier and Ellen Kefford a Health Inspector, he would have been working for the same company as Samuel but how Ellen became caught up in this remains a mystery."

"What happens now Tisha?"

"The plan is for Ross and Susan to fly to China and in particular to visit the Shanghai Bell company together with the hospital to try and get some lead on how and why this started or whether even more are involved."

"Yes it's a good start but impress upon Ross he will need to be very careful." David considered carefully what Tisha had been saying. He had picked a great deal from her mind already. Now he was establishing how the words fitted into the puzzle. Ditton, for the manor where the patients are, the hospital for the clinic and again where they are and treated.

He learnt of Samuel and Ross, Connectiqua for the connection word and at a guess for Ford read Ellen

Kefford, one of the patients at Ditton Manor. What had not come out were the words India and Setna. He guessed they are probably in Tisha's mind without her knowing it. Another concern, strange, that feeling welled inside again, he found himself thinking of Shyam Rosha, shuddering he started to sweat at the thought.

"Tisha, Tell me why have you come to see me?" he asked seriously wanting her to put into words what she truly felt and wanted. "How do you believe I can help you?"

For a fleeting moment, she wondered whether what she needed to say would sound foolish. She knew in her heart, the man sitting in front of her was probably the only person of this world and the next, who could possibly help them. She struggled to put into words the feeling she had, the distress of Samuel's plight and her sheer despair, when looking at both Matt and Ellen, even though she did not know them.

"I want you to help my Samuel and his companions deal with something or someone who is attacking their minds. I don't know what its, but I feel it is evil and if they don't get help soon I know it will destroy them to their very soul." Tisha was clearly panic stricken about what she thought was happening tears welled in her eyes as she spoke.

"Everyone is treating it as a physical condition that might be affecting his mind. I disagree, I believe there is a presence that is out to force its will or kill Samuel, at least attempting to control his mind and in turn I believe is going to start to harm him physically. Help me to help them David," she pleaded. You're only person who can understand and fight it."

"You put it as strong as that?" he said sympathising.

"Yes I do!" she exclaimed. "Some evil is playing with their minds, I'm not sure how or why but we have to stop it, put up some defence against it."

"Tisha you have written a number of books about psychic defences and I've been quite interested in them, what would you have me do? Individual's need to build their own internal defence mechanism and this through much meditation and practice. I fear we do not have the luxury of time. You tell me they cannot function mentally anyway. Any suggestive conditioning will not help. Some paralysis or hypnosis appears, from what you tell me has already taken place. I would have to see how far this deterioration has gone personally before I could suggest a course of action."

"Please, please come and see them David I beg you, they desperately need you. I know you have helped others through their problems at the psychic fairs, I do not know how but you manage to penetrate people's minds and remove harmful stuff," Tisha continued in the hope of convincing him further. "I don't have not a clue how you do it but you have helped so many people."

"I will agree to see them Tisha, but know I believe we're about to go on a long dangerous journey together without knowing the implications or what the outcome will likely to be," David stressed. "You need to consider the risks and the likely outcome involved. We may end up in trouble ourselves and not helping Samuel at all," he went on. "If we left the problem alone maybe whoever or whatever it is may just give up and move on to something else."

"David, it is not an option, I cannot sit by and do nothing, besides the prognosis is that Samuel will be dead or mindless within a month, we cannot afford to let it go on much longer," Tisha responded, considering his point.

"Have you had Chakras training?" he innocently asked.

Tisha nodded. "Some time ago, I do try to practice each day."

"Then you will be aware of the teachings where we each have a special place to put our problems? Somewhere we can use or go to get peace of mind letting our spiritual guides help us," David watched Tisha closely and saw her physically relax and close her eyes, her thoughts were deepening. He would help her to find the peace of thought she needed. "Let me walk with you through your own special place."

He had to calm her down she had taken on the responsibility of Samuel's wellbeing. Very quietly gently and holding her two hands, he asked her to keep her eyes closed, and to focus on where she was.

He joined her mind at her childhood stream, her father sitting on a canvas chair at the stream's edge. He was throwing a line hoping to catch a sprat fishing was his favourite pastime. Close by two boys from the local school appeared to be struggling with the extended pole they held as they guided their wooden punt together up stream. The spring sunshine caught the yellow of the daisies blooming Californian poppies and a Sierra shooting star complete with frogs their bulbous eyes peering out from the stem, complimented by an array of purple lupines.

The sky blue in its yellow hue of the sun beating down through the occasional cloud of the season, with the sun darting in and out of tree branches as the gentle sway caused by the breeze pushed them from side to side as they lined the riverbank. A wooden bench overlooked the stream, holding the toys of the young. They were seated upright watching over their charges, a one eyed teddy bear with a stitched scar down its forehead, a result of being involved in a past child's tantrum, looked on relaxed in the knowledge his little lady was sitting colouring in by crayons, a picture of soon to be a multi-coloured parrot. The young girl occasionally glancing at her father sleepily nodding under his loosely woven cane hat, the line throwing had obviously taxed him the fishing rod loosely held in his hands.

David sat on the bench by the teddy bear watching as Tisha ribbon in hair, dressed in a pink and white chequered dress, coloured her parrot. They could hear her father gently snoring.

Quietly David spoke. "Do you know me Tisha?"

Without hesitation, Tisha answered childlike. "You're David, my friend you have come to help me. How long will we stay here together?"

"Just a short while, my dear, I need to look around in your world for a moment and then we must go. This is your dream and special place where I have no part."

David looked behind him at the beautiful cottage with its thatched roof and chocolate box windows, truly idyllic, he heard a noise it was coming from the punt, a splash. One of the boys had fallen into the stream and began shouting for help, flapping arms furiously in an attempt to stay afloat.

They couldn't, shouldn't be able to see David, for he didn't exist in this world, only in Tisha's thoughts. It was time for him to leave. Just then, he looked at the other boy in the punt holding the pole, stretched out towards the boy in the water. He knew then he had found what he was looking for.

He saw an Indian boy in the punt grinning directly at him. Once again, unease welled inside him even here, in the private place of Tisha's mind. She not aware of their presence at all. Somehow, the grinning boy had planted himself in her mind for his benefit. Fear washed through him again. He shrugged away the feeling.

Quietly he asked Tisha to wake up and released her hands from within his. "What do you remember from your special place?" he asked softly.

Puzzled, "You were there, weren't you on the bench?" Tisha said, surprised at her recollection.

David nodded. "Who were you aware of?"

"Just my father and you, how did you do that?" Tisha enquired.

"I truly don't know. I have always had the ability to walk through people's minds, it's a great responsibility," he ventured.

"You could catch all the criminals of the world, find out exactly what people are up to, it's endless," Tisha suggested.

"No, there are limitations and the parties have to be willing. Having been a priest I know only too well not to play God with people's lives," he continued. "Think of it like a virtual reality adventure, each person has a history and that history is in sections or compartments within the mind. By tapping into those areas of the mind where there are problems. I can help change, not history, but the impression of events that a person remembers."

"Wouldn't that unbalance a person?" Tisha ventured. "What about a family death or an accident."

"Actual reality doesn't change therefore, history stays the same, but a change of perception in recall could make all the difference to that person. For example removal of unnecessary guilt that had plagued a person throughout their lives. By playing out the happening whatever it had been could change the view of it, therefore a person could deal with the circumstances better than before," David was becoming tired, it was normal after such a session. Unknown to Tisha there was a purpose in looking into her private mind place. He found what he needed to see. He suppressed those feelings of fear once again. He had found the Indian in her mind in the form of the boys. Just the name left.

"What happens now, David?" Tisha asked noting that he looks older than his years and obviously very tired.

"Make arrangements with everyone I need to see Tisha. We must let our adventure begin." Laughing aloud to Tisha, the unease washed through David's veins like a waterfall. He hoped she had not noticed his fear. Someone powerful was playing dangerously with people's mind and could destroy them, he knew he would have to confront it head on, but for now, he needed as much information as he could get.

Chapter 5

The blue screens above the waiting areas of the departure lounge highlighted the delayed notice for the Air France Flight leaving for Charles De Gaulle airport in Paris. Flight AF2171 due to depart London's Heathrow airport terminal 2 at 19:15 British time now scheduled for 20:15.

The hour delay was a blessing in disguise helping Ross to compose himself as he considered the task before him. He looked forward to travelling with Susan the chemistry very real between them. The prospect of getting to know her more excited him.

Susan had yet to arrive in the departure lounge.

Watching the entrance constantly checking the time, not late yet. He wanted her with him to make sure she was actually going to spend time alone with him on this trip, try as he wished he could not stop thinking about her. Last night was fresh in his mind, but he realised they must stay focused for the sake of Sam he was finding it difficult.

He kept looking at the blue departure screens above him impatiently he suddenly felt a presence alongside him.

"Hello to you," Susan flirtingly cuddled up to him, her perfume pleasantly invading his space, the air around causing his heart to miss a beat, his face reddened glad to have her so near him again. He kissed her cheek naturally, the waiting over.

"Our flight is delayed for an hour I'm afraid," Ross informed her needing to say something serious, she played along knowing that their time will come soon.

"What's our flight number?" she asked looking at the departure screens.

"AF 2171, Air France to Paris," he looked into her eyes losing himself in her beauty, shivering at the intensity of his feelings for her. He knew he was forever lost in her soul.

"Are we staying in Paris?" she ventured searching his face, her eyelashes deliberately flashing at him. "That would be so romantic of you," she emphasised.

"I'm sorry not this trip," Ross replied enjoying his attempt to ignore her teasing. He went on to explain the travel arrangements and wondered if he was being too stuffy, the freshness of the relationship overwhelming him.

They were to arrive in Paris Terminal 2F Charles De Gaulle at 22.15 if the delay stayed at an hour. They needed to connect to the outgoing flight bound for China at Terminal 2E which meant they only had an hour to change terminals and connect to the 23:15 Air France flight AF112 leaving for Pudong International Airport.

"How far will we be from Shanghai?" queried Susan purposefully looking deep into his eyes." Where will we be staying?"

"At short notice, we are staying at Pudong's Airport there is a conference holding hotel so it should have everything we need, it is quite convenient and Shanghai is only about nineteen miles or thirty kilometres away."

Luckily, the delay stayed at an hour. Terminal 2 was Heathrow's first terminal despite it called number 2. The Queen opened Terminal 1in 1969 so it lost some of its status although it is still the home to 28 airlines. They were sitting on a red patterned bench in what was originally, the Europa building. Since opening in 1955 and despite the many refurbishment's it was showing its age. Once on the busy Airbus 321 and realising all two hundred and ninety six seats were taken, each passenger angling for their own space on board Ross was thankful the flight was short.

As the evening progressed, they found themselves settling down on the long haul flight AF115 an Airbus 343 for their onward journey to Pudong this time in business class. The aircraft half full this time, more comfortable, the flight would take about seventeen hours. Drinks and in-flight meals arrived in front of them without asking as they talked about their individual lives before they had met.

Part of the research for her degree in Psychology, Susan had taken in meditation, paranormal and psychic evaluations, not in depth but an awareness of each subject. This experience led her to believe the likelihood of unseen forces at work in the cases of all three patients.

Ross was a financial master of the stock market with a fierce logic to compliment his business ambitions. he made money out of the smallest of opportunities and was very good at it. Now he felt out totally of his depth.

Warming to each other both excited they shared confidences likes and dislikes, genuinely interested in each other's point of view, enveloping themselves in the promise of a new relationship. During the long flight, they dozed holding one another comfortingly.

Ross looked down at Susan's face quietly asleep her breathing rising and falling gently hoping this moment would last forever. Guilt interrupted his thoughts realising it has been the first time for over a month that he had not been thinking of his best friend. In his mind, he walked through all that had happened during the last few weeks glad he was now doing something positive. He wondered what Tisha was up to, she went off mysteriously on her own mission. He hoped she was successful. Susan stirred beside him, looking up she smiled and spoke softly to him.

"Hi my love, we will find a way to help Sam you know, we've just got to work at it." She'd read his mind looking at his strained features, hoping that one day their relationship would move forward without worry for others. She too felt guilty.

Gently kissing him, she put on her headphones and settled down beside him to watch the in-flight movie hoping it would help her to fall asleep again, it did.

Ross knew he was falling in love with Susan and did not want to stop himself. It was the most natural feeling he had ever, jumping at the opportunity to be with her, he also began worry for her safety knowing they could be facing similar dangers Sam must have done. He promised himself, that he would look after her always.

Susan slept on as Ross fumbled for the in-flight magazine quietly charting their flight route.

Ross, a partner of a Canadian group of Accountants had studied for his Bachelor of Commerce at Queen's qualified in Ontario as a Chartered Accountant. He'd moved to Canada when much younger with his father's brothers family, having previously been pushed as a young boy from one relative to another after both of his parents had died in a skiing accident in Switzerland. Sam and his family helped him come to terms with his grief, but he could not stay with them forever.

He had worked since qualifying for various organisations building his experience in trust and tax planning and along the way discovered his fascination for the stock markets. He made money, lots of it and luckily, it allowed him able to help Sam.

Following spells working for Deloitte's and KPMG international. A group of like-minded colleagues set up on their own. They tempted him with the offer of being responsible for the firm's computer audit and consulting practice. Best of all his office was set up in London, England.

Jumping at the opportunity to return to his native land, Sam and his family, now he was older, welcomed him into their home as their long lost son. He built a business that supported 100 staff working globally linking the other partners of Craig, Keen, Burrough's and Mansell into a financially strong business. It was how he came to know Connectiqua as a major client. He had introduced Sam to them and now began to doubt the wisdom of it.

Ross checked out Connectiqua, prising information from them the basis of client confidentiality and involvement in the welfare of the people they had sent to China. He found nine people had contracts linked to the major national corporations in China and Sam headed their list. Armed with enough information he gave the list to one of his own trusted staff to work with while they were away.

Penny Whitmore loved working for Ross she had done so for many years. She had heard of the problems his friend had and welcomed the opportunity of helping. Highly intelligent and despite her overtures toward him Penny realised Ross would never be interested in her. He liked her, respected her and that had to be enough. Since arriving in England from Australia on a year's sabbatical from her post office job in Canberra, she had stayed mainly because of her fondness for him.

Although mid-twenties, her years belied the maturity and resourcefulness she had. One of the main reasons Ross had fought many a battle with the authorities over her visa extensions. Finally, she had been able to stay permanently. She missed home but loved England and working for Ross.

Ross had given Penny a paper with nine names in a column and alongside each was a company in China. He had asked her to try to speak to each individual by telephone to check if OK. If not she was to speak to the company officers to find out where they were, establishing who is still working and more importantly still alive and well.

The second task was to contact the British Embassy's in China the British Consulate has three sites specifically in Shanghai. They could help with visa information for those not connected to the Connectiqua 9, as well as check how many other foreign nationals are working in China and have become 'ill'. Penny did not like needle in haystack tasks and told him so.

About halfway into their flight to Pudong Ross felt Susan stir beside him, he waved to a flight attendant for coffee as she went off to the washroom to freshen up. On her return, Ross asked if she had contacted WHO the world health organisation.

"Yes I have and I'm not sure whether it's good news or not. They have not received any information about any type of epidemic at all for that region. Although they qualify it, by saying any information I could give them may well be the beginning of one. They were interested to know how the three so far were affected and would certainly look at any matches they may have in their files."

"Was that encouraging?"

"I believe so," she ventured not wishing to degrade her investigations. "It means our cases are isolated however, they could find some match and if we find more people then they will be aware of the problems."

Ross unconvinced it only confirmed what they had been thinking. It is not a normal illness, but something controlled affecting all three, he hoped they did not find anyone else. Though they needed to otherwise they would draw a blank.

Sleeping, walking and eating seemed all they could do by the end of their seventeen hour flight they were exhausted. Gratefully they learnt so much about each other and liked what they knew.

The tannoy confirmed their arrival as the airplane touched down on the runway at Shanghai's Pudong airport and immediately they became two people with a mission.

Ross reflected on what he had read in the in-flight magazine, Shanghai, China's largest city with a population of over eight million people. A major port and centre of industry Pudong itself contained many high-rise towers where foreign and Chinese companies locate their head offices. One such company is the Shanghai Bell where Penny had arranged for Ross to go the following morning to meet the Chief Executive.

Settled in Pudong airport's hotel far away from the hustle of the overwhelming number of people their flight arrival met with, the evening welcoming for the peace and quiet both needed. After a short flight delay, customs and searching for baggage, there had been time for a brief snack before both welcomed the tranquillity of their own rooms, the twenty-four hour journey taking its toll.

Ross before retiring investigated the facilities of the hotel. Realising he could have been anywhere in the world, he decided to return to his room, adjacent to Susan's.

Both refreshed, they met the following morning at breakfast to go over the likely day's events.

Ross would visit the Shanghai Bell Company as arranged with Susan intending to turn up at the Huadong Hospital in the suburbs of Pudong.

Penny had prepared the way for Ross's meeting by emailing ahead and fortunately been able to waive the normal protocol rules for a quanxi to obtain an introduction.

She discovered, talking to the Embassies what the levels of protocol require where connections and relationships known as quanxi in China. This applied for sending a letter or email to the most senior person in the company. However, because of the time constraints a Chinese translated e-mail worked for them.

Ross arrived surprised at the modern building rising high above him. Black glassed steel structure kept the rays of sunshine outside the air-conditioned environment inside. Met by security officers with some suspicion, he was finally, after some wait, shown into the office of the chief executive.

Hudong Hua a dark haired slight build man greeting him by giving Ross a slight bow of his head followed by a warm handshake. Ross was careful to be early arriving for his appointment as this showed respect to his Chinese counterpart.

Hua gave him his ming pianr and expected Ross's own business card as a response. Hua informed Ross he spoke good English so no translator would join them. The Chinese normally conduct business over a lunch or dinner entertaining being a key part of sharing information, but Penny had left them in no doubt, Ross's mission was an urgent one.

As each assessed the other, Ross hoped the man in front of him would be helpful to his cause and made a decision to tell Hua everything. Slowly Ross unfolded the story as Hudong Hua listened carefully. The CEO knew and liked Sam and knew of his disturbances. He felt Ross was telling him everything, but knew he could not, would not be quite as open in return.

"Thank you for being so open with me," said Hua. It was refreshing he thought, recognising the trust afforded to him.

Ross pressed on he had several questions. "Any information you could give about when and where you or your people started to notice problems with Sam would be very helpful," He ventured. "Are you aware of others who have been affected in this way, in yours or other organisations?"

"Was Sam working on anything particularly special or exceptional, which could have affected him?" Ross carried on regardless taking fully the opportunity to get all his issues out in the open.

"Did anything unusual happen prior to Sam becoming sick?"

Hua let out a sigh. "I fear you ask too much of us, but I will check and let you know as soon as I can. How long do you intend to stay here in Shanghai?"

"A few days at least or as long as it takes to get some answers for us to help Sam."

"I will try to get back to you before you leave," Hua tried not to commit himself to a time. He knew the work Sam was doing had some bearing on his condition. This was a personal matter and knew he could not supply the answers Mr Mansell required.

Hua already knew about Matt and Ellen and expected Ross to mention another name. Before telling Ross about the other person, he would first check this with his people and the consortium he worked with.

Hua watched as Ross left taking one of the glass lifts downward to the ground floor. He signalled to security below to escort him off the premises. Disturbingly, Ross had triggered thoughts in his mind and not welcome ones.

A project had come through several months before from Alcatel his parent company. A new piece of computer software provided to them allowed their business consortium of ten to link together all the services they offered via the internet. It meant they could each offer specialised areas without competition and overall agree the prices to be charged. This provided a seamless route for any organisation to access their ranges within the consortium to select best offer and price. It literally meant all ten offered similar services and prices but only one would be destined to supply the goods or services already agreed within the group.

Each member would then get its own core business work no matter what company or price the buyer chose. They had formed a trade cartel, where each could dictate what the bottom price of an offering would be. The consortium as a whole would be sharing the profits without any risk as they fixed the best deal price and then the right organisation in the cartel did the work. Hua had to be careful, not only is the cartel illegal, if Alcatel realised their subsidiaries were operating this way he would be finished.

The thought playing on Hua's mind was the software package they were using had originated from an Indian organisation who had failed to patent the product properly but was now holding them to ransom because of the trade cartel. He wasn't about to make this publicly known least of all to someone investigating the state of mind of one of their ex-employees. Samuel Thornton had altered the source code of the package supplied by the Indian company only then to patent and license worldwide as the cartels own software.

It is not possible for an Indian company to sue a Chinese one. There is no treaty in existence between the two countries, so despite threats from his counterparts in India, Hua and his company were selling the product to any groups of organisations that wanted to work trade and communicate together in private throughout China. His Shanghai Bell Corporation were laughing all the way to the bank. It was a money-spinner for Hua and his consortium colleagues. Alcatel never knew and that was his risk.

Hua was not about to take the blame for Thornton's condition, especially as it was happening to others. However, once Ross had left he could not help feeling the problems he had may have an Indian connection. He would have to look at damage limitation and reduce any connections he had very quickly.

When Ross left the building, conscious he had been politely ejected, despite explaining the position truthfully to the Chief Executive he was unlikely to get any information in return.

The short oriental middle-aged registrar greeted Susan in the Huadong Hospital's private wing of its smart busy reception area. Grace Tsai introduced herself by apologising for being dressed in green operational theatre scrubs, knowing Susan Brackden would understand being a doctor herself.

She introduced Susan to the receptionists who gave her a visitor's identity card. Grace ushered her into a small clinical nurses office filled with cabinets jammed full with notes and results of patients passing through this busy department. She offered Susan vending machine coffee.

Declining the coffee, Susan thanked Grace for seeing her and began to prompt her memory for any recollection of Sam she may have.

"Sam's is a strange case it was too easy to make a diagnosis. He had shown almost all the signs of Schizophrenia," she paused.

"Does it mean you disagreed with the findings?" she prompted.

"Considering it further, yes," Grace continued acknowledging the interruption. "Difficult though it is to believe, I would say it was controlled."

Grace went to a four drawer grey upright cabinet in the corner of the office and pulled a folder from the second drawer down. She opened the file in front of her on the desk and began casting her eyes over the contents as Susan spoke to her.

"You're saying controlled Schizophrenia?" Susan looked confusedly at Grace.

Grace sidestepped the question and began walking her through the many tests her team had run on Sam.

Grace raised her hand as she skimmed the papers stopping Susan from asking more, she needed to explain.

"The sickness in Sam manifested itself in several ways looking back it appears a show was being put on for our benefit."

Interrupting her Susan was horrified.

"Are you saying Sam was, is faking it? Only this is certainly not the way it looks to us."

"No, no, no! You must have realised Sam or at least his mind is being driven, being led by an outside force?" Grace was confirming both Susan's and Ferral's original thoughts.

"Sam is ill, but it is a forced mind trap being played out."

"Ferral Goldlay, the Medical Director at Ditton Manor and I had the same conviction, but we could not prove it and didn't really understand, nor do we know how to deal or cope with it and what it is doing to Sam himself," Susan admitted hoping Grace had some answers.

"What do you know of Ellen Kefford, how does she fit in here?" Susan asked shifting the emphasis away from Sam for the moment.

"She came to us purporting to be an inspector working for the US department of health. As I recall she kept asking about her deceased father Jack Kefford. He died here recently. She was also interested in Sam, because of confidentiality we wouldn't talk to her about him," Grace continued. "With Jack, we were at a loss to know why he'd suffered his heart attack."

"Do you still hold his body?" Susan considered re-evaluating the post mortem.

"Unfortunately the body has been returned to the US and the family. As his death was unusual, the family shrouded the findings in some secrecy.

"Susan, I cannot talk to you about it either," Grace stated apologetically.

"Did you explain the circumstances of Jack Kefford's death to Ellen?

"We never got the chance. By the time, we had collated the facts for her she began to act strangely. Within a week, Ellen began accusing us of a cover up, naturally people willing to help her at the start began to back off. Doors started to close towards her," Grace shrugged dismissively.

"What you're saying is she may have gotten near the truth about Jack or Sam and was stopped by her own enforced illness," Susan suggested gravely. "I just don't understand the link between her father and how she knew Sam."

"I gather Ellen had found Sam's name and details when she was going through her father's papers, shortly after his death," Grace recalled. "It appeared on one of the last neurological cases Jack had been asked for an opinion on, appearing on a scribbled note as if he had taken a phone call."

"Is it likely it was to do with a case Kefford was working with?"

"It seems unlikely, but there did seem some connection between them, though I couldn't tell what it was," offered Grace. "Jack Kefford was known to us, our clinical director and I regularly consulted the Harvard medical school man where he was a professor, whenever we had problematical neurological issue we needed help in solving. It was during a consultative visit Jack was literally struck down and subsequently died," Grace looked tired and felt drained the professor had been a friend. The day was taking its toll. "Sam had visited Jack a couple of times, in fact, within the last two hours before his death."

"Ellen came out here on the spur of the moment to talk to Sam, only to find out about his illness and decided to use her position in the US health department to get some answers," suggested Susan. "She must have had a shock when she found out about him."

"You're right," accepted Grace. "You know the rest she's ended up with you!"

Apologising for constantly asking questions, Susan pressed her. "Tell me what you can of Matt."

Susan followed Grace to the vending machine for more coffee, the main reason why Grace was still awake, twenty-five straight hours on duty taking its toll.

"Matt came to us through Alcatel the largest communications group here in Shanghai, he too displayed similar symptoms to Sam," Grace responded. "Trouble really came with Matt. He is such a prominent well-known business man a key figure in our local trade consortium.

"What happened to him?" asked Susan recognising Grace's tiredness, accepting she would have to cut short her questions until another day.

"Matt had collapsed during a visit to the Shanghai Bell organisation. This was the company who only two weeks before sent Sam to us for treatment," Grace paused for effect. "You've no idea the widespread panic Matt's illness caused across the companies he's been dealing with, nine or ten of the most powerful in Shanghai if not China itself, not least because of who he was, but the confidentiality demanded by the varying businesses!"

"A word of warning, Susan, please be careful, something's not right," Grace offered. "No-one wants to part with any information, which is unusual and certainly suspicious to the point of dangerous.

Susan saw Grace physically shudder at what she saw as a rising epidemic. "You think there's a pattern emerging?"

"Oh yes, certainly," confirmed Grace. "Sam no, Ellen maybe, with Matt definitely! I was given no choice but to move them on to England as quickly as possible, for their own sakes if nothing else."

"Why do you think?" asked Susan.

"To avoid embarrassment mainly, Matt's profile being very high could not be linked specifically to the other two. There would be investigations and no one here wanted that," Grace suggested.

As the pressure on Grace's time ended their brief meeting, the weary doctor embraced Susan. A common enemy to be faced they bonded leaving each other as friends. Susan hoped to see Grace again before she left China for home.

It was quite late in the evening by the time Ross and Susan were able to swap notes on each other's day. The dining room where they sat was an informal affair, the choice of whether to have a waiter constantly attending to them or deciding their own courses by buffet style arrangement. Opting for the later, they huddled together like partners in crime plotting their next escapade.

Their first course passed in silence, each at last, happy to relax in one another's company appreciating the closeness lost during the long day. Susan eagerly listened as Ross described his day meeting with Hudong Hua at the Shanghai Bell. The Chinese introduced by surname first as is their custom and so Hua is the Christian name. Ross explained he had been very open with him but left feeling Hua was keeping something from him, and regretted his own honesty.

It was Ross's turn to listen to Susan talk about her time at Pudong's, Huadong Hospital and her meeting with Grace Tsai, the medical registrar, she went through the worries they shared and told him of Jack Kefford Ellen's father.

Susan explained how Ellen had forced herself upon the hospital claiming to be a health inspector and how she gradually become a victim. Grace feared the worst and was prepared to help all she could.

As they, each considered the others day Ross started to plan what they should do next.

"Tomorrow our enquiries need to be stronger, now we have introduced ourselves. We can turn up unannounced and hopefully catch people off their guard," Ross suggested firmly.

"I agree Ross, but frankly I'm at a loss to know what to do or ask," Susan worried. "Brick walls come to mind I don't want to create the same barriers Ellen had."

"Nonsense!" admonished Ross. "Let's consider what we need to know and share the tasks."

Susan felt Ross could be strong in will, but had not seen it of him until now.

Ross continued. "I need to talk to the people Sam worked with, his expertise is writing software program source code. I have to find out who is doing the same. We have to understand how he was thinking and what exactly he was working on."

"You believe his work could have some bearing on his illness?"

"It's likely it will lead us to what they're trying to hide from us," his mind racing as if trying to get his thoughts aired in case he forgot them.

"Call Ferral and ask him to check Ellen's status with the US Health department," Ross continued. "Let's get him to look closely at Jack Kefford's death as well and to try to find a link with Sam somehow."

Picking up his flow Susan offered. "Both Jack and Ellen had obviously gotten onto the right track, so we need to find and follow their path. I will talk to anyone I can at the hospital to see how Sam and Matt were when first admitted," with more enthusiasm, she suggested. "We need to find those who knew Ellen. If she told them what she was doing there."

"Yes, but be careful, I suspect she had to have spoken to the wrong person," Susan felt his protective instinct wash over her.

"Penny should have some more information by now on the names I gave her, somehow, we need to get hold of Matt's papers to see what he was working on, there must be a clue in those," he considered.

"I'm sure when Matt came to us there were two full boxes of papers, I could get Ferral to send us copies although I recall they were in very large boxes and both were quite full," Susan remembered.

"No, let's not wait ask Ferral if he personally could go through them. It may be of help to us," Ross determined what else they could do.

"As you're going back to the hospital I need to get back to the Shanghai Bell as it's also a key place, we must get more from them because I'm not convinced the guy at the Shanghai Bell will be forthcoming with information even if he bothers to get back to me. He is heavily involved, I am sure of it," he pondered.

It was three in the morning China time when Ferral called Susan, another victim had been found at a different Chinese company and been referred to them by Connectiqua. Vijay Ahuja a specialist in systems security was apparently in Huadong Hospital awaiting his transportation to England.

Barely awake Susan yawned trying getting her mind clear from the deep sleep she had been in. "Why England, his name sounds Indian to me."

"Your right Susan, he is Indian but lives in England. More to the point he is one of the contractors on the list of nine that have been sent out there by Connectiqua," Ferral wondered how his fellow doctor and friend had been holding up.

"I'm fine Ferral, don't be soft, Ross is taking good care of me," Susan felt touched by his concern. "I'll get Ross to check with Penny about Vijay apparently there were three she couldn't get in touch with, he could be one of those," she said. "By the way do you know what the time is?"

"Of course, just gone seven, it's a nice pleasant sunlit evening. What's it like where you are" She heard him smiling.

"It's cold, dark, three a.m. and I was asleep, goodnight Ferral." She hung up the phone on him. She heard him laugh as she did so.

At breakfast, a tired Susan told Ross of Ferral's call and about the new patient admitted to the Huadong Hospital from the Shenzhen Seg Company, here in Shanghai.

Ross went over their plans again. "Now you have legitimate questions for going to the hospital," he considered, he guessed this is what Hua did not tell him!

Penny had checked with all three embassies finding all nine people on Ross's list checked out with visas, medical certificates and work permits. She confirmed the organisations they each currently worked for in China.

The embassies had been helpful and she had obtained the addresses of where each were staying in China. Of more concern to Penny, she had not been able to contact three of the nine names. With Samuel Thornton's name on the list, it left eight she was able to contact five of them who were working quite happily.

In each of the other three cases, they were simply too busy or not in the office, she found herself being interrogated over the telephone. Who was she to ask? Who was it she worked for and why did she need to speak to them and what information would she expect to gain?

Each company suggested they would pass on a message for the person to contact her. She knew this would never happen. All three were working on confidential matters for the company concerned and they could not be disturbed without an official request from his contract company.

Ross told Penny about Vijay Ahuja referred to the clinic in England he had been one of the three she could not contact. Ross stressed to her she must continue to try to find out about the other two contractors on the list. So far, seven of the nine accounted for. Penny had done well it meant four people were affected and possibly six. It was time he, Ferral, Susan and Tisha got together again quickly to share information.

"Penny, try and find out what Vijay was working on," Ross had telephoned her again. He had forgotten his China time midday was four a.m. her time. Apologising as she reminded him he continued. "Tell them, you know about his situation as you are working for Connectiqua. Quote Anna Jacobs, she would have set up the contract if they want to check on you."

"She's aware we work together, so they may feel more inclined to help us," Ross sighed. "Keep digging Penny you're doing great this is getting to be an epidemic and we are no closer to finding the cause. Time is running out."

"Do you want me there with you?" she offered aware of his growing feelings for Susan. "It's difficult prising information from people who don't know you, especially the Chinese with their customs and a healthy mistrust of anyone western."

"No, at a distance is safer, I want you to find out details from Connectiqua for lengths of contracts, when started and how long each person has been living in China," something was nagging at Ross. He had to wait, his instinct never wrong.

"I'm looking for common threads, what they've been working on, does it cross over, will it affect each other, anything to give us a lead," Ross had been aware of Penny's crush on him for some time and felt he had been drawing closer in friendship to her. Meeting Susan had changed him. Penny was firmly a colleague and friend, Susan was more, much more.

It was the second evening in Pudong. Ross waited for Susan to arrive for dinner in the hotel restaurant. She was late he thought, checking his watch. It gave him some time to reflect on his day.

Ross had been determined to talk to someone who knew Sam so he went back to the Shanghai Bell Company. The dark glass panelled building presented a barrier of security to him as he walked through the automatic sliding doors. Bag checking, metal detection was normal. He bluffed his way inside, past security, so he could speak to the reception staff. He said Hudong Hua had given him a name in the computer department to talk to about Samuel Thornton who had previously worked there. Apologising, he explained his mistake by not writing down the person's name, but he must speak to him today.

Sheepishly, Ross said he felt too embarrassed to ask Mr Hudong, could they help? He was sure he would recognise the person's name, if he saw a list. The staff, feeling sorry for him were helpful and busy. They handed him a departmental telephone list to look through, not wishing to become involved too much. As he browsed the list, he spotted Sam's name still there.

'Samuel Thornton, IT Systems Programmer, Extension 8546 was listed under Information Technology, the company's Computer Department.'

Just underneath Sam's name, a Bei Aolun is listed as a programmer with the same extension number. Ross was betting they had worked together. Asking the reception staff if he could call the person as he recognised a name, they pointed to a silver telephone booth he could use just off the reception area.

By dropping the Chief Executive's name into any request, he gained the required response and a meeting arranged for Aolun's lunchtime break.

With an hour to wait until his lunchtime meeting he sat in the recreational park just opposite the Shanghai Bell building. The small man-made lake gave the lunchtime sandwich eaters a place and watch the parade of bird life feed off the guilt of those with more food than them.

Ross had no wish to draw attention to himself as he sat reflecting on his brief sight of the organisations telephone listings. His instinct working overtime again, he had seen something that did not quite add up. What is it? This was the second time this happened. He had to get himself a copy of the telephone list.

"Ross Mansell?" A voice questioned behind him. Ross turned to face a fresh faced youth who was sweating nervously, despite the cool morning breeze offered up by the lake.

The young Chinese man carefully scrutinised the naturally taller westerner as both stood, so each could go through the ritualistic custom of the meeting of east with west, one bowing, the other shaking hands.

Bei Aolun seemed uncomfortable he had not told anyone he was meeting this man, who had said the Chief Executive wanted him to speak with. Cynically, he doubted Hudong Hua even knew him or if he existed. What was important is the mention of help he could give to Samuel Thornton. Sam had been his friend and had taught him how to write software code in just a few short weeks. Any mention of his friend's name since his illness strictly forbidden within the company, and no word as to how or where he was. If he could find out how Sam is and help him, he would be pleased.

"How may I help you, Sir?" Aolun deferred to the older man. "Will you speak of Sam, he's a good friend, he had, of late, been acting very strange."

Ross restricted information to the facts he felt would be commonly known. Nor did he link Sam's problems to others. Ross was wary of trusting anyone from the Shanghai Bell Company.

Aolun wanted to trust this man even though he knew he was not going to get the full story. Never mind he told himself, he did not need or want to get too involved. He could lose his job and he had a family to support, those who relied on him. He believed Mansell was looking after Sam's interests.

Aolun spoke of their time together, Sam had visited his family, had taught Aolun many things about the western world. How to program and develop systems and in particular, about western culture.

"Tell me what you were both working on Aolun?" queried Ross, measuring the friendship with Sam.

"We had been given a software package to break its coding for the source."

"What does that mean it sounds technical?" Ross was confused.

"Most software is locked so the patent is protected. It means no one is able to change or correct it. A program is written in code called the source," advised Aolun.

"You're saying, you and Sam were asked to change someone else's source code of a program?"

Bei Aolun nodded.

"Isn't that illegal?" Ross ventured.

"We do as we are told. We were given a software program and asked if we could hack into the source and change it sufficiently to make it work exactly the same and to make it unrecognisable, if we were challenged as to the ownership," admitted Aolun. "It is called in Information Technology as reverse engineering."

"Sam was a part of this?" Ross would not believe it of his friend.

"At first, he did not realise what he was doing. It was why I worked closely with him for the company."

"So you knew?"

"I have a family to support. If it help's, by the time Sam found out the true reason for altering the code he wanted to stop, but then he became ill," offered Aolun.

"What's the true reason?" pressed Ross.

"Shanghai Bell wanted to free itself of the tie to the Indian company and in particular the writer of the software. That's all I know," he stressed. "I do not know if this was in some way the cause of Sam's illness."

Ross kept his thoughts to himself. As he continued to question Bei Aolun, he began to understand what Sam had been involved in, the young man before him seemed unaware of what could be wrong, but listening to him, Ross believed he had found the first link between the patients, particularly Matt and Sam.

Ross decided when he discussed his day with Susan he would leave much unsaid, believing his information would be better shared with the whole group.

Aolun relieved to have spoken to Ross about his friend but immediately he returned to his office the head of security called on him. Aolun's family would be the poorer for Ross's visit.

Ross looked again at his watch, concerned Susan had still not arrived back.

The taxi had picked Susan up from outside the station's Pudong hotel as expected in the morning to take her to Huadong hospital. It smelt inside of stale tobacco. She had positioned herself on the charcoal coloured rear seat, trying to avoid the floor trash of fast food burger packaging. The drivers grime ridden, part toothless grin, served to make her retch. She considered getting out from the cab but the man drove off at speed immediately she entered.

She fumbled for the right amount of money as he drove erratically through the busy city streets, narrowly avoiding an accident at every turn.

Taxi drivers here she knew, liked the fare paid with RMB10 bills. Anything larger they tended to refuse, as they do not want to change the money at the banks. Susan didn't want confrontation. With the fare of 35 Yuan ready in her hand as they turned into the hospital grounds.

Susan strangely felt very, very tired as they pulled up in a free parking space a short walk from the entrance.

She closed her eyes for a brief moment.

Immediately as Susan passed through the automated entrance doors of the hospital she had the impression her arrival had been expected. Met by a tall thin Asian man, who introduced himself to her as the hospital's Clinical Director. His stare fixed above her causing a shiver to pass through her. She noted a similar smell as in the taxi surrounding him like body odour. Odd, she thought, the reception staff never acknowledged her and they had been so friendly when Grace had introduced her to them as they walked past only yesterday.

She assumed they had expected her to return, following Vijay's admittance and his referral to Ferral's clinic in Ditton Manor. She pushed aside the thought of how they could have known and the strangeness of the staff to her.

Sanjay Hammad led the way to where he said Vijay was. Susan was aware she seemed to be walking in a tunnel, the bowed walls arched above her. A decaying tiled surface, bare bulb lights swung from their cords creating shadows in their wake. She touched the tiled walls feeling sick in order to steady herself, they were tacky with rubbish lining the walkways, uneasy and now afraid, she found herself walking faster and faster, never quite catching up to the giant of a man in front. Turning, he produced a wide grin, his breath smelt and she noticed the gaps within the decaying brown teeth, his eyes still fixed and cold, made her shiver once more.

He opened a door to a ward with six beds, hit with a nauseating stench that filled her nostrils causing her to retch, five beds she noticed were empty and made ready for patients. Walking to the far corner of this grey, badly lit room, she became conscious of her feet dragging they felt like lead sticking to the floor as she was guided slowly to the patient writhing in the last steel bed in the room. In front of her, the giant now at the side of the bed ushered her to come forward. As she drew closer toward the bed, she noted the four leather straps holding the patient down tightly the body writhing trying to break free, buckles taking the strain down the centre of the body.

Feeling the pressure of hands on her shoulders, she shuddered seeing no-one. The director was standing on the opposite side of the bed. The weight becoming unbearable, manoeuvred to face the person in the bed trying to stop the pressure bearing down on her the weight becoming progressively worse. There was no one behind her, no one forcing her, yet the pressure intense.

She believed this had to be Vijay Ahuja. The grip on her shoulders grew firmer the pressure beginning to tear into her shoulders she could feel her muscles splitting under the weight. It forced her to look at the writhing patient clearly for the first time. Blood was trickling from his ears and nose. His eyes bulging in terror fighting violently against the restriction of the straps holding him. She screamed violently as recognition dawned.

She turned and ran through the doorway the shoulder pressure instantly released. Into the hall tunnel it stretched far as she could see, she kept running. The tunnel began closing in, suffocating her, getting smaller and smaller drawing the very breath from her, feet sticking to the ground. Struggling she still kept running until finally she collapsed, images of the bed ridden, blood harnessed patient, invading her thoughts, the stench still with her.

Ross refused the waiter's offer of food and drinks for what must have been the fourth time and decided, he needed to find Susan he was worried. At the hotel's reception desk, he called her room getting no response. He waited for the lift, intending to check her room. The receptionist at the front desk beckoned a call for him.

"Susan, where are you," Ross spoke immediately he picked up the white telephone from its cradle.

"Is that Ross Mansell? this is Grace Tsai at the Hudong hospital, you had better come now, it is about Dr Susan Brackden," Grace left the words hanging in mid-air as Ross, without questioning dropped the telephone and rushed out of the door of the hotel to a waiting taxi.

Grace met Ross as soon as he arrived at the hospital's reception. He tried to keep calm as she explained Susan was found screaming in the back of the taxi which had brought her to the hospital, the driver had only left her for a couple of minutes while he checked if he could park in the space he'd pulled up in.

"She's had some sort of breakdown, I've given her a sedative and she's calmer now but will not stop sobbing," Grace could not understand what had happened, Susan wouldn't speak to her at all.

The clean faced smart young cab driver met Ross and took him out of the hospital to his pristine taxi to explain how he found his fare behaving after leaving her for a few minutes.

Paying and tipping the young man, Ross thanked him and went in search of Susan.

Ross entered the private room where Susan looked at him in horror from her hospital bed, her instinct to shy away from him. Words did not soothe her he moved nearer taking her blocking hands raised at him pulling her closer toward him and holding her gently in his arms.

Struggling, she was edgy, in his embrace, touching him, holding his head in her hands, almost stroking him disbelieving.

"Hello, my angel, my heart is with you, relax I'm here by your side," Ross spoke softly, only to invoke more tears. "Tell me if you can what happened to you," Susan shook her head not wanting to remember.

"Susan, tell me as much as you want to," Ross said gently, she shook her head in defiance not wanting the experience to return.

When Grace joined them Susan felt safer and told of how she initially stood in reception and been met by the Clinical Director Sanjay Hammad. She assumed he was taking her to see Vijay Ahuja, the latest victim and one of the 9 contractors on Penny's list. All the time she was speaking, she kept touching Ross refusing to believe it was really him. Continuing, she spoke of the staff's coldness toward her when she arrived and how she followed the Director down a long arched corridor like a tunnel to a ward. Suddenly began to shake the ordeal getting the better of her, she stopped speaking. She waved her hands in front of her face, flatly refusing to talk anymore. Her mind had been invaded she knew it and wondered if the patients back at Ditton Manor had been through a similar trauma, at least she had come out the other side.

"Let me tell you, we have a problem with your story Susan," Grace looked at Ross for support as she went on. "Our Clinical Director is a Japanese woman called Nahoko Koriyama and the reception staff say they never saw you at all this morning," Susan was shaking her head from side to side in disbelief. We have no tunnels as you call them but normal corridors and you couldn't have seen Vijay he, with two of our medical staff, were boarding an Air France flight as you arrived at the hospital," Ross felt Susan grip his hand tightly as Grace continued. "Furthermore, the taxi driver said you didn't get out of the cab because you hadn't yet paid him."

Susan groaned. "It's not true, not true," she exclaimed.

Grace looked directly at Susan and pointed to the top drawer of her bedside cabinet. "Look in there Susan, please."

Looking in the drawer, she reached and picked up what looked like a paper ball. Susan realised exactly what it was and what it meant.

Ross was confused and turned to Grace for the answer.

"As Susan knows, it's 35 Yuan. She was still clutching the taxi fare when she was found in the back of the cab."

"Get me the driver he can explain," she begged.

Ross went off to find the driver who luckily hadn't left the hospital favouring coffee before continuing his next shift.

Susan shook her head in disbelief when Ross stood with the driver in front of her in the room.

"No, no that's not him," the young man shrugged and left not wishing for any involvement with a mad woman.

Both Grace and Ross left Susan with a nurse tending to her as she started to cry again. "Is she able to travel Grace?" Ross asked the registrar who nodded.

"Then it's time we went home," Ross acknowledged.

Chapter 6

Ferral looked at the two boxes, both the size of tea chests he was daunted by the prospect of opening them. The boxes, numbered one and two, were brimming with files, papers and photographs.

He'd determined the best way to piece together Matt's time in China prior to him arriving at Ditton Manor, was to take all his papers whether in files or not and put them in date order. He was careful to photocopy them, in case, the way Matt had filed them had any relevance. He didn't believe it significant but was not going to take any chances.

A date order pattern was emerging, diary notes of people he was supposed to meet and agenda's for meetings. He recognised names of individuals and organisations listing Chief Officers and Alcatel's subsidiaries in the region of Shanghai, ten companies in all.

The papers, bound in manilla files, each assigned an alphabetic letter. Within each package or group of files, a specific organisation identified. The location, the type of organisation, the service or goods supplied, the people running the business with each person listed having an attached profile. Each package also had a listing of whether individuals or organisation was in favour of the proposals being put forward by Matt on his hotel projects for the region and a reporting sheet for forwarding to the main board at Alcatel with an attachment on costs and likely financial involvement. There were pictures of the proposed sites and people who were involved.

Ferral was impressed, Matt was clearly very thorough and organised. He soon realised the papers needed a trained business eye and felt Ross should also take a closer look at them.

The alphabetic order of the papers puzzled him, the key being there was no order just a letter at the start of each bundle. He listed all the letters in the order of the removal from the boxes. The papers in box two followed the same letter pattern of the first.

Half of the box contained Matt's personal effects presumably placed on top by the hospital staff.

Newspaper cuttings, photographs he presumed were family, an address book, wallet with money, credit and business cards. A gold watch, a signet ring and an engraved gold pen completed the find. His clothes, Ferral remembered sent in a green hospital disposable plastic bag.

He repacked the boxes carefully retaining the order and placed the photocopies in a file ready for when the group met again.

His thoughts returned to Susan. He'd been alarmed by the telephone call received from Ross yesterday evening. He was bringing Susan home following an incident at the hospital in Pudong. Ross, briefly outlining what had happened, he felt it could be a warning for them to back off from their investigations.

It was better to make sure Susan was OK and to bring the group together immediately to decide the next move. Ferral did not expect them to arrive until early morning the following day.

Meanwhile, he spoke to Tisha she wanted him to meet a friend of hers who may be able to help them. God knows we need it, Ferral thought.

By the time the group got together two weeks had passed, with each day raising concerns about the patient's welfare. During this time, Vijay Ahuja had arrived at the clinic weighted down by his own mental torment. He appeared to be suffering the same fate as Sam, Matt and Ellen.

Shortly after Vijay's arrival, Susan returned with her own demons to deal with. Ferral noted thankfully, it did not appear she had suffered the same fate as the others.

During the last two weeks, David Bareham had spent many hours working with the patients and staying at the Manor. Introduced to Ferral by Tisha and had been so impressed even after a brief meeting with him he asked David to start working with the patients immediately.

Each patient is given a basic room within the clinic section of the manor, devoid of luxuries with only a bed, bedside cabinet, chair and table, these surrounded by white walls dominated by a single locked nine paned window looking out to the rear of the park across the woodlands. The bare light bulbs hanging down from the ceiling gave the impression of a cell rather than a patient's room. The rooms distinguishing themselves from a prison cell only by the quality of their furnishings and view of the outside grounds.

Of the five, Susan was the one able to communicate properly and David began talking to her as soon as she arrived back. She slowly went through her ordeal in Pudong. She kept wringing her hands nervously and wiping her sweating brow with tissues placed in front of her on the table. David held her hands. She felt awkward at his touch, not meeting his eyes. He asked gently, if she would close her own.

She became conscious of him walking through her mind, him talking quietly and moving through her perceptions and the situations, she had encountered in China. He realised some of her perceptions did not happen to her in reality, but unfortunately were lodged firmly in her unconscious. He learnt through exploring her fragile mind what did happen and what she thought she had to hide from him, for fear it could be true.

David became very concerned at the silent force presenting itself with her. He stood beside her at the hospital bed of the writhing patient. He felt her rise of fear again, as he took in the facial expression of the doctor. He had to step back and immediately and remove both of them from the bedside he was shocked he knew the Clinical Director. He backed away from this area of her recall quickly as he could.

Gradually across the next few days, he set about changing her view of events, knowing the final correction had to come when the group would meet.

With Vijay, he came against a solid wall. Physically a weak man, slight in actual build, a tall man of thirty. He tended to lean to his left side, a humbling stature. His eyes darted up, down and sideways with uncontrollable panic present within. David held his moist sweat filled palms and realised, mentally a barrier existed which he found very difficult to penetrate.

The psychic defence put up by Vijay was so strong and completely at odds with his outward physique. David suspected Vijay was, somehow controlled by a powerful force, it could not live in the physical or the spirit world at the same time. Suspecting he was being ruled by a dead being. He needed time to consider how he could move forward with Vijay, and suspected here was the key to unlocking the minds of all the five.

He noted the same unease creep through him, drowning him. He shuddered and shrugged off the feeling immediately. This was happening too many times now. Fear designed to stop him interfering. He would press on despite beginning to feel it would not be long before the force turns on him.

He turned his attention to Sam as his next patient. David believed he had to halt his deterioration quickly, so decided to take a different approach. Like the other's he began by holding Sam's hands, attacking his mind with such a force through any barrier that existed and quickly realised it was too easy, whatever had gripped Sam's mind had relaxed or was just dormant. He'd made good progress searching for Sam's special place. He quickly realised it had been almost purposely destroyed.

Great torrents of deep grey clouds hung over an alpine setting, high above a Tyrolean village, set near Innsbruck in Austria. Raging like a hurricane with barely an outline left of this idyllic creation within Sam's mind. He reconstructed Sam's mental state, areas, doors and pathways, opened or closed like a jigsaw according to the pain the individual stress point was causing. Unusually, he felt there were barriers at each step of the way, these were weak and not been nurtured for quite a while. They had been left to push the mind into a drift downwards, with the effect left untreated, damaging. Although slow, the decline would be continual and eventually be a complete and final shutdown of the mind. Death would occur naturally beyond.

David considered why the strength of the psychic barrier could be so different in Sam as opposed to Vijay. It had to be something more than Vijay being the most recent casualty. He realised he was making a judgement on physical rules, rather than the limit of the dead to inflict immense pain.

Stripping away each layer from Sam's mind, he created areas of stress and calm weighting each evenly and gradually moving the stress out of his mind. He continually referred to Sam's private place and noted at each stage more and more could be seen the storm itself subsiding. David knew any special place cannot be destroyed the memory is the hook to survival while the person is alive in the physical world.

Once dead, the soul has this as its root and if it is weakened the soul can be caught in another's path for their use and not as an improved being for future reincarnated birth.

He worked tirelessly night and day with Sam, knowing, he had to bring him mentally back a long, long way.

Building powerful dreams of good, happy, joyous times, revisiting friendships. Gently lifting the dark clouds, the sorrow of life defeated, by giving the path of light shining in the distance. Sam needed something for his soul to reach out to. He felt his mental strength growing with each day he spent with him. He knew Sam better than he knew himself and realised the importance of both Tisha and Ross in his life.

In Ellen's case, significantly, there is one major stress factor bringing its own barrier in her mind. The ultimate fear, she could be responsible for one of her parent's death. It had closed her mind to all her father held captive in a prison. This being all the information his trawling through her mind will allow, the shutters were up and her stress levels extreme. He needed to know more of her before he continued.

He also decided not to get involved with Matt, from what Ferral had told him, he was quite a complex character and it was best he concentrated on the quick wins he could gain with the others.

David hoped the group meeting would shed some light on both Matt and Ellen, particularly, on the way they think.

Ferral arranged for a lunchtime buffet in the drawing room where the three imposing windows overlooked the park. Expectantly, he stood looking out onto the manor grounds willing his guests to arrive, only David meanwhile had been staying at the manor during the past two weeks, Susan herself becoming a patient. His wait was for Tisha and Ross bringing his colleague Penny who had been doing some research for him.

Tisha was the first to arrive by black taxi from the local station. She gave Ferral a greeting hug and kiss as he met her on the driveway, paying off the cab she promptly enquired where David was.

"He will join us shortly Tisha," gesturing towards the windows of the drawing room, he said. "Why don't you wait in there and I'll bring the others in presently."

As she entered the manor, Ferral turned toward the smooth engine tones of the Panhard gliding up the drive, the gravel, sounding all the richer for its arrival.

Ferral greeted Ross like a long lost son and turned to the ravishing blonde standing beside him. It had to be Penny who made his heart skip a beat, she was stunningly pretty. When she spoke her Australian accent soothed his very soul, he was smitten immediately. Stuttering he ushered them both toward the drawing room as quickly as possible, to avoid embarrassing himself. He noted the wry smile on Ross's face. He excused himself leaving them to find David. Muttering as he walked down the hallway. "God, she's beautiful."

"Hi Tisha." Ross greeted her. "This is Penny, she's found out some stuff, so I suggested she join the group today."

Penny smiled and Tisha patting the red leather sofa welcomed her to sit beside her.

Ross noted there were three red sofas instead of two as before, shaped in the style of a horseshoe with the open end offered to the fire burning a gentle glow, he suspected Ferral had lost one from his office. Ferral entered the room apologising for leaving them alone, he walked to the long table that stretched the length behind one of the sofa's, it was waiting to receive the lunchtime buffet.

Tisha facing Ross heard behind her the sound of the drawing room door, its hinges yawning as it opened gently. She saw his jaw drop in surprise turning excitedly she rose to her feet and ran to the doorway followed swiftly by Ross.

Each took an arm of Susan's and helped this willowy shadow with dishevelled hair and sunken eyes. Softly, Susan smiled into Ross's eyes and gripped his arm so tightly as if she could not believe it. Almost fainting, she dropped onto Tisha's arm for support who led her to the sofa directly facing the fire.

Susan quietly spoke to both of them catching her breath by doing so. Ross just surrounded her in protection, as if she would break without him. Amazed to see her so improved and talking, she quietly kept stroking Ross staring at him lovingly, not letting him move an inch from her.

David watched Susan, her mind registering closure of her anguished thoughts he noted, screaming Ross is alive. Written across her face, she sneaked a glance at him and nodded in thanks, her eyes tearfully, glistening with joy, her ordeal rapidly coming to close.

Tisha broke the spell of endearment and praised David shouting. "What a clever man you are, I love you so much."

Ross turned toward David grabbing his hand and shaking it fiercely, thanking him profusely for helping Susan.

David shook himself in embarrassment and made light of the praise. He held out his hand to greet the most beautiful exquisite woman he had ever seen. Penny who had been sitting there quietly watching this all unfold, stood to his greeting. As he held her hand, a moment briefly flashed between them. She felt herself blushing at the tingle the contact gave her. Their eyes searched for the depth in each other.

Stunning he thought to himself. He did not recognise the feelings building inside him. Feeling awkward like a young schoolchild would, he too blushed.

Penny confident enough to know how men viewed her felt different, strange. It was impossible she thought, reluctantly, she let go of his hand.

After the initial euphoria and introductions, they settled down with their drinks to discuss what had happened during the last few weeks. Ferral enjoyed seeing the group together.

For the benefit of David and Penny, He went over what had happened so far starting with Sam and the connection with Connectiqua, the Chinese angle and the need for Ross and Susan to go to Pudong.

Ross picked up the story, highlighting his meeting with Hudong Hua. He had not gained much information. He told of his discussions with Sam's work colleague Bei Aolun, who had been afraid to talk and did so only out of the friendship he felt toward Sam.

Ross determined to get the phone listings, which he had a brief sight. He called back for Aolun the second time and was told he no longer worked for the organisation. At the time, concerned by what he saw on the listing rather than not getting in touch with Aolun. He still could not remember what it was.

Caught up in Susan's problems, Grace Tsai had contacted him. Ross felt Susan grip him tightly. He led the conversation toward her so she could tell her story to the group.

Susan looked for confirmation from David before she started speaking. She explained her travel to the hospital and the twist it took when she had arrived, her horror at seeing the patient who she expected to be Vijay Ahuja. Quietly she explained the sight she saw and the blood seeping from the patient, clearly in so much pain and wishing to die. She closed her eyes at the remembered sight of blood oozing from the eyes, nose and ears of the once handsome face.

She noticed a tattoo on his right arm above the elbow an unusual landscape of a family home perched on a hillside with children playing. She drew breadth and stiffened, explaining what she saw as she looked at the patients face.

Her eyes fixed steadily on David, noticeable by the entire group, because of the rigidity she displayed and strength of purpose she seemed to be mustering.

"It was Ross!" she exclaimed, her voice stammering. "It was my dear, dear Ross," she swiftly turned and strengthened her grip on him, smothering him as he sat beside her. She still did not understand, but she trusted David, when he had told her to have faith that it had not been him.

In her heart, she felt he was right as Ross had brought her home, but the moment she spent any time alone or asleep, the images of the hospital bed and the occupant came flooding back. Each time serving to convince her, Ross was in terrible pain or dying.

David broke the silence that had fallen amongst them. "Your journey is over now Susan. Your lives will go forward together," he reassured her. Mouthing words of thanks, she settled down in Ross's enveloping arms of comfort.

The buffet's arrival broke into the intensity of the moment they were all sharing, each chatted as if this had been a business lunch and filled their plates from the platters of sandwiches presented before them. Ross excused himself to make a phone call, much to the dismay of Susan. Penny promptly took his place beside her. She could now see how much they meant to each other.

Penny explained who she was and what she had been doing for Ross, while he was in China. She had traced the Connectiqua contractors working there and attempted to find some link to Matt and Ellen. Of the nine contractors, five were ok and were working fine one was Sam which made six.

This left three. One turned out to be Vijay and two were missing.

"Nothing sinister there either," Penny offered. "I couldn't get hold of them because they had both gone home, fed up with their jobs, although the organisations they are with were somewhat reluctant to tell me that!"

"The only connections I could find, Sam somehow knew Jack Kefford, Ellen's father. One other interesting fact, although Vijay is a Connectiqua contractor, he was the only one of the nine that had not actually started any work. The gap between him being sent out to China and turning up at the hospital is just over a month. Anna Jacobs at Connectiqua has received the normal signed contractors timesheets, but according to the Shenzen Seg Company, the organisation he went to work for, say he hadn't turned up at all," Penny raised her eyebrows in obvious frustration at this result. "I cannot tell you what he's been doing and I have no address for him either."

"Who signed his timesheet for Connectiqua? Enquired Ferral.

"Illegible unfortunately," she responded.

The session was taking its toll and they agreed to have a break, a walk around the courtyard or even the park itself.

Penny determined, rose and positioned herself by the side of David. Tisha joined them as they made their way out to the manor's grounds and took David's arm naturally.

Ross and Susan stayed together sitting in the central courtyard, while Ferral went off to check on his patients. Tisha and Penny walked with David outside the manor on the gravel path that circled the building, where once, a century ago, had been the moat. The air had a chill to it on this bright sunny day. Taking her lead from Tisha, Penny also entwined her arm in David's giving him, as he expressed two fine looking roses adorning his thorn bush frame. Like young girls, they both giggled at the charm of this grey haired man in his early fifties, who had not yet lost the twinkle of youth when confronted by the female sex.

With ease, they strolled discussing Penny's homeland of Australia and the developing closeness unfolding within the group marred only by the concerns for the patients. Like Tisha, the more Penny talked to David, the more in awe of him she became. She began wondering what type of private life this charming man had, resolving to finding out. Oblivious, David enjoyed their company and greeted the way back to the drawing room with some sadness.

Ferral had brought before them two large boxes with several files. He identified them as Matts, stating that he had been through them all as finely as he could.

He had photographed all the papers as he came to them, believing, they may have been in some sort of order, however, if there was a key, he could not find it. The order alphabetically spelt out SETNADEWANG and did not make sense at all.

"I've been overwhelmed by the business content of the papers," Ferral frowned. "I don't profess to understand half of it. Will you help me Ross?"

"Better than that, both Penny and I'll go through them together and see what we can find, have you any thoughts on what you have read or seen?" Ross asked expectantly.

Delicately, Ferral offered. "Not being an experienced businessman I may well have gotten this wrong, but feel I've been looking at an established Chinese trade cartel. So many links to ten businesses, each offering the same in terms of products, but only one is capable of specialising in each of the products offered."

"We'll dig deeper into the paperwork as it could be our problems links to protecting business interests.

"By the way," Ross spoke solemnly. "I learnt during our break, the person I'd spoken to at the Shanghai Bell Company, the one who'd been Sam's colleague, has been involved in a fatal car accident," he sighed deeply. "I feel I may have been the cause," Looking at the group, he said. "From what Ferral has said about the Trade Cartel, it's as illegal there in China as it is here. If true, they would want to hide the fact and may have felt Bei Aolun had given me information." Each in the group nodding considering it a possibility.

"What made you try to contact him today?" Queried Tisha. "Is there more you need to tell us?"

"Yes, two things, first Aolun had a landscaped children's tattoo on his right arm above the elbow, just as Susan had described, she'd noticed on me at the hospital. I needed to find out whether it was the same. If so, how did he get it and where from. At the same time, it crossed my mind he may be at risk. I needed to check if he was alive," he paused. "You know the result."

"Secondly, I realised the phone listing I'd seen at the Shanghai Bell reception had my name on it, this could have been written by the security people when I arrived, so it didn't register too much with me. What was strange is, why the listing I was given had been in English and not Chinese, unless they knew I was coming."

"Which means someone was bugging your rooms or following you around," put forward Tisha. "You and Penny had better start delving deep into Matt's papers and see just how much they were trying to protect themselves."

"Bit dramatic isn't? Are we talking about the killing of people?" Penny considered.

"I doubt from what's been said, they would go so far as murdering Aolun, maybe, there is another cause which links them all," David offered his thoughts.

"What could it be?" responded Ross unconvinced.

"Let's work through this in a short while, please wait while I go and see one of the patients," David left the group, nodding to Ferral as he went.

"There is one other thing I've remembered," Ferral looked at Penny and pondered. "Vijay Ahuja figured prominently within Matt's papers, particular in the meetings on certain dates with the varying companies. I'm willing to bet this will coincide with the dates that you cannot account for his whereabouts."

"When Ross and I go through Matt's papers, I'll check on them," Penny volunteered.

"Who is David, does anyone know? He has obviously done wonders for Susan but what do we know of him?" Ross questioned the rest of the group.

Affronted, Tisha sharply retorted. "Nothing wrong with David, he is just a private person and I do know him and trust him completely. We all must do the same, if anyone's going to sort out this mess he will."

Penny flushed also affronted and found herself mentally siding with Tisha. For the first time ever she too was angry with Ross.

"Calm down Tisha, I was only thinking aloud, I'm glad for what he has done, but he's a mystery to me, that's all," Ross responded apologetically, noting Penny's upset as well.

Ferral interrupted. "I had that same feeling, in the beginning. However, over the last couple of weeks I have watched David closely. "I feel, what we must do is to trust him implicitly. He knows exactly what he is doing even if we don't," he said smiling.

Chapter 7

The door to the drawing room gently creaked open causing the group to take notice. In the doorway stood a frail, stooped smiling man, who was holding on to David tightly, in case he should fall.

"Hi people, I'm back!" he beamed at the familiar faces.

"Samuel!" screamed Tisha. Already taking leaps toward him, to be at his side.

Ross was dumbstruck at seeing his best friend and followed a short pace behind.

Both Tisha and Ross took over the support from David leading him toward the trio of sofas. Sam settled alongside Tisha, as Ross re-joined Susan who, along with Ferral saw the obvious progress David had been making with Sam.

David broke the spell. "We must try not to tire Sam, I will explain all without him having to. It was important for him to see you and for you to assess how he is."

"Tisha, you may recall, I'd been interested in Sam's strength of character and I'm pleased to say it helped him tremendously." Tisha nodded as Ross interrupted David.

"David, we cannot thank you enough for what you have done for Sam and are doing for all the patients. Are we any closer to understanding why this happened to them in the first place?" Ross asked his scepticism over David vanquished.

"I believe I do understand how it happened, as to why, that is in the mind of someone else, whom we have to find," David assessed. "Let me explain."

As the group took in what had happened, more refreshments arrived and each group member began appreciating, the role David had played knowing without him, they would not have gotten both Susan and Sam back.

Ross overwhelmingly voiced the opinion of them all again, thanking David generously, each in their turn joined in. Questioning, Ross asked David what he could do for the others and whether Sam or Susan were in danger of a relapse.

David recognised it was time to let the group know what they were facing.

"You are all so gracious and I know there is scepticism amongst you, but without the patient working with me, I would have been unable to succeed," he said noting the acknowledgement of Susan and Sam. "I'm sure Tisha, with my blessing, will tell you what you wish to know about me personally later."

"Uncanny, how did you know I…..?" The words trailed as a totally bemused Ross, listened to David.

"We have, I believe a wealth of future to learn of each other however, for the moment, I should tell you I am peculiarly blessed with being able to look into people's minds," an amazed audience listened to David intently. "Translating this into the practical, means I've been able to read both Susan's and Sam's minds," David paused nodding to Sam before continuing.

"In Sam's case, his view of the world was distorted much the same as a spirit or soul is once they have departed from this physical existence."

"You mean dead, don't you?" Ross blurted, ever the blunt instrument.

"Yes, but Sam would not have realised. He could see the world as he knew it, only more so, and in much greater depths. He understood his condition to be spherical vision," David suggested. "I believe Matt, Ellen and Vijay are experiencing something similar."

"Spherical, isn't that something ball-shaped? What's that got to do with vision?" Ross asked confused.

"You're quite right Ross, it is ball-shaped and if you think about it, a ball is three hundred and sixty degrees in circumference, so vision is at all possible angles and not the usual two hundred and twenty."

"David how is it possible?" queried Penny reddening at the use of his name. "A person would literally be able to see out of the back of their head."

Ferral felt he understood and addressed the group.

"David described Sam's case as distorted, much the same as a spirit. The key here is the vision is not physical. Its spiritual where differing rules apply," he looked to David for confirmation.

"Ferral is exactly right the spiritual being is free of the constraints of the physical. Those who could not hear, can. Those that could not see, can. Hear all, see all, it is normal in the spirit world," David confirmed.

"Forgive me am I missing something?" An alarmed Ross blurted. "Medical problem yes, mental issue ok, which is why we are all here, but spirits, spooks, what's that all about?"

Susan spoke quietly. "Ross, if you remember when I first met you, I said someone is messing with the patient's minds, well this is it."

David saw Ross had understood and continued. "This is, in itself, totally unnerving, but for the stress levelling."

"Stress levelling?" It was the turn of Tisha to question David.

"This is the most interesting of conditions, we all suffer from some aspect of stress, but crudely this is a form of mind trap," expecting a question, he looked around the group, it did not come, he went on.

"Does anybody know the number of thoughts a person is likely to have in a day?" Smiling at the group, he did not expect an answer. "The rate of thought, during waking hours is said to be ten per second and amounts to some thirty six thousand thoughts per hour. Add this to three thousand six hundred per hour when asleep the average thoughts in a day is over six hundred thousand. So consider the maximum number of genuine worries at any given time is about four, where the varying spins on any given problem could amount to thousands, this can control a person's stress levels."

The disbelief amongst the group was quite expected David held his hand up to be allowed to continue.

"Think of these possible scenarios. The child left quite safe at school in a morning. Let us introduce a worry or suggestion, while you are at work the child walked out from the school at lunchtime and has gone missing. Add to this an earlier problem over the breakfast table, a financial issue escalated, causing the likelihood of the very fabric and structure of your home life to come crashing down. Perhaps a job loss or redundancy, for instance. Only two so far, each in isolation are normal," he paused knowing they were linking this to some of their stresses.

"Fears and worries, together they represent a breakdown waiting to happen, most of us cope. Press a button here or there, turn up the worry into a crisis, add a third a reported death in the family and where that could lead, add a fourth with the husband or wife playing around with other partners. Suddenly, you have stress at full levels constant worrying and searching for answers or solutions. Stress starts to control the mind, which equals a mind trap. It only takes a second to suggest the spin and most people are hooked, over a very short period, each area can be built to a greater of lesser degree with the right buttons pushed."

"Most people's minds predominately work on suggestive influences, so this appears simple enough to achieve on the face of it, but how do you get people to believe in each scenario?" asked Ferral.

"How can that be, people cope with stress all the time?" Susan spoke, gaining confidence to speak within the group, Ross by her side.

"Susan you're right, most of us look on stress as part of our daily life, but how do people really cope when worry after worry builds."

"If it was me David, I tend to take a break, get away for a couple of days and think things through." Ross suggested. "It's the logical way, stop thinking about problems."

"OK, let us work it through, Ross," David considered. "Problems, worries seemingly so bad. It is unlikely you stop thinking of them, unless you are a very special person with a heart and mind of steel, escape, if you're lucky," he mocked. "If not, what's the answer?" He looked at Tisha, Ross, Ferral, Susan and Sam listening to him without comment, he continued.

"Most of us retreat within ourselves where every person has that special place within their mind a memory of a time at peace. Perhaps even the holiday where that last look carries them through to their next year holiday until they can relax again. Comfort of a childhood memories safe and strong within the family unit. This becomes our escape, the only real place for us to work through and deal with stress, whether conscious or unconsciously," David went on.

"Find this sanctuary in someone's mind then use it for harm or to control the mind. Keep dropping them in and out of their comfort zone to think about each issue or problem."

"This is a good thing isn't it?" suggested Penny.

David agreed. "In normal circumstances yes. However, if as happened to Sam, someone encroaches on our private space or through dropping in a worry or two where each like a building block actively increases the stress. The stress gradually gets worse."

"Remember in the safe place, the unbelievable becomes true and peace of mind itself, now becomes stress." David breathed deeply noting he was tiring he had not spoken this long for many years to anyone, let alone a group. He suddenly became conscious of himself talking.

Tisha spoke recognising his feelings. "I've a question," she said. "But we mustn't go on for much longer as we must all surely be tired. The special place I have tends to be where I leave or lose my problems not build them, so how do I gain stress?"

David bowed toward her, acknowledging both her question and her understanding of his restlessness. "It's governed when you increase the comfort state of mind to a level, where one or two major worries go away. The person retreats to it whenever the problem is greatest in reality it is the real hook. The person locked in the safest, peaceful and worry free place they know. It is a hiding place as problems increase, they are gradually trapped in make believe, their comfort zone. They want to stay longer where the stress is less. Left alone, this in reality will become a nervous breakdown.

"Generally, our normal mechanism is to unconsciously put our problems into different compartments in the mind. Hence, the clichés "sleep on it," and "will seem better in the morning" are relevant. However, by gradually building up a person's stress levels in their comfort zone, the safe haven in their mind starts to be lost to them, manipulated, where there is no safe haven, they snap! Luckily, the hook at this key stage another path purporting to show a small element of comfort opens up to them. Human nature opts for a way out, by then of course it's too late."

"Good God!" Exclaimed Ross. "I'm not clear, you're saying, on the one hand we have a safe sanctuary, a place in our minds. On the other is full of stress," Ross discussed. "I don't get it, your suggesting someone is actually doing this to them, as I said earlier, I thought we were looking at this as an illness that each had caught. Mentally stressed I grant you, Psychiatrists, Psychoanalysts and the like have to unravel their minds but the suggestion they are being controlled is surely very unlikely."

Ross pressed Susan's arm tighter and looked toward Sam and asked. "Are you two able to talk about what happened to you or...?" He tailed off deferring to David's acceptance as he spoke.

Susan spoke first. "I felt I was locked between two worlds, one moment I remember being fine travelling in my hired taxi and the next, I was walking down a darkened tunnel. It reeked of stale breath multiplied, the walls arching above me seemed to have a nicotine stained hue. Recalling, nothing had proper dimensions, a doorway would be arched not square, a table not quite level or flat but uneven and lumpy, ceiling light just a bulb swinging fiercely on cord but dull.

Grey shadowing, lurked in corners as if crowded, but no one to see. Faces, deformed some bulbous and red some with pointed features so sharp that to touch, could cut you. People were bent double, sideways, backwards, but never normal. Teeth pointed, stained, unwashed and although strange, held together a level of reality because I was the odd one out. I didn't feel normal, so were they normal?" Susan began to shudder, her voice rising with each thought, panic not far from the surface. "I was led into a room, each corner triangular in shape. I paid no attention. Someone was screaming from the only bed in the room, knew him I did." Her voice tailed off, she was visibly shaking.

David leant across to her and said in a low soothing voice. "That's enough for you Susan, relax now, we won't call on you again today." He looked at the others in turn, each nodding their agreement. Susan shrinking beside Ross, she began to drift into a deep sleep.

Tisha looked at Sam who seemed to be holding his own better than Susan. "What can you tell us Samuel?"

With a deep breath, he struggled to speak. Stammering at first but needing to tell his story. David had prepared him for this, but his nerves stretched to breaking after hearing Susan's ordeal.

"Pudong and in particular Shanghai, is such a great place to live and work, full of hustle and bustle with an energy and purpose for living. At the Shanghai Bell, I had been given a programming job to work out, what some source code could do, with a Chinese lad named Aolun, we became friends.

The group unwittingly looked at David for support.

"Sam about Aolun, he's had an accident, I am afraid he's dead," David's expression displayed sorrow.

Visibly, Sam retreated within his fragile mind unable to cope with the news. Forcibly, David spoke to him, gesturing silence from the others with his right index finger to his lips.

"Sam, stay with me, look directly at me," David commanded. "He had an accident, remember him well as your good friend, not as someone who has died. You will know him again, I promise."

Samuel relaxed and David comfortingly put his hands on his shoulders whispering. "Let him go, it will help him, you must continue."

Stammering, Sam fought back tears. "My good friend and I worked on a computer program where the code had already been written, we were told our task was to make it usable for a whole group of organisations.

"Sam I remember Aolun had a tattoo on his right arm, do you know how he got this?" Ross pressed him.

"Yes I do, I vaguely remember an Indian guy coming around the office offering free tattoos, bit of a zombie like character as I recall. Aolun was the only one who decided to get it done, why?" he asked.

Ross explained some of Susan's nightmare to him.

David drew breath at Sam's comments the same feeling again arose within him. Feeling he recognised his apartment visitor, he kept quiet.

"Who did the code belong to Samuel?" Tisha gently queried.

"We didn't know, except throughout the documentation with the code, the initials DS were present like an artist's signature which we could not understand."

"Sounds like the author, but what did the program do?" It was Penny asking the question.

"As far as we could tell the software had the hallmarks of being written in India by this DS person," Sam paused as Ross asked.

"How did you know it was written in India Sam?"

"Major programs tend to be recognisable by style, much like a radio handle, with experience you can feel it and know how it flows. A program structure follows a route, does particular actions until a condition occurs and so on," Sam explained further.

"Each program code is also designed to generate messages for error. Say a user presses a wrong key or enters a wrong figure the system code throws out a message. Only the English know English, Americans do not. There is in American English where Centre becomes Center and so on. Indian "isn't it" becomes "init" or they write in English, but leave out proper phrasing, that's how you tell."

"Why weren't the messages written in Chinese?" asked Ross.

"Makes sense of course," Sam said thoughtfully. "However, English is the common trading language."

"The program allowed multiple organisations access to a single level of data and shared work amongst each, according to the workflow coding," Sam's face lit up while discussing his favourite subject.

Scolding him, Tisha said. "Samuel, it's great to have you back with us but if you could just talk in English it would be helpful!" The whole group began laughing, easing the tension, which had been building in the drawing room for some time.

Sam bowed acknowledging. "The idea is that all the organisations involved offer the same products, as if competing against one another for price, quality and timescales for delivery etc. However, this hides the fact that each organisation focused on producing, only part of the whole and sub contracts the work received to the party that will do the work, or supply the products for the group. Meaning the customer always thinks they have a choice, but only one organisation does it for all. This saves money, guarantees work and they share the rewards amongst themselves."

"This fits in with what Ferral was talking about earlier. It is a Trade Cartel and it could be they assumed Aolun had been supplying information to

Ross. It has to be breaking some international rules surely," Penny suggested.

"I am not convinced this had led to Aolun's death though, but I wonder where Matt is in all this, did he find out, was he stopped we have to explore those papers of his in more detail," Ross considered. "He surely would have known."

Tisha glanced fleetingly at David who looked troubled and wondered, what he knew, he did not want the group to know. She would ask him later.

David was deep in thought not for the first time had he felt genuine fear of the unknown triggered by another connection the group are oblivious to or appear to be missing. DS? What or who could it be it was another Indian connection.

"Sam, old mate, we need to ask you some more questions are you up for it?" Ross inquired kindly looking for David's approval.

"Sure, I'm OK, go ahead," Sam spoke just a little too convincingly which David and Tisha noticed but Mr Blunt continued.

"Tell us about Jack Kefford?"

A short, audible gasp from Sam causing him to start swaying from side to side. He looked intently at Ross.

"Sam, why would Ellen Kefford try to find you in China, before she was taken ill?" Susan questioned. "How did you know him?"

As Sam glanced around the group, David quietly urged. "Tell them Sam, It's time they knew."

David shook his head at Ross, who was about to interrupt and raise a question, he took the cue and kept quiet.

"I tried to see Jack Kefford the week before I went to China I had known of him before this."

"You went to Massachusetts where he lived?" Ferral interrupted realising this is where Ellen his patient lives in the United States.

"Mmm, I found some papers in an old shoe box in the attic when I was looking for a suitcase for the trip. Family pictures and letters, I read several of them describing a lost childhood, money obviously paid in guilt." Stammering fast, Sam rushed out the words as if he would forget them. "I had to see, meet him for myself, it was my duty. He had family, a child of his own, most of all I wanted to know why he had abandoned a small boy who so desperately needed him."

"Sam, I don't understand what are you talking about, who was the boy?" A frustrated Ross asked.

"Jack Kefford had an illegitimate son and left him to grow up without knowing.

Sam considered. "To be fair, he thought the boy knew he was his father. Unfortunately, by the time the boy had grown up Kefford had realised he had never been told and stopped writing. Sadly, I didn't get to see him in Massachusetts he'd left for China to work on a neurological case, which had been referred to him."

"You are going to tell me this was in Shanghai aren't you Sam?" Ross pressed his dear friend.

Sam nodded and confirmed it was Huadong Hospital.

"What a strange coincidence," offered Tisha. "You're going to China and all the way from Massachusetts Jack Kefford had gone as well and to the same place, Shanghai."

David gestured for Sam to continue.

"Take your time Sam," urged David. "The coincidence is not lost on me either, Tisha."

"Someone is messing with our minds," reminded Susan.

"When I arrived in Pudong, I called the hospital asking for Jack Kefford and was told he'd had an accident and was not able to speak to anyone, however, I could visit him," Sam paused collecting his thoughts. "I told them he was my father."

Ross looked sharply at Sam and considered his comment. It was a possibility.

"I remember asking for his ward and room number, before heading off to my assignment at the Shanghai Bell organisation, but it wasn't until a few days later I was able to get time to see him."

"You're doing very well Sam," encouraged David.

"He begged me to make sure both Ellen and his "boy" knew he loved them and to do all I could to bring them together."

"So you weren't his "boy" then Sam?" Ross asked confused.

David sidestepped the interruption for Sam and softly whispered to him. "What were you feeling Sam? It's important."

"I'd been to see Jack a couple of times before, but the last time I recall the room seemed oppressive, heavy in atmosphere, dark even." Sam struggled with his emotions at the thought.

"I felt Jack drifting away from life and his strength was somehow transferring to me. Difficult to explain, mentally his weight of thought passed to me there were images of Jack's childhood the pressure inside my head forcing me to be still," Sam was sweating at the recall.

"My brain seemed split in two. One side me the other him. Jack held my hand to almost breaking point, through my mind I heard his screaming," he shuddered. "I remember feeling it to be natural having him there inside my head on the other side. Only we were not alone there was someone else a presence, it was a feeling no more. I became afraid and had to force myself to leave, otherwise, I am sure, he would have died there and then," Sam stopped to catch his breath, the thought raising anxiety within him.

Penny poured him some orange juice he sipped it gently.

Solemnly, Sam looked at the attentive faces of the group, bowed his head, quietly he spoke. "Jack died two hours after I left him."

Tisha asked about Jack's widow and how she was coping not only with the loss of Jack but Ellen's illness and did she know of the son?

Sam looked to David who confirmed he had spoken to Lecia Kefford with Ferral. She has been to see Ellen and Sam and asked that we should help and do what we can for them both at whatever cost. Both David and Ferral confirmed, she did know of Jack's son, not who he is.

"I will make sure I go to see her myself," Tisha offered kindly.

Noticing Sam's difficulty, his agitation and obvious feeling of discomfort. He had held on to this information for so long. David asked for calm from him.

"Oh Sam I am sorry I didn't know, growing up with you I never guessed Charles was not your real father," Ross sympathised reading Sam's discomfort as pain of realising he had a different birth father and having lost him.

Ignoring Ross, he continued. "Ellen read her father's papers and believed as you do wrongly that he was my father so she followed me and that's why she came to China."

The group grasped the significance, a piece of the jigsaw in place.

"Ross, don't you get it, this is not about me but you my friend. I believed I had found your real father and had to investigate before you were told," Sam observing an astonished Ross pressed on. "Jack Kefford was your father, not mine, he arranged with Mum and Dad when your father died that you be told and looked after until you decided you needed to see him."

"You're serious aren't you?" Ross was stunned. "I never knew."

"One huge mistake by mum and dad, you were happy with the memory of the parents you thought you had, a father certainly. They were different times and attitudes when you were born and Jack was married. Only when your mother died did Jack start to consider he needed to think about providing for your future. How could I tell you without making sure myself?" Sam stressed.

"Ross, can I explain?" Sam looked around the group who were mostly confused.

He nodded.

"Firstly when Ross was a young boy his mother died following a long illness and within six months his father died. His mother Geraldine had an affair soon into her marriage with his father Edward "Teddy" as most knew him and that person was Jack Kefford. As both Geraldine and Teddy were an open couple most in the family knew of her indiscretions but Teddy brought Ross up as his own even though they and their friends my own parents included knew," he watched Ross's reaction carefully.

"On his mother's side from what I could piece together from the papers I found at Jack Kefford's house and at home, when they died Geraldine's family effectively disowned Ross as not being true family which led to him being passed around, even my own parents couldn't take you at the time. Finally, Teddy's brother Keith although unrelated to you, took you in to live with his family in Canada.

"How did you find all this out Sam?"

"My parents, Jack and Teddy at least kept in contact and I saw some educational papers which suggested it was Jack who funded your education in Canada, so I started to ask myself the question why?"

Tisha spoke quietly to the group. "In her grief at her father's death Ellen could have reacted to the same information she had found and assumed possibly Sam caused his heart attack."

"It's a possibility," Ferral injected. "She had to have found responses to letters."

Ross faced Sam and asked. "Why didn't you tell me sooner, I could have known him," sadness overwhelmed him at his own loss. He was unclear whether his feelings were for a lost father who died or because he never knew him. Both, he concluded.

"You had a father and he'd died, I had no idea Jack would die or he was for real or this problem would arise. Just like my parents I left well alone," Sam responded strongly surprising everyone. "I'm so sorry Ross!"

Penny crystallised their thoughts. "Ross, you have lost a second father, one you didn't know of but, you've gained a sister who had been searching for you indirectly. Family, flesh and blood you never knew existed, be thankful and help us solve her own crisis."

"No wonder you were so insistent on having a week's break before you went to China, Sam!" Tisha added.

"I need to see her now," a distraught Ross demanded.

"I'll take you to her," Ferral responded and both left behind a silent group.

Tisha and Susan stayed with Sam while David followed by Penny took in some fresh air from the manor's central courtyard.

"Will Ross be OK David?"

He nodded. "You're very fond of him Penny, aren't you?"

"Yes, up to now he has been mine alone although at a distance. Now he has two more women in Susan and Ellen. He will always cherish them both more," she admitted sadly.

David kindly said. "To find a soul mate is divine, Ross and Susan have found each other. To find unknown family is precious and to have a true friend like you is priceless. There is room for you in their lives I'm sure. We must work to deliver Ellen to Ross as quickly as possible."

Penny marvelled at David's goodness of thought.

The group reassembled. Tisha asked Ross for his thoughts on Ellen.

Ross had followed Ferral down the corridor to a small clinical white room softened by the fair-haired Ellen herself.

Ferral guided him to one of the chairs at the table and left him to it closing the door behind him.

"Hi Ellen I'm Ross," He stood up from the chair and went to sit on the single iron posted bed beside her. She did not move.

He took hold of her hands frail in his grasp and spoke softly to her.

"We are trying to get you well, try hard because you and I have a lot of time to catch up on when you find out who I am," She stared straight ahead shifting uneasily.

Ross touched her face gently stroking. "You're my family," He said holding back a tear. "I love you already."

He wiped his eyes as he left the room. Unknown to Ross her eyes followed him to the door watching, wondering who he was.

Ross, a ghost of his previous self, smiled weakly and nodded. "She's OK, there's a likeness, I can see it," His voice strained, shaking at the memory. "I had this feeling I had seen or knew her from somewhere. I now know why, she's very beautiful."

"She would be Ross," Sam suggested, they all laughed.

"Maybe we ought to call it a day?" The group agreed with Susan.

The breakfast room of the manor peacefully faced the fifty acre wooded enclosure set at the rear of its grounds. Many times used for executive team building either for war games, paint-balling or trekking parties. Today it just provided a tranquil backdrop to the opening meal of the day.

David wrestled with the scrambled egg server, placing it's find on his already plated buttered toast. Unexpectedly, the breakfast room begun filling with staff. The clinic forgotten, in the hub of business life that is a dominant feature of each day life at Ditton, most unaware of the clinics existence amongst their activities.

When the group reassembled in the drawing room later that morning, David knew he had to take the lead and tell them what was really happening. They were locked in the belief each problem was separate, individual. Looking around the group, he wondered whether he should be sharing the burden. Ross, Tisha, Susan, Sam, Penny and Ferral were helping themselves to coffee and sorting through the packet biscuit favourites placed on the table in front of the red leather sofas, in another life this could have been a training course break.

David smiled to himself assessing the group before him. Ross a powerhouse of a young man everything black or white with him no grey at all, Tisha, an open and enlightened soul, Susan of high intellect, fragile as an individual and a great match for Ross. Sam is a brotherly person and impulsive. With Penny, he struggled with the feelings growing inside him for her. He looked at himself as an old fool even so it did not stop him liking her very much. Finally, Ferral who had become a good friend he had never experienced this before.

The group concerned themselves with the wellbeing of Sam and Susan, their sleepless night evident for all to see. Watching the group David knew they had dropped into a comfort zone, they were forgetting about Vijay, plus Ellen and Matt all needed his attention, as well as him continuing with Sam and Susan's rehabilitation. He wanted help and within this group he had to, needed to, find the person strong enough to work spiritually with him in the journey ahead.

Penny gazed across at a troubled David, above the chatter she spoke kindly. "Share your thoughts with us David," intuitively she knew what he was thinking.

"I believe I have to, it's not easy, once I do we'll each become targets," he suggested.

"Whatever do you mean?" jumped Ferral. "We are surely halfway there with our problems. "Sam and Susan are getting better, the others will take longer but I know you're able to help them."

"The problem goes much, much deeper than you all believe, for example, what are the connections do you all think we have found?" he questioned.

"China, hospital, family, the same symptoms across the patients," Ross offered.

"What's wrong David, Please tell us!" Tisha asked, panic not far from the surface.

"It may astonish you," he said speaking to the entire group. "But this last month has been the most interesting, I've had for quite some time," holding his hands up to prevent interruption, he went on. "I truly feel the pain we're all going through, as the group of friends we have become. Before Tisha came to me with her request for help, I was feeling quite sorry for myself. I'm a very lonely man without friends however, within this group I have grown close to each of you and would like to count on you as true friends."

As the group fondly expressed reciprocal feelings and acknowledgement of their growing friendship, he made the conscious decision to share his life if they wanted it with them.

"Look, we are all getting too complacent, comfortable with what' going on," By scowling at them, he made them sit up and take notice. Let's look at what has been happening to us and our friends," he spoke solemnly. "Tisha, you came to me asking if I could help you and your friends and I can, but believe me when I say we are just beginning our journey together."

"Sam, Susan both of you, do you think it's over," the group instinctively focused on the pair.

Tears welled in Susan's eyes as she gripped Ross's hand tightly and shook her head negatively. "I'm struggling to keep it together."

Sam looked around the group. "I've tried so hard to be positive and believe I'm free from the torment I've been under, but David knows full well as Susan obviously does, there is a darkness deep, deep inside me waiting for it's time to come to the surface.

Alarmed, Tisha begged. "David, I know spiritually you are far more advanced than anyone here, tell us what you know, so we can help each other.

"I'll take you through the journey I've personally had since the first day you came to me and you can judge for yourself what it means," he considered it time to tell them all.

"Before I do tell you we all need to do more research, which will take a couple of weeks," David noted their disappointment.

"Ferral and I need to work more on Matt and Ellen to get them back with us like Sam and Susan and I need to personally work harder on Vijay."

"I'll use the time to go through Matts papers thoroughly," Penny offered.

"It's China again for me, Ross said, followed by an audible gasp let out by Susan.

"You cannot go it's too dangerous, please, please don't go," her voice faltering in defeat.

"Susan, I have to go, I have to know what's happened to Aolun, I've questions still unanswered from Hudong Hua at the Shanghai Bell Company," Ross pleaded with her.

"Sam and Susan, I suggest you both rest as much as possible and instead of Ross, help work with Penny to go through Matts papers, but both of you must reflect together on what happened to you," David continued almost begging.

"There is a link, a key that began this and I have yet to find it, work and think together, something, anything, however small, will help."

"Ross, while you are in China you must attempt to trace Ellen's steps for the time she was there. Penny, if anything in your search of Matt's papers is of use to Ross or myself, let us know immediately," continuing David asked. "Ross, check on the others out there, make sure they are still OK. I am sure Penny has the details. Check out, if you can, Vijay's last week as well.

Tisha appreciating finally David taking charge of the group asked him. "What do I do, each has something to do except me."

"Shyam Rosha, do you know him Tisha," David questioned.

"Not that I'm aware of, why who is he?" she asked responding.

"He came to see me on the day you needed to talk to me and introduced himself by way of knowing you," he said.

"Do you want me to find out about him?" Tisha asked.

David nodded. "See if there's a link to Vijay, and one more thing, Tisha and Penny, check on prominent Indian people who have died in the last five years."

The group collectively quizzed David. Raising his hands up to them. "A hunch," he said smiling. "Just a hunch."

Chapter 8

Ross had flown on the Air China flight CA 938 to Beijing International. Darkness began to settle on the terminal three building. They had just left on the ground at Heathrow.

The earliest flight at 8.25pm meant his arrival at Beijing would not be until the next afternoon scheduled to land at 1.15pm.

He realised he was already missing Susan and during the long night flight knew he would be going over all that happened the last time they had travelled together. He was comforted in the knowledge this time she was safe.

His seat in economy on the Boeing 747 400 was not very comfortable. The aeroplane looked full of all 568 passengers it is supposed to hold. Stuck with the 544 economy passengers wondering what sort of luxury the other 24 first class passengers had.

Like everyone travelling on long haul flights, the first task was to check and agree the number of seats to the pocket magazines statement. With rows of ten across, three either side, rows of four down the middle. He began working out the numbers to check, easily giving up his mind becoming bored with the trivia. He fidgeted with the radio and TV controls becoming increasing frustrated and uncomfortable.

The plane ascended from the runway, he closed his eyes.

His mission this time to re-trace Ellen's week before she became ill. Another visit to the Shanghai Bell would help him understand what happened to Aolun, he hoped to find where he lived and talk to his family. Ross hoped to find out about Matt as well, he had much to do.

His sister, how strange the word sounded to him, had to have been in contact with Grace. He decided his first call would be to Huadong hospital.

The hours drifted by with Susan never far from his thoughts joined by Ellen in them as his new sister. He looked forward to getting to know her as family.

His connecting flight another Air China flight CA 1515 to Shanghai was on time and would depart Beijing at 3.20pm and arrive at Hongqiao Airport at 5.15pm. By then he would have been travelling for some fourteen hours. He would book into the same Pudong Airport hotel, as the distance from Shanghai's older airport was forty kilometres and judging by taxi it would take about forty minutes he would arrive early evening at around six.

As he settled on the final two-hour flight, he realised unconsciously having picked up the flight magazine. This time, he was in the business class section of the much smaller Boeing 777-200 with 336 passengers. Again a full plane, but he shared the business section with 44 other passengers so this time he was far more comfortable. He avoided the seat map section of the magazine.

After a restful night at the hotel, he marvelled how he could hear the aircraft despite being able to see the runway from his room.

He arrived the following morning at Huadong Hospital. Penny previously made sure Grace Tsai would be around to see him.

On entering the hospital and reminded of Susan, the terror she had gone through and his desire to get out of the hospital to take her home. If Ellen had been through a similar horror, he needed to understand why.

A smiling Grace walked toward him he remembered the help this small but dynamic oriental woman had previously given him. They greeted as long lost friends embracing each other fondly.

"Come along to my office Ross, I have Ellen's file on my desk," She led the way through the hospital's maze of corridors to finally end with a small but functional room. "I get the broom cupboard these days but it helps with the paper work," Grace realising she had said this several times lately, I should stop! She thought amused.

"Ellen's my sister," Ross offered.

"Yes I know, Susan rang me while you were travelling, in a way it helps as it seems you're next of kin and means, I can discuss her condition freely with you," Grace told him of her surprise. "I had actually assumed she was Sam's sister as she was trying to find him."

"We all did," Ross acknowledged. "It's strange how glad I've become about having a sister."

"Susan sounded good is she?" asked Grace, thoughtfully.

"Yes, she's better now," he said somewhat guarded not wishing to elaborate.

"Tell me what happened to Ellen please, Grace."

In her cupboard of an office, Grace made some instant coffee for both of them. "Like she told Susan, Ellen said she was a US Health Inspector. We have some American patients from time to time so we generally welcome any reasonable inspection," Grace went on. "Ellen was interested in both Sam and the circumstances surrounding her father's death. While they were not able to give details of Sam's medical problems mainly of course, because they didn't understand them, they could with her father. The circumstances surrounding both Ellen's and Sam's illnesses and as we now know, your father's death was unusual."

This hit Ross like a bolt, He really hadn't considered Jack as his real father until right then. New sister yes, she had a father but not the same as his." he buried himself in the instant coffee.

"As was the custom in difficult neurological patients, a long standing arrangement existed where the hospital could tap into the resources of the Harvard Medical School in Massachusetts, in particular, it was Professor of Neurology, Jack

Kefford," Grace suggested, she had explained this to Susan.

"Just before Jack Kefford's death he'd been called in to assess a patient who had died. Jack had responded by travelling to China immediately because of the strangeness of the case."

"What was so strange about the case to have to call him in?"

"The patient himself, although clinically dead and his heart had stopped beating. When the attending team removed the monitors, the patients head shook so violently they reconnected them," she paused. "This immediately showed the patient seemed alive mentally without any bodily functions working."

Bemused Ross asked. "This isn't a normal occurrence when someone dies then?"

"Certainly not!" Grace replied surprised at his naivety. "Three days further passed since his death and the monitors were still registering brain activity. Meaning any routine post-mortem could not begin."

"How was his brain surviving?" Ross was confused.

"Jack's practice was to formally confirm the patient's status by hooking them up to the monitors. After three more days on monitors, no physical activity registered as expected. CAT scans, CT perfusions, brain oxygen and cerebral blood flow and EEG were the varying types of monitoring taking place with the results suggesting the brain was in part active without oxygen fed into the body.

"Wouldn't that starve a brain and cause damage rather than help it survive?" Ross suggested.

"You're right," Jack even attempted to revive the heart, which had given out because of the massive attack causing this state. It was very clear the patient was physically dead and would in fact stay dead. This of course led to investigations into whether the patient was initially misdiagnosed," she frowned as she considered what the scenarios of being under a microscope could bring. "Readings from the checks and tests were considered and found to be correct. The right decision being made, brain activity was still strong in the patient despite Jack's own assessment," Grace went on.

"It was on the seventh day after the patient had "died" where Jack was becoming increasingly agitated. He had hardly slept since arriving and it was obviously taking its toll on him. He decided to switch on all the life support machines, pumping oxygen and drugs into the body," Grace breathed in deeply. "He wanted to force life into this poor dead soul. He knelt on top of the steel trolley on which the patient lay. I was watching him from the gallery above the operating room with several other Doctor's, Nurse's and administrative staff, fearful of the state the patient on waking could be, opening up the hospital to a minefield of litigation."

"Presumably it wasn't Jack's decision alone?" He questioned.

"Mostly, he was an eminent man the board listened to him. Jack decided to boost, shock the patient into life with one huge volt surge, probably enough to execute someone." Grace recalled the moment carefully.

"When administered an unease, no I have to say a darkness hung in the air, the emptiness, an abyss as this was done, several people watching, describing the tremendous shudder running through them followed. Likening it to an earthquake but only within themselves, as if consumed totally by a violent force never before experienced." she drew breath in recall. "Me included."

"Within seconds for each watching, the feeling died within them, but we soon realised they were looking at Jack journeying through quite unbelievable pain, so much so we were in a state of shock, unable to help him. Watching helplessly as spasms literally erupted within his head," her head bowed in sorrow at the thought. "We noticed the physical bulging of his brain within the skull."

His screams of pain echoed, chillingly, as Grace recalled for Ross, never wishing to witness it again. After seemingly hours but really minutes, Jack collapsed on the floor, still but alive. His patient though was dead, completely dead. Physically, mentally, truly dead.

"What happened to my father," he felt uncomfortable referring to him as such.

"Jack was taken to a side room for recovery and the patient monitor's, no longer active, were switched off. The patient's spark of life finally extinguished." Grace's voice tinged with sadness.

"It was weeks before Jack was well enough to even speak, but his experience was lost to his memory," Grace continued, taking in more instant coffee. "As Jack recovered he explained what he had tried to do. Although there had been brain activity, the testing they had performed following the patient's death was against each primary functions.

All, but one of the six primaries were not registering and clearly not fed by oxygen, however, the right frontal lobe was undamaged and perfectly active.

Ross confessed he was lost.

"The frontal lobes are considered our emotional control centre and home to our personality. The frontal lobes are involved in motor function, problem solving, spontaneity, memory, language, initiation, judgement, even impulse control, social and sexual behaviour. They are extremely vulnerable to injury. There are important asymmetrical differences in the frontal lobes. The left lobe is involved in controlling language related movement, whereas the right frontal lobe plays a role in non-verbal abilities."

Ross picked on the last point. "Is it likely it was the right frontal lobe which was registering, considering in all other respects he was deemed to be dead?"

"It's a fair assumption and one we all lean toward," Grace accepted. "We suspect this part of the brain survived because of the initial trauma of the heart attack."

"Is it important why he had the attack?" Ross queried.

"We understand he was running fast and had a seizure, why he was running we have no idea. As he fell, he must have encountered a blow to the head, which could have resulted in a bubble of oxygen inside the brain prolonging an active state. Unfortunately, it still leaves the question of blood flow or rather the lack of it to the brain. Sadly, it will remain a mystery how the brain could survive, but evidence shows it did," Grace filled her mug with coffee again and topped up his.

"What happened to Jack, er, my father?"

"Jack had suffered a mild brain haemorrhage and his progress went extremely well until the final day of Sam's visits," a troubled Grace saddened. "Sam had visited him a couple of times and all seemed well until the last time. As Sam left him, almost immediately the will and the life seemed to drain from Jack."

The tears welled in Grace's eyes the pain still fresh. She had admired the Professor greatly.

"I'm sorry Grace I've no wish to upset you." Ross said apologising, unclear of his own feelings.

"No! No! It frustrated us all, when he was doing so well. His rich and full contributively life just vanished almost as soon as Sam left the hospital," she felt angry at the loss. "One moment Jack had substance, the next, an empty shell from which he never returned. Within two hours he had died." Grace uncontrollably sobbed for the lovely man she had known most of her career.

Ross helped himself to more coffee and refilled Grace's mug.

"What of Sam?" he asked gently sharing her pain.

"At first, Sam had asked to see Jack on the pretext of being a family friend to Jack's son. It had been clear from the outset that Jack was quite troubled when asked if he wished to see Sam. In fact, he'd refused several times, always explaining he didn't have a son, only a daughter," Grace recalled.

With some reluctance, Hua agreed to see Ross Mansell. The problems with Samuel Thornton just would not seem to go away. Despite getting rid of Bei Aolun who was a liability.

He vowed to provide the minimum of help to Mansell. He had started to have his own demons to fight. He would have smiled to himself, but it was true, he'd begun to have nightmares. The problem is he knew who was coming for him. He wished he had never tried to steal the code from Setna, he had to keep his nerve the organisation is doing good business and he took credit for the recognition it afforded him within the cartel.

Ross shown into the boardroom on the fifteenth floor of Bell house, the offices of the Shanghai Bell Corporation. Waiting for him Hudong Hua looked a greyer man since they last met.

As each bowed and greeted one another in their traditional way, Ross made a conscious decision not to be quite as open as he was the last time they met.

"How is your friend Samuel?" Asked Hua. "Well I trust?"

"Improving slowly," Ross offered, looking for any sign of weakness. "He is starting to speak and is remembering well."

"We were looking through Matt Shanahan's papers and several references to the Shanghai Bell made interesting reading. Did you know he was with us as well as Samuel?"

"I wasn't aware he had become sick," Hua lied and unsuccessfully tried to hide his shock at the news. Shanahan knew everything. He had assumed after a short hospital spell he had gone back to Alcatel to assess his progress in Shanghai for his hotel project. He had not expected him to go back to the UK for any treatment. This disturbed him greatly.

Ross decided to bluff. "Oh, I didn't say he was sick, just that he was with us and talking quite a lot."

Ross for the second time noted Hua face reddening and not prepared for this. Hua knew Matt had become sick, and been taken to the hospital by his company's own personnel staff. He also noted Mansell economy with the truth.

What surprised Hua, Matt had left China. The key question being what was he saying. This was not good news at all.

Ross decided to push him carefully.

"You have some interesting trade arrangements," Ross suggested to him. "Does the software Sam had been writing now work?"

"What do you know of his work for us Mr Mansell or indeed our trade arrangements?" Hua addressed him formally leaving Ross in no doubt of his displeasure. "I would suggest humbly, this has nothing to do with you." Hua bowed.

"My humble apologies," offered Ross, also bowing he had touched a nerve, time to try another approach.

"What do you know of Vijay Ahuja, only he too is with us too and he had meetings with Matt Shanahan and possibly yourselves."

Hua decided to get himself off the hook and try to explain. "Matt and Vijay were working on behalf of Alcatel our parent organisation. We hardly knew what Matt's brief was except, he was looking to secure finance for a coastline of hotels in Shanghai and any discussion we have had always included Vijay.

"I came back to see one of your employees following our first meeting a colleague of Samuel Thornton's. I was sorry to hear of Bei Aolun's untimely death," Ross bowed in remorse.

"Yes sad business, terrible accident I understand," Hua reddened again. "The family will be taken care of."

"Yes, I gathered he met with an accident," Ross deliberately phrased it this way to gauge his reaction. "How did he die? If possible, I would like to visit his family to offer my condolences on behalf of Sam."

Hua was expecting this one. "Yes, very unfortunate a good lad who worked well with Samuel as I understand. He collided with another car and forced off the road. His car turned over on impact with a crash barrier."

"The other driver, what happened?"

"Sadly it was a hit and run." The police are unlikely to ever discover who it was." Hua closed the subject. "I'll give you his family home address." He found it in his desk drawer giving himself something to do, not wishing to look Ross in the eye.

Immediately once Hua had given Ross the address he made it very clear this would be the last time they would speak.

"I believe that concludes our business Mr Mansell, my best wishes to your friend Samuel and have a pleasant trip back to the United Kingdom." Ross bowed thanked him for the address and was soon ushered from the building by two men who were not the tallest of Chinese but certainly the widest he had ever encountered.

Basha Miao village, in the Guizhou province, bordered on the Yangtze River. Here, Ross bowed politely on greeting Aolun's mother, Bei Kailten.

She was clothed in a makeshift dress, bright patches of green, red and several shades of blue coloured, with many different types of neatly stitched woven material. She wore her hair in typical Miao style, coiled with a comb as an ornament at the top. Her weathered face welcomed him and although Kailten did not speak English, her daughter Caara in similar attire, standing close to her side, at school, had learnt enough to help her mother understand.

As they spoke reverently of Aolun, Caara took his hand and they led him to their sons and brothers burial site. Throughout time, Chinese people were fond of giving their food and money to the dead. His graveside showered in such gifts, many of the villagers gave, and Caara explained by tradition, the rice is put inside the mouth of the dead so they are not hungry in the afterlife.

It was a deep-rooted belief the spirit of their loved one had to be looked after constantly. Paper money, clothes given to the dead, their offerings burned. Although these traditional ways were once condemned by the communists troops who took over China in 1949, these rituals were still carried out firmly embedded in outlying wood rotting villages, despite the communists disapproving of the idea of a supernatural world, branding their homage as superstitious.

Ross quietly paid his respects to Aolun as Kailten tugged at his jacket to follow her. He looked at Caara, who told him her brother had sent something home for him.

Ross pulled from his pocket a symbol given to him by Aolun's mother. He showed the group two small wooden perfectly carved arrows, bound by reed in the form of a cross and coloured dyed in bright orange.

When Ross left the Basha Miao village, he decided to go back to the hospital as the only place holding the connection with Ellen or Matt.

Not having a clue where to turn next to trace the paths of Ellen and Matt. Thinking to himself she had to have stayed somewhere locally to the hospital and decided to try the area of Van an Zhong Lu and found a Four Seasons hotel. Several hundred Yuan placed with the concierge revealed a small suitcase in storage and an unpaid bill, which he settled.

The small green case had a pull handle used as a pull trolley, it had small locks linked through the zippers which Ross forced without a key.

He found a small book tied with a red ribbon. Untying the ribbon the book opened, he realised it was his sister's diary, he felt closer to her, but stopped short of reading it feeling he would betray her confidence. David would know what to do.

He wouldn't get any more out Hua about Matt's journey that avenue was effectively closed. He decided it was time to go back home and to the group in the hope Matt would be better and could tell them himself. He is not going find out any more about Ellen.

Chapter 9

Eagerly, the group reformed after a long two weeks apart and in the now, familiar drawing room at Ditton Manor. The three majestic windows seemed to welcome them with shafts of brightness bearing down as each helped themselves to coffee and croissants this fine early sunlit morning.

   Like a family re-union, each looked for the well-being of the others, especially noting the vast improvement in both Sam and Susan.

Watching David the group developed a sense of unease as he began to speak.

"As I mentioned before we broke up it's time to take you through my journey since first meeting you all, it will help you understand what we are to face together," David reminded them.

"There are no rules, it's like a parasite resident in the mind," anger swelling inside him as he spoke. "A leach gripping seizing on any stress point twisting and turning, the process constantly darkening the thoughts, the more stress the more hold it has."

"David, I don't understand," she looked around the group. "Nor do the others," Tisha was scared, she had learnt of something strange and it matched with David's mood. "Tell us, explain, I beg you."

Since you first came to see me Tisha, I have been aware of the presence of evil. Its manipulating the very thought patterns of all of us," David offered.

"Us?" Ross questioned.

"Yes, are we all not affected by this, including the patients as well as…..?" David's voice tailed off, as he was deep in thought.

"My dear, dear David, tell us we need to know," it was the turn of Penny to feel frightened by his tone.

"As I said, from the moment I knew you were coming." David began to explain. On the day he was due to meet Tisha, he spoke of Shyam Rosha, explaining his unfathomable fear and the strange conversation he had with him about being India's messenger arriving from China.

"The person who called himself Shyam Rosha had to have used a false name," Tisha interrupted.

With questioning looks from the group, she went on. "You will recall this is the person whom David asked me to find. Shyam Rosha actually died some two months prior to his visit to David's home. Apparently, an unexpected suicide death, his family gave this photograph of him swimming while on a recent holiday. Is this him David?"

Looking closely at the picture, he recognised a much happier Shyam his complexion had lost the greyish hue evident when they met in his apartment, he said so to the group. Looking closer he spotted his first real connection.

Before giving it back to Tisha, he asked Susan to look at the photograph. He watched her face carefully, she went pale realising she too had spotted the link.

Susan's mind went crazy, bringing to the surface memories left buried deep inside her. The man in the bed, she placed her hand across her mouth, the same tattoo.

"What is it?" Ferral asked picking up the photograph dropped by Susan. "Good God," he cried. "He has the same tattoo as Vijay. The landscape, house and children on his right arm."

"I assumed the person I was looking at in the bed at the hospital was Vijay." She was disturbed. "Then as you know I saw Ross."

"I believe we all did but if you think about it Vijay was on an aeroplane travelling toward us at the time. You saw the person in the hospital bed," David offered. "If not Ross, then it had to be someone else. Now we know."

So you're saying the person I saw in the hospital bed in Pudong is Shyam Rosha?"

"A strong possibility Susan."

"Let me look at the picture," Sam froze as he recognised the man offering the tattoo to his departed friend Aolun and said so to the group.

"Wait a minute Tisha, you said he died at least two months before you and David met, over three months ago in fact. How is it Susan saw him in the hospital bed during the last three weeks?"

"That's exactly what we don't know!" offered Tisha.

David continued with his explanation, with Tisha's permission, he told of her mind search to a favourite place and to her surprise highlighted the grinning Indian boy on the punt in the lake.

She smiled as she recalled the happy moment in her mind.

"What you're saying is the Chinese connection may not exist?" Ferral questioned. "But there are so many links."

"Yes, all red herrings designed to throw us of the scent, India is the real threat or at least an Indian person," David acknowledged. "Except China is where this all started and we need to consider the part the cartel has played in this."

"That's it of course." Penny exclaimed. "We have been working through Matt's papers line by line, so much detail. We could not understand why the papers weren't filed logically, alphabetically either by date, by meeting, by anything other than Ferral's original order."

"I don't understand what have you found?" Ferral asked, feeling her excitement growing.

"The order is a name, a bloody name!" The group looked at her quite vacant in their understanding.

"If you break up the letters you get two Indian names, Matt was trying to tell us who is causing this," Penny looked at David. "You knew and that's why you asked me and Tisha to look at prominent Indian people who'd died recently."

David astonished at her insight, felt an immense burden lift. Up to then he felt that he and he alone had the capability to solve this puzzle. "You're right we are a step closer thanks to you. No, it is a leap. Looking at Tisha and Penny, he asked. "Do you have your list of names and does one match against the order of Matt's papers?"

"Would someone like to explain this to me?" moaned Ross. "I'm now totally confused."

Penny took the list to Ross and fingered her way down the list explaining as she looked. "Each subject had a letter, was categorised. For example, S equals Sessions or meetings, E for Environment, T for Travel inns or hotels, N for Notes and A for Actions and so on."

"S-E-T-N-A D-E-W-A-N-G." Penny spelled the letters aloud to the group as Ross was searching the list.

"Why is there a gap in between the letters?" He queried.

"Because there are two boxes with sections in each box representing a letter," she became depressed knowing the name was not on the list.

"Hold on a moment, Indian people put their names the other way around just like the Chinese, don't they? Even if they didn't the Chinese definitely do and Matt was in China, so let's check the list again," Ross began spelling out the letters.

"D-E-W-A-N-G S-E-T-N-A," Penny now becoming agitated working her fingers down the pages containing some five hundred names. It was there, a male. She sat relieved soaking in the achievement, the group congratulating each other.

Quietly in an almost sinister voice, Ferral asked of David. "What does this mean? This particular person is dead yes? If what Tisha says is true so is Shyam Rosha. He has already been pronounced dead long before Susan supposedly saw him in the hospital bed, but somehow they are terrorising Ellen and Matt, not to mention whatever's going on with Vijay.

What is going on David, I don't like it, and just what have we got ourselves into?" Ferral was getting nervous and unusually gaining some of the fear David had been alluding to earlier.

"Hang on a minute, I know that name he actually died in the Huadong Hospital," Ross exclaimed. "That's the Indian person whom Ellen had gone to find out about!"

"Now I'm confused, what did Ellen do?" Susan asked.

Can we all rewind, I too don't understand," It was Tisha this time.

"We have our first true links," offered David. Remembering his journey into Tisha's mind the very first day she came to him.

"Let's look at the Indian connection. Three Indian names Vijay Ahuja who is with us, Shyam Rosha who, as Tisha has investigated, we believe is dead and Dewang Setna, who is also dead according to Penny's list.

Quietly, Sam raised his hand. "There is another link."

The group questioning looked at him.

"DS, it is the signature, the program coding signature, Dewang Setna's initials," Sam offered.

Astounded Ferral agreed. "Well done Sam. Link that to the boy on Tisha's punt, we now definitely have the Indian connection."

"Why though and what do we do with the knowledge?" Susan enquired.

"Good question," David surveyed the group each wondering whether their newly gained information would make a difference.

There seemed a chill in the air hanging over them. Subconsciously David considered clothing, observing Tisha in a full length cotton dress enveloping herself within a large shoulder woollen navy blue shawl, pulling it around her tightly for comfort and warmth. As each sat on the red leather sofas knowing each other better, they realised they had dropped into a kind of comfort zone appearing happier in the group rather than as an individual, but there was a danger they could not fathom and literally out of their depth.

"Let us hear how Ross got on with his trip," David suggested attempting to settle the group down.

Ross talked through his journey and spoke of his discussion with Grace. At this point Ross turned to Sam within the group.

"Although Grace told me what she believed happened, perhaps Sam you could pick this up and tell us about your meeting with my father er...Jack," Ross stammered.

"I was finally let in to see Jack and although ill, he had an authoritative air about him. His manner was one of resignation, he knew he was about to die," Sam faltered, knowing he could have been the cause.

Sam had spent a lot of time considering what he would say to Jack Kefford on his treatment of Ross and lack of contact. He intended to remonstrate with him. He should have supported Ross during his own parental loss. Unfortunately, all the anger felt on his friend's behalf dissipated on seeing Jack lying in the hospital bed. He could barely move and only speak in spasms.

The best Sam could offer was the assurance of love and thought held for Ross, deep guilt and profound regret they never actually met. Jack was sad that he had never seen brother and sister together.

"What of my mother?" Ross asked. "How, what were they to each other, was it an affair?"

"Ross, my dear, dear friend, I don't have all the answers and fear we never will. Yes, I gather theirs had been quite a passionate affair, he regularly visited Quebec on medical seminars, where their love grew strong during a time when, to follow his heart, would have meant breaking with every family tradition he held dear," Sam gauged his friend's feelings and considered his words carefully. "Both were married but your mother wouldn't leave your father Steven. She loved him too much," Sam comforted him and addressed the group.

"Jack had pleaded with Olivia, Ross's mother," he said to the group. "To leave Steven especially when she was pregnant, despite the likelihood of destroying his career, which was so interlinked with his wife Lecia."

"So they used to work together?" Tisha posed.

"Jack and Lecia had taken faculty positions together in Michigan they published over one hundred neurological articles. He would have given all that up for Ross," Sam assured them.

"Within three years, Ellen was born and life became a habit where the pain eased for everyone. A name on a card or letter, a passing thought, life went on. No one was supposed to get hurt."

"What did you feel at the time Jack was speaking to you Sam?" David enquired.

"Felt strange, we were not alone, a presence always seemed to exist. Although up to now I never thought of it in those terms just something, not right, we were being watched, listened to even."

"Please explain Sam," asked an intrigued Tisha.

"When I shook his hand, touched his arm, it was like," he paused considering. "I was an extension of him or him of me. Chemistry, flow, thoughts, feelings passed through us like veins joined together as one. At the time, it felt right, not strange, but natural between two human beings. Later, I realised

I was bleeding the very life from him, how or why, remains a mystery to me even now. I remember, on about the third visit panicking, realising I was gradually killing him, I felt drawn towards him with no way out," Sam began to sweat at the recall. "Forcing myself away I ran from the room, from the hospital. A sudden heart attack, I never saw him alive again," Reflecting, the thought saddened him.

"Where did you go when you left him, Sam?" It was Ferral's question.

"My office, in the Shanghai Bell building, the hospital rang almost as soon as I sat at my desk." He shuddered at what he was about to say.

"I remember saying to myself how sorry I was at his passing. To my surprise, I gained an answer it was natural and said. 'I am within to guide you, Jack and I are here'." The sweat pouring from his brow as he told the group.

"My response was acceptance until the pressures within my head began." Sam started to remember the pain.

"How long after this happened did the pressure start Samuel?"

"Only a day or two passed and then I was asked about the programme I'd been working on, had I nearly completed it," his voice rising with agitation.

"Hold it together Sam. Remember you're free, please be calm." David said intervening, his voice tone having the desired effect.

"What did you gain from the experience Sam?" The comment surprised the group as each looked at Susan. They had forgotten the psychologist so quiet amongst them.

David nodded assurance to Sam as he wrestled with his deepest thoughts.

Bitterly he began. "I gained a voice inside my head, constantly arguing with me, against everything I wanted to do. Constantly bickering about the computer program, I was changing rewriting, suggesting different ways of using the code. Each time I followed the advice systems would crash like the voice wanted failure. I couldn't cope I was afraid." Sam's tone was getting higher and higher as his recall was beginning to scare him. "In the end I was stopped from working completely. The voice was trying to sabotage any programming work I'd been involved in."

"Think carefully was it Jack doing this to you?" Susan queried.

"I recall thinking how I had become like this and when the point of feeling well and not well had occurred. Rationally, I knew it was at the point of my third visit to the hospital to see Jack." Sam surveyed the sea of faces looking out from his group of friends. "It wasn't Jack and no, as I have previously discussed with David I don't know who either!"

Lunchtime arrived for the group in the form of platters of sandwiches and fillers designed to satisfy even the most discerning palettes with beverages flowing throughout.

Penny grabbed David's arm and pressured him to walk with her in the manor's vast gardens needing to recapture the first time she met this lovely man.

In the quiet breeze of midday they strolled together deep in their thoughts enjoying each other's unspoken friendship.

After fifteen minutes of silent strolling, Penny ventured. "We're fighting someone or something, aren't we David?" he nodded.

"It is the something that has been controlling Sam?"

Again David nodded, comforted by her insight.

What are we going to do, David? Are Sam, Ellen, Vijay, Matt and Susan still vulnerable?

Nodding he responded. "Each to a greater or lesser degree, the trick is finding the key if we don't one by one they're going to die."

"But Sam's OK, yes?" She was horrified.

"Currently Sam is the most vulnerable, it is not over for him and he knows it."

She held him tightly, she already knew she loved him and that she would have to wait for their time together, she sighed, there were bigger things in heaven and earth.

They both walked back into the drawing room. "I have saved you both lunch," Tisha held out an assortment of plated bites for them to try.

"Ross will you continue, about Ellen?" Ferral asked.

"That's just it, we don't know. She'd found out from Grace most of what I've told you concerning her father, but still wanted to see Sam who by this time was already in the hospital being treated. Within a week she too was being erratic and showing all of Sam's symptoms."

"Did you ever meet Ellen?" Susan asked Sam.

Sam did not recall, he knew he connected to her when originally brought to the manor they seemed to understand what each other was feeling. He remembered not hearing her but sensing her thoughts, asking for help.

"I gather Ellen had bullied those at the Shanghai Bell to tell her where Sam was so my next call was to Hudong Hua. Primarily to find out about Ellen and Matt. However, the death of Aolun had concerned me. I don't believe in coincidences," offered Ross.

"What coincidences Ross?" Sam asked.

"Sam you worked for the Shanghai Bell. Aolun worked for them. Matt was involved somehow with the cartel through them and both Ellen and I asked questions of them. Ross looked at his friend directly. "You, Matt and Ellen end up here. Aolun ends up dead because of the questions and just maybe I was getting close and had to depart because of Susan's horror."

"All good points, Sam," suggested David.

Sam agreed.

Ross continued telling the group of his time in China.

"I thought I would try and locate Bei Aolun's family for the sake of Sam's friendship with him."

Sam thanked him it meant so much to him.

"What do you make of these?" Ross offered the wooden carved arrows to David who in turn passed them around the group.

"Sam, he was your friend you must have them."

"No Ross, you must keep them with you always. It is a message for you only. My interpretation would be crossed arrows, signify spiritual union and with the colour orange, conveys facing your challenges."

"You are saying it's a good luck charm David, for me?"

"Yes it suggests Aolun has become your spiritual helper," David posed.

"But are you sure they are for me and not for Sam?"

"Time will tell Ross, but you should hold on to them." David assessed. "You will know what to do given time."

"You can tell all that from two pieces of coloured wood," Ross was truly amazed.

Seriously, David looked at him. "Ross it is a talisman, you're right a good luck charm if you like, but look after it. We may have need of it before we are done."

Tisha wholeheartedly believing, urged Ross to continue with his story.

"I didn't have a clue tracing their varying paths until it occurred to me Ellen, not Matt, particularly had the original purpose to go direct to the Huadong Hospital, I assumed she would have stayed in a nearby hotel." He told of his finding Ellen's suitcase and showed them the small book tied with red ribbon, which he had found within the case. "This was the only significant item in the suitcase. Clothes, shoes and toiletries made up the rest."

"I tried not to read some of it but I became bored on the flights home, there are letters CD-SH but they don't make sense to me."

"May I take a look?" David held out his hand.

Penny studied David's expression as he was reading the diary he had found something.

When the group busied themselves with the latest refreshment supply, she observed David talking quietly with Ferral. He left the room in quite a hurry.

"Susan, come bring your coffee and sit with me," David spoke to her quite firmly causing the group to notice. He patted his leather sofa.

He gently took Susan's hands and looked into her eyes. The group mesmerized.

"Have you ever met Vijay?" he asked the simple question provoking a shaking of her head. Penny noticed a touch of fear flicker across her eyes like a dark shadow. Susan trusted David completely.

Behind Susan, the drawing room door opened, David raised his hand ushering Ferral in with Vijay almost a zombie by his side. Quietly whispering to her, he asked her again. "Think carefully Susan, have you ever met Matt, Ellen or Vijay?"

At first she nodded, then shook her head. "Matt and Ellen yes, they were here when we, Ferral and I were treating Sam in the beginning, Vijay no, I don't think so, never have."

Still holding her hand and whispering he urged. "Susan I want you to turn around and next to Ferral is Vijay, don't be afraid I'm here." Gripping her hands tightly he helped her move. "You will not be harmed in any way, I promise."

Penny looked at the wizened weak man supported by Ferral. Stress tight, showing within Vijay's staring expression, almost vacant but life, distant, just, in the wets of his eyes.

As Susan gradually turned herself around the deafening scream rang out loud seemingly shaking the very walls of the manor itself. Penny ran to her as David enveloped her within his arms.

When Ferral walked Vijay from the room both David and Penny noticed a brief flicker of a reaction in his eyes. David knew he had broken through the barrier, exactly what he had set out to achieve with him and also laid a ghost to rest within Susan feeling her gently sobbing on his chest as he held her close.

"What the hell happened here is someone going to explain?" a rapidly exploding Ross questioned. All he could see was someone he loved being upset, he blinded by his love for Susan.

As Ferral re-joined the group, he urged them all to be calm.

"Ross you brought back Ellen's diary and there are several references in it which I felt could help Susan. The letters you read out were those I needed to help her."

"I don't follow David, why did she scream so?" Tisha asked.

"SH stands for Sanjay Hammad."

The group bemused shook their heads.

"CD is for Clinical Director Sanjay Hammad. The person who greeted Susan at the Huadong Hospital just before her nightmare began had been Vijay using a false name," David highlighted.

"David had realised by the letters, what they stood for, thus providing the link we needed for Ellen, but had guessed about Vijay. It had occurred to both of us, Susan had not met him," Ferral explained. "She needed to face her final fear and we needed some breakthrough with Vijay."

"Wait a moment this is not right. Susan couldn't have seen Vijay he was supposed to be on a flight back to England when this happened. Wasn't he?" Ross asked.

"Yes he was physically Ross," David responded. "However, in spiritual terms he was actually in the hospital as Sanjay Hammad. I am willing to bet he'd spent most of his flight fast asleep."

"Surely Susan is not making the whole thing up?" Ross suggested protectively.

"Ross this occurred, not in reality, but in Susan's subconscious. She was abused mentally by Vijay on instructions I guess," David discussed. "This is why she had been found still in the taxi cab and had not moved from it even the hospital staff had no recollection of seeing her that day."

"I have to say it does seem more logical." Susan herself offered looking at Ross. "But it seemed so real."

"I saw him react to Susan's scream," Penny acknowledged.

Several looked at Penny confused.

"Vijay," she explained. "He reacted David I thought you should know."

"It gives me something to work with for both Vijay and Ellen," offered David.

"How will this help Ellen?" queried Penny.

"I'm not sure yet but it shows with the diary entry she could've gone through a similar trauma as Susan," David discussed. "I can see a business link with Matt I couldn't see a link with Ellen or Vijay. They're outsiders without any direct link, now we've established one."

"What about all three of them David, has there been any progress, is there any hope?" Tisha feeling for the trio, asked.

David explained how he had tried to break through with Vijay many times, his expectation rose higher with the confrontation with Susan. With Matt, he was slowly getting through to him.

David also had the key he was looking for and it was Dewang Setna. David avoided sharing this yet with the group.

"Ellen still worries me," he shared. "She's still locked in her own world."

To the group he spoke. "My friends I need a few more days with our patients and then I suggest we could meet at my apartment in London. It will be time for us to go to work, in the meantime, relax rest your minds as much as you can."

As the group dispersed, Ross held Susan and Ferral escorted Tisha and Sam to the door. Penny moved toward David and hooked her arm close in his touching him gently. "I'm here for you David, always," she said softly, she hoped he felt the same.

"Penny come and stay with me, I would love your company," he smiled into her shining eyes.

Her heart skipped a beat. He had made a commitment to her and both wondered where it would lead them.

Late into the evening David decided to begin with Matt, he went over in his mind what he knew of him.

A middle-aged Irish financier well respected for building and troubleshooting ailing businesses. Up to the present day, he had been working with Alcatel the major energy and communications worldwide conglomerate, which owned major shares in a number of Shanghai businesses including the Shanghai Bell organization. Matt's objective was to get funding through the cartel for Alcatel's hotel venture and to make it work to buy in what was needed from the local businesses.

David could not establish if he'd known about the illegal trading agreements and been working with the cartel. It would explain why he had suffered the same fate as Sam. Matt a good business man by all accounts, but that's all, the cartel would give him an added edge.

Looking through Matt's box of papers carefully maintaining the order of them, he glanced at each skimming purposefully through them. David unsure what he was looking for since Penny, Sam, Tisha and Ferral had all been over them, he needed something to shock, to try to gain a reaction from Matt.

The more he read, the more he understood the man, meticulous in his notes, researched every meeting he was to have, always prepared fully. Everything covered, so what went wrong?

He picked up Matt's diary hoping it would highlight something similar to Ellen's but it was not to be. By 3 a.m., he had emptied both of the boxes, 6 hours after starting on them. Resting on the newspaper covering the base of one of the boxes there was a small packet, it was the last item, the padded envelope stared up at him it contained photographs. Inside were twelve prints.   Laying them out onto the table, he assumed they were prints of possible hotel sights along the coast of Shanghai, each print marked as a place on the back. Nanhui, Chongming, Henshai Island, Jiuduansha outside of Pudong airport and the remainder of the Yangtze River and Jinshan Island.

He felt disappointment and discarded the boxes. He rose frustrated to get himself a hot drink. Something bothered him, he looked down at the photographs again on the table and again at the diary, nothing.

He stacked all of Matt's papers in their right order and began to put them back in the boxes. He filled box one, still maintaining the same order of filing and then filling the second to about half full, he stopped. It came to him, emptying the box quickly, realising he was right.

If Matt had been working in China, why had he lined the base of his packing box with an Indian newspaper 'The Times of India' carefully, he removed the tape edging the paper holding it down, sticking it to the base of the box.

The headlines reported on Indonesian bombings, two killed and four hurt in a train robbery at Guj. Unidentified gunman kills two soldiers. Talk of India cricket and the advertising of its E-Paper, offering Bollywood news.

Turning over the single sheet of newsprint, the page concentrated on business, financial matters. The bottom left hand side of the broadsheet showed a picture highlighting three Indian men locking arms smiling at the picture taker.

At first, the significance not registering with him, he read the headline. Dewang Setna poses with partners to celebrate the financing of a new software package and a new trade deal with Alcatel's subsidiaries in Shanghai.

Underneath the descriptive element went on, Matt Shanahan who put the deal together on behalf of a

Chinese Consortium takes the picture of three successful men. The software program expected to take two years in the coding is one of the largest in the world, offering synergies amongst Chinese trading partners, offering very real, cost saving benefits.

Against a backdrop of a dark glassed Shanghai Bell corporation building, a lake and recreational park fronted the building where the three men posed proudly for the picture. David searched for a magnifying glass within Ferral's desk drawer, often working at night in his office at the manor, he was sure Ferral would have one.

In smaller type, those in the picture named in left to right sequence. As he read them he froze, time stood still, he was in shock, not understanding his feelings, his mind blank.

For a while, he just stared at the picture, moving the magnifying glass back and forth, pushing up and down on the instrument as if it would show a different result, it never would.

There was another figure in the distance standing in the doorway of the building, looking directly at the camera, obviously Chinese, but he was unable to make out the features. He would ask Ross to have the picture blown up in size.

He found himself shaking his head in disbelief, the same fear on the first day of this journey welled strongly inside him. He knew it would help in his confrontation with Matt. He expected to shock him in the same way he felt now.

He read the names again and searched the faces hard trying to find a mistake but none presented themselves.

Dewang Setna held centre ground in the picture, a face he hadn't seen before, full of character, eyes focused in control flanked by two men. David looked at him closer studying the man's features. The eyes followed him no matter which way he looked at him, he could not read his character. To the left a tallish thin man of about thirty years of age, easily recognisable and stated as being Vijay Ahuja. The patient he knew at the manor, a shadow of the person in the newsprint. On the right, making up the threesome and stated as being Shyam Rosha. He sweated at the recognition.

The newspaper he noticed had gone to press some six months earlier and since, both Dewang Setna and Shyam Rosha had died.

Chapter 10

The white windowless room housed two upright chairs and a table, David had one of the storerooms cleared out for these sessions with the patients. Clinical, without distractions, no focus, except for the thoughts of the mind.

An expressionless Matt sat opposite David across the table, a man nearing his sixties looking much older for this experience. His unkempt, unshaven appearance, belied the previous status David knew he held in business.

Speaking softly and greeting him, David reminded Matt who he was, why they were there and assured him of no harm.

He placed the newspaper broadsheet in front of him and asked him if he knew what it was. There was no reaction.

David turned over the 'Times of India' broadsheet, highlighting the picture and asked him to look at it. He maintained the staring expression until David forcibly took hold of his stocky hands and placed them on the newspaper, causing Matt to look down at what he had touched.

Matt visibly gasped at the picture. Keeping the momentum, David clapped his hands hard making him jump.

Shouting loudly at him, David's voice reverberated around the empty room, just short of an echo. "Wake up, wake up Matt, trust me, you must trust me." David implored. "Peace is here, in this room now. Break free, speak to me."

Shaking uncontrollably Matt began to sob, David stood and walked around behind him and put his hand on the balding crown of his head, firmly pressing down. It began to have a calming effect.

"I am so afraid, so very afraid." It was a whisper but a breakthrough and the first time David had known him to speak. David considered as he went back to his chair to face Matt he had expected this reaction, feeling Matt was strong in character and was fighting within all the time, he just needed a shock to shift the focus and it worked.

"Tell me of the picture Matt," asked David calmly attempting to keep his attention. "Do you know who took the picture?"

Matt pointed to himself, quietly stammering he spoke. "It was meant to be a great deal, heralding Indian and Chinese cultures working together forming solid business relationships, Setna was wronged, he swore revenge."

"Did you believe that Matt?"

"Oh yes, without doubt," Matt nodded.

"Come on let's get out of here and walk together in the fresh air. Now you're back, there is much to discuss and much to repair in you," David comforted him.

As they strolled around the courtyard, a gentle breeze pushed at them, Matt made a conscious decision to trust someone, this man the first in a long while. He felt safe. He openly cried, he was overwhelmed with fear. David naturally held his hand until he was ready to talk.

Matt began to explain how he had been a powerbroker for Alcatel, strong arming the small Chinese corporations by inferring supply restrictions and suggesting a step up of competition through the Shanghai Bell if the rest of the cartel did not buy in to the hotel chain. There was business for all but on Alcatel's terms. It was mostly good deals for all. What they needed was the right systems infrastructure to handle the transactions, the processes involved. There would be financial restructuring, sharing the business among all in the cartel. Through his contacts, he found the best person to supply and build the systems to manage this. This person was a well-respected Indian man with global connections.

"Dewang Setna?" David offered to Matt's surprise.

"Setna himself drove hard bargains and wanted to know everything possible. He ended up getting too involved in the cartel to an extent where he wanted to manage it. The more they worked with him, the more irritated the Chinese Consortium were becoming with him," Matt considered. "There appeared to be a dark side to him, his capacity for knowing people, remembering their names, ways and problems. He seemed to know what a person's weak points were and tended to play on them, using it to his advantage. His powers of persuasion knew no bounds." Matt shuddered at the thought.

"Were you aware of the cartel arrangements?" posed David.

"Afraid so, you could say I engineered most of it, encouraged it. Alcatel knew too because I told them, after all I worked for them, they were my paymaster, but they didn't want the consortium to know. If they suggested the withdrawal of goods or funds then this would make them agree to fund my project," Matt smiled for the first time. "Just company politics, happens all the time."

"Were you able to work with Setna?" David asked.

"Yes I was his paymaster and backed by Alcatel. He used my influence with them." Matt considered. "Naturally, he began gaining enemies, certainly those that feared him. He was backed up by a man called Shyam Rosha and another Vijay Ahuja."

"Did you fear him Matt?" asked David simply.

"Not at all, too thick skinned, I suppose."

"What went wrong Matt?"

"Setna made the mistake of assuming he controlled the Chinese consortium he wanted too, but he was a rough diamond knowing little of the Chinese protocols which bind them together. He had begun to get his way on many things." Matt considered. "They allowed it simply waiting for him to make a mistake."

"Did he?"

Matt shook his head negatively. "The consortium decided to hire someone independently to work on the source code of the software, changing it sufficiently so they could dispense with Setna's services. They asked me to find the best person. I contacted Connectiqua who arranged for Samuel Thornton to come. It took a week for him to get there. The result being they were very, very pleased. Sam went to work directly for the Shanghai Bell Corporation."

"So what happened to Setna?"

"Shanghai Bell's legal team poured over the contract without finding anything to dismiss him for, so they tried to buy him off. They offered him a substantial amount." Matt whistled at the thought. "With Setna knowing they were trying to get rid of him and they were already trying to steal his software code or at least rewrite it, he resolved to get revenge. Money meant nothing to him he wanted control. Typical problems followed, him threatening to tell the world through the media about the consortium, the cartel and their sad private affairs," Matt discussed. "Setna said he would find a way to destroy the software and their reputations. That did it, the Chinese are, of course, very big on reputations, not something he understood."

"How was this affecting you Matt?" queried David mindful of the trauma he'd been through.

"Oh, I was ok, quite enjoying the battle of wits between differing cultures," Matt was growing stronger the more he remembered. "All three of the partners were set for deportation. It never happened because not long after, we learnt Setna had died.

"Do you know how or where he died?" David posed. "Did you know what happened to the other two?"

Matt shook his head negatively.

"Never mind, we will find out in due course." David made a mental note for Penny to do some research for him.

David recognised Matt had mentally come a long way in just a few short steps. He needed to take him into a differing mind-set, where his subconscious needed attention. As they continued talking, it was clear Matt's personal mind retreat centred on his birthplace in Ireland and in particular, riding stables in Dingle, County Kerry where as a young man he helped the stable hands groom the horses it was where he learnt to ride. The memories had been shattered and needed restoring. Matt took great comfort in recalling the bygone days.

Such was Matt's demeanour he wanted to get back to China, Alcatel and the cartel. David's advice to him was to wait for a few days until all the group including him got together, then he would be free to go wherever.

David told Matt what he knew of Shyam and what he suspected had happened and told him of Vijay being very close to him in the manor.

The following day it was the turn of Ellen, again he tried to think of shock tactics.

The white room enveloped them David held Ellen's frail hands in his own. He knew it was now he had to act because she was becoming a fragile, tragic creature. Her soft moist hands a tell-tale sign of her inner stress.

Ellen a trained Psychologist had set out to find a brother and get some answers on how her father had died. She had a different agenda to the rest of the patients and been caught up in the same web of torment, a by-product to stop her interfering, getting in the way.

David believed all that held her mind was a simple spell, wizardry no more. The problem out of the many, many thousands of them used throughout time by differing cultures is to know which and how to undo it.

Most spells worked on beliefs held by the subject, a person believes it is true, therefore the results are expected and right. The person then goes with its flow, embraces it, no matter how painful.

Proof is all, he suspected with Ellen, Sanjay or Vijay had shown her, not Ross dying in the hospital bed like they did with Susan, but her father Jack with the penalty of death befalling him if she had tried to find Sam.

She was terrified of the consequences, with the price too unbearable being her father's death. Her belief she had killed him, forced her within, hiding inside her mind completely. Another trap.

David wondered what her special place had been because he struggled to find it as he gently held her hands while pushing his thoughts through the barriers of her mind. Fortunately, the strength of block relies on how strong the mind is. It works in such a way, the more strength of mind a person has the more likely the barriers of belief are very strong. Thus the weaker or fragile the mind the barriers are weaker, easier for short term manipulation, unfortunately, longer term it either breaks down or destroys the victims mind.

As he travelled through her memory of events, he watched her sorrow at the loss of her father, she reading through his papers and supporting her mother Lecia, who was arranging for the body to be transported back home. He found it strange, still no sign of her special place.

He saw she believed Sam was her brother and this had shocked her. Lecia had assured her of her father's love and told her she knew of his son but where and who he was, she never wanted to learn. Jack had kept it to himself.

Ellen had travelled to China and arrived at Huadong Hospital in Pudong where she had spoken to Grace Tsai, she went to see Sam believing he was her brother but he was fighting his own demons. She never had the opportunity to talk with him.

It aroused Ellen's suspicions that her own father's death may not have been as straight forward as she believed. She demanded to see his records and talk to the varying hospital staff involved. She also wanted details of the patient her father had travelled there to consult on and met with a blanket refusal because of confidentiality. Due to her demands, the barriers to her questioning started to go up. She started complaining, someone was hiding the truth.

Knowing her diary as he did, David linked this to a time when she had the appointment with CD-SH the Clinical Director Sanjay Hammad – Vijay. It appeared he took her through a similar route to Susan, the tunnel and the sweat smelling hospital grey room. His bad breath seems to pervade everywhere even David visiting her mind sensed the stench. In the bed, her father is pleading to her to help him and to stay away from his son Sam.

David immediately realised whoever was manipulating them had read her mind without any evidence and was acting on her believed knowledge rather than the truth.

At this point, David suggested through thought, she should look again. He showed her it was, is, an ordinary hospital room, flowers by the bedside and the person in the bed she would not recognize.

This shocked her and she began panicking. Where was her father, she had lost him, he had been taken away, been disposed of.

David assured her although he had passed away and been transported home to her mother Lecia, and there arrangements had been made to bury him. She screamed inside her head, she had killed him, she cried physically.

He held her hands tightly. Jack had died before she arrived in China. She helped with the arrangements to get him home. David struggled to gain her attention. She must remember. Becoming calm and looking directly into his eyes speaking with him in her mind, trusting him, his soothing voice helping her pain.

"Sam my brother, what of him?" she said in thought.

He explained as briefly as he could of Sam not being her brother, but he was alive. She saddened quite abruptly. She spoke of her mistaken belief that she had a brother and should never have gone to China, making things worse.

David asked her to talk openly to him still disturbed he hadn't yet found her special place. She was looking all over the room and not looking at him at all.

He decided to hold her head to force her to look directly into his eyes. Mentally he was attempting to read and plant questions in her mind. Who is she? Where is she? Is she now safe or still scared? She answered surly each question as a matter of fact. By suggestion, he moved her onto a stairway and described the base as fear and she needed to climb the stairs to safety where a friend would greeted her and help her to be forever safe.

David had tried the technique before with some success. She counted on his instructions the number of steps as she rose up them fifty at the top.

Ellen smiled at him gripping his hands voicing a greeting to him.

David himself brightened.

"Welcome Ellen, I am David," bowing to her.

He began by telling her of Ross, confirming she had been right about a brother just a different person to get to know. He decided to push her further and began to ask of her special place, this confused her and she struggled to understand him. Surprisingly for him he could not find any peace for her. Her memories of childhood seemed to have a cloud over them. Although loved well enough, but special moments or places she found them difficult to recall. He decided he would have to create a special time and place for her not yet visited in the hope, this would finally allow her to break free of her mind trap.

He described the manor, the drawing room she knew, he told of her brother and what he looked like and how he was looking forward to seeing her. He created excitement in her, of looking forward to meeting him and how wonderful, it would be to get to know each other. David told of Ross's love for Susan and how they all, expected to share their lives together.

He asked her to close her eyes, be silent in mind and to think of the future with her brother, a time to create her own special moments. When her eyes open he expected her to completely trust him as he would be with her forever.

A few minutes past and he eased his hands from her, she opened her eyes slowly and smiled into his eyes.

"Thank you David, thank you for giving me back my life," she struggled to mouth the words that made her stronger. He held her close to him and took her from the cold white room back to her own comfortable one, suggesting she should now sleep without fear for as long as she wished. He would be sure to be here when she awoke.

"One thing, remember those special moments you've created and planned to have," he suggested. "Let nothing damage your special place."

David loved to walk the grounds of the manor and its courtyard it helped him clear his mind as the wind rustled through the trees high above him.

He was pleased at making breakthroughs with both Matt and Ellen.

He worried Matt would continue as before, opening himself up to further risks, but at least he agreed to come to the next meeting of the group and be made aware of the risks and exactly what is happening. It will be up to him how he played out his life from there.

With Ellen he predicted a bright future, especially with Ross to look after her, he was convinced even Sam would make sure she was happy as the brother she never had.

His own uneasiness still existed to him he had gone through a normal process where to others it was unorthodox. He felt they had been too easy to fix, although convinced they both were good for the future, the hold on them had been superficial appearing to be weaker as time went on, the mind power spread too thinly. He did not know what to make of it.

Reflecting on his time with the group, he began to appreciate how lonely his life had become. He'd been happy enough with his daily prayer, psychic readings and festivals and he maintained through much reading a certain level of astral or nirvana travel in sleep. Unfortunately he realised friendship, human contact in groups and love were outside of his life until now. He hoped for a time when they could all be just a group of friends passing time and enjoying each other's company instead of dealing with problems. He was grateful for the time he spent with them.

He was also becoming quite fond of Penny, she is a lovely organized Australian girl so totally open he felt he loved her already, but he wasn't sure of the protocol these days. Perhaps he was just being an old fool. Tisha was truly a Godsend he was grateful to know her. She supported him totally and was very knowledgeable about psychic matters.

In Ferral, there was a strong down to earth character he looked forward, knowing they would become close friends. With Susan now back alongside him in the clinic they were formidable. Ross a true friend, with his love for Susan and respect for Penny, he fought hard to get help for Sam, it had caused him more pain than the rest. He recognised but for Ross the group r would have got together. Sam for all his brashness was quite reliant on Ross like a brother, but Sam was not yet free of the problems somewhere deep inside their lurked a danger and when it resurfaces the whole group could be facing real issues.

Matt and Ellen were set to join the group soon.

Next, it was the turn of Vijay and he did not look forward to the encounter.

Vijay stronger of the three who had a direct connection with Setna whom David suspected of causing the near death experiences of the others.

On a human point, he worried for Vijay, because he was a living creature manipulated willingly or not, by an evil force.

The white room offered clinical privacy, the humble table and chairs the only break of colour the occupants now sat facing each other.

David looked at Vijay, a cool stare emanating from a strong mind with a body suffering, bent like an old man. Originally, a tall lean handsome man, he resembled a vagrant old in stature and weak frame. His will enough for him to survive eating but a few scraps of food and minimum drink, the purpose seemed to be just to waste away and die, a far cry from the picture in the newspaper.

David attempted the penetrating probes into Vijay's mind without success many times. However, the episode with Susan screaming helped him. It meant on some level, he could hear them.

"How are you today Vijay?" David asked not expecting a response. Vijay staring ahead looking through him almost.

Without touching Vijay, he laid the picture in front of him on the table. All three faces stared up at him from the newsprint.

Watching him carefully he asked.

"Do you recognise those in the picture Vijay or should I call you Sanjay?" A blink, slight, imperceptible, but a blink.

"How did you get your tattoo of the house and landscape? Shyam has one as well doesn't he?" Again a blink. He knew Vijay had to know of Shyam's death.

David pushed his thoughts toward Vijay hard, breaking into his mind. As before, he came across a grey mist, almost black barrier. He pushed, forcing his will on Vijay.

David well practised in this art, began darting from side to side, top to bottom, corner to corner constantly keeping Vijay busy putting up barriers.

He went from each point faster and faster and varied his pressure, almost like a firing range or invader game. The break came slow at first Vijay was weakening, tiring because of the constant protective barrage. David pushed and pushed determined this time he would finally get through after several nights of trying. A ray of light, small, shone in a corner barely noticeable. It was rare he had encountered such a force to stop him seeing into a mind.

Confidently he continued day after day. More light shone through, two corners.

He kept battling with him using tremendous will power and mental energy.

Pushing and pushing, harder and harder. Rays of light began bursting through the grey matter, a tenth, twenty, fifty percent, David got through at last. This was not Vijay; this was a strong will unseen as his barriers gradually broke down.

Vijay shocked, mentally stumbling, confronted with the live picture David positioned on the table in front of him. Losing ground to David, Vijay immediately built another layer, the picture itself. This new layer as David gained strength was a stronger barrier. David came face to face with a laughing Setna and recognized Shyam. It was enough for them to repel him. The instant shock dropped his guard and he felt his own pressure hard, the pain like picks hammering against his very skull, noise so loud to be indecipherable. Three brains working against his. His energy drained to a point where he could lose his sanity if he did not break free.

They gripped him, forcing him to look around him. He was in the picture watching them. The building behind them, the Shanghai Bell Corporation's recreation area, the lake, even birds twittering as they flew. The same Chinese figure stood at the door, concerned, no his face showed fear. He turned looking for Matt knowing him to be the picture taker, just darkness where he should have been.

David fought for closure dispelling thoughts as they hit him. He searched for London Bridge and his favourite church, La Salette. Praying loudly, he found them instantly and pure white replaced the picture of darkness in front of him. He sensed this surprised them.

Opening his eyes he looked across the table at Vijay, a shadow of a wry smile crept across his features and then disappeared. The picture torn in half in front of him, David picked up, folded the two halves of newsprint and put them in his jacket pocket.

David led Vijay back to his own room. He decided this was the wrong level to take the fight to Setna. When he was ready, he knew there was a different mental plane he would have to tackle him on the feeling of unease touched his very soul. The force of returned attack was unexpected and of concern. He needed to seek solace in the church before attempting any further journeys. His nerve ends prickled with the fear he had come recently to recognise.

David spent the next day back at his own apartment in London, among his familiar items his rooms and his own space. He walked the bridge to his church and did much praying and thinking.

From the way Matt had described Setna, he had been a major force for the technological growth of India and been respected worldwide. His own corporation had spread like tentacles around the industrial world.

Setna had truly been wronged by the Chinese cartel, they had constructively set out to steal the software code written by him personally. It bothered David as to why, if they wanted something similar or different why could they not just get someone like Sam to write from the beginning. David felt they had deliberately set out to destroy the man himself. With reluctance, he accepted Setna would have been right to feel aggrieved but the degree of the revenge pursued is questionable. He recognised he was in danger of feeling sorry for him, but for the anguish he caused, only the puppets of the cartel were being punished not the Chinese themselves, he felt either Setna was missing the point or very scared of the history and power spiritually of the Chinese. He suspected the later.

Before David had left the manor, he contacted Penny to ask if she could get as much information on Setna as she could.

Penny learnt Setna had died of a massive heart attack running away from the Buddhist Yufoa temple belonging to the Chan sect not far from the Huadong Hospital in Shanghai. He appeared to have been making his way towards either the railway or the bus station, in the opposite direction to the hospital.

Penny had called Grace Tsai and asked as a favour if she would look up the file on Dewang Setna. Grace told her he had died after running from the temple. Apparently, he ran so fast he collapsed. He died in the ambulance taking him to the hospital.

There was a line in the coroner's report, Grace highlighted. It read "A weak heart near exhaustion probable cause of death, heart failure."

However, one further comment, 'The demeanour and facial expressions of the deceased appears to be consistent with the patient running rapidly after suffering a shock'. In particular, in the coroner's opinion the patient had been literally frightened to death.

Chapter 11

Dewang Setna knew his path would one day cross with those sitting by the river watching him in the punt. To make the older man remember him he rocked the punt and his companion had fallen overboard into the shallow waters.

The man looked across at him and he understood. The little girl he knew as Tisha, by his side, playing on the grass in front of him. She held a one eyed tan teddy bear while colouring a picture book sketch of a large bird in front of her with her crayon.

Dewang Setna always felt his life had been blessed his spiritual development in the ways of Shamanism gave him a power beyond his dreams.

The key to Shamanism is the ability consciously to move beyond the physical body to the higher spiritual levels with ease. Dewang Setna was a traditional Shaman a trained initiate with years of guidance and stubborn learning to master the art of psychic travel to the depths of existence and to the height of wisdom. Through his heritage, he gained what appeared to others to be magical powers, control of a fire or flame, the wind and an extraordinary healing ability. He developed journeys of the soul, which immersed him in the mysticisms of religious and spiritual life supporting and healing, offering himself freely for the good of the community surrounding him.

His psychic role offered him the opportunity to help literally the lost souls of death accompanying them to the proper resting place in the next world. He spoke for God in his preaching as he journeyed to the altered state of consciousness similar to self-hypnosis. In this state, he would be in total control visiting the heavens and hells of existence, communicating with spirits, controlling them and retrieving souls making mind changes, which alters people's reality of the physical world. A high priest, working for the general good of others. He was happy and content, feeling both one with nature and with God.

In India, Shamanism coexists with Buddhism more used as methods for talking to and controlling the spirits. It comes from a belief in Animism, one of man's oldest belief where every object has a spirit or soul whatever its creation even if it is inanimate. Trees and plants worshipped for years. The intoxicating Soma plant of India worshipped because of the products made from them.

Dewang's belief of spiritual life in everything was at the heart of his soul. He had been a good man striving in business using his spiritual knowledge and wisdom to make the most out of situations and became a wealthy entrepreneur supplying software solutions in different parts of the globe promoting the Indian culture and its benefits to the wider world. A subservient race where he constantly sought status for them amongst the world in equality. It was his mission and one he took on with relish.

All things have their opposites and Dewang came across the goddess Kundalini essentially through exercises involving Yoga. It caught his interest and like Shamanism it involved some form of spirit possession with the difference of temporary or permanent insanity and this intrigued him. He began to evaluate his belief in the methods of Shamanism and began delving into Hindu mythology and then the occult such was the influence she bore on him.

The myth of Kundalini thought of as a female serpent, lying dormant at the base of our spine. Through yoga meditation, she can awaken to uncoil and travel to her lover Shiva her masculine counterpart in our brain. Known to be bloodthirsty and as a destroyer carries a garland of skulls around her neck drinking the blood of humans.

Her arousal found not only in Yoga, but also in many religions, occult practices and used with new age health techniques. A form of energy creation, it purports to be a warm living conscious presence spreading throughout our being and occupies our minds in a trance like state. Normally through Yoga, the energy creation leads to a trance like possession by those who experience it. It is dangerous, destructive to humans, to morality and social life. The practitioner controlled by Kundalini who forces her will by their compliance. This leads to her ownership of the soul's personal spirit by deception and demonic means. A person becomes frightened thinking this to be a mental illness or evil spirit.

In the village of Malajpur, a tiny place nestled in the hills of Madhya Pradesh in India, once a year at the end of January, during a full moon, tens of thousands of souls congregate at nightfall.

A ghost fair in and around the temple of Malajpur traditionally held hoard's of believers who were pushed and dragged from side to side, chanting mantras. The procession of the weird and freakish.

All coming to be exorcised at the shrine of a long dead, Hindu holy man, Guru Maharaj Deoji.

Belief in ghosts widespread in rural India and fodder for the occultists. Possession talked of throughout the region, where it could have been epilepsy or psychiatric illnesses such as Schizophrenia or clinical depression. Most of these villages have not heard of these as illnesses, such is the ignorance.

Dewang had found a more subtle way of 'helping' his subjects in the Soma plant.

The belief this plant had been used for four thousand years and existing for some twenty thousand. The Shamans use it as a hallucinatory drug, similar to magic mushrooms causing psychedelic experiences. The spin off these days are abused in the form of E's on the dance and rave scenes in so called trendy clubs of the west, a designer drug.

The Shaman practiced in its use as a way of healing. Dewang used a spin off mixture called Ayahuasca which when translated means the vine of the dead or vine of the souls. He used heavy doses to bring on in his 'patients' visual hallucinations and astral projections where he would guide them into his path.

Shyam Rosha had once been Dewang Setna's friend. Although always quite apart in his upbringing from Dewang, they schooled and played together in the same village. His belief in Setna and in their early life meant his trust in him was absolute.

Early life recollections by Shyam had led him to remember following his leader, being the tool carrying Setna's word to others. Like all boys, he enjoyed the protection afforded to him by the Shaman. Dewang tested him in all things. He often tried and succeeded in hypnotising him. Whatever the command Shyam followed his master despite being of the same age, not from fear, but total belief in his master.

'One day this will matter'. Shyam complained about being 'rocked' off the punt into the river after falling in the water. The splash attracted the attention of a nearby family on its banks. Shyam lifted himself from the water and dutifully awaited Setna to paddle toward him and pick him up. He climbed back on to the punt without question.

Shyam always there to do his bidding he was good and productive in all tasks until Kundalini.

She changed Dewang his control became obsessive to the point of causing both their deaths. Shyam had been pressurised into awakening Kundalini.

The balance between good and evil in Setna was changing fast and Shyam started to fear him he was in his grip and would never get out of it.

Dewang decided to experiment with Shyam and used Soma plant extractions on him to create hallucinations. Kundalini's awakening, through dedicated yoga practice, should take an average of twenty to thirty years. Unfortunately for Shyam, Setna couldn't wait this long, through his Shamanic upbringing and the use of the drugs created from the Soma plant he brought about the right emotional state producing the necessary shocks through hallucination to evoke the energy of Kundalini within Shyam almost immediately.

Ordinarily, through the right preparation, Kundalini yoga can be a good thing, but without, it becomes a nightmare. Shyam's mind exploded in rages, spiritually he became tormented to such a degree he never closed his eyes for fear of demons. Kundalini power turned inwards and began to destroy his immune system. He became debilitated, unable to talk or think rationally, slowly driven insane.

Tired he closed his eyes and Kundalini or Kali Ma the destroyer as she was also known, appeared to him in a vision, a goddess of overwhelming beauty mesmerising him as his eyes looked deep into her third eye, she imposed her will within him. Her eight arms adorned by trinkets, her neck held a garland of skulls, her waist a band of severed arms and hands of previous conquests. Fear shuddered through him unable to look away from her.

Kali Ma held the head of the smiling demon Raktabija dripping blood from his severed neck. She thrust it into his face he screamed in terror and looked at her for mercy. Kali Ma licked her lips tasting the blood.

Shyam jerked awake he vowed never to close his eyes again until he died.

The thought of death was his answer knowing he would have to get away from both his lifelong mentor Setna and Kali Ma. In his mind he believed to decapitate would be to separate mind and body, spirit and soul.

His severed head, hung by a thread, after he attempted decapitation to save himself from an eternity of spirit possession and dominance. He had purchased large sheets of thin plain glass and placed them neck height on blocks in an empty aircraft hangar, he especially hired for the purpose. The building blocks were set parted in the middle, the glass placed flat down edges weighted and clamped tight, not for moving. He had to be careful that Setna did not suspect him.

The hangar, cold and grey this early morning, every sound echoing. Mist edging through sky lighted sunrays.

He sat on a borrowed motorbike and panicked he realised he needed to raise the blocks to allow for the difference in height the motorbike gave him. Finally, the preparation was complete. He hoped he could get up enough speed. He sat majestically on the leather seat, his bared torso thrust forward in defiance. Head held high proud of what he was about to do. Revving the engine, he engaged the motorbike's gears. As he gathered speed towards the blocks, he hoped the hundreds yards distance allowed, would produce the right result at the right height on impact. The split second he travelled, his mind clarified in the moment as wind pushed hard against his chest.

Like a sharpened blade gently pressing down on hardened bread, the glass slid through his windpipe, severing his vocal chords, onwards slicing his arteries. The force of impact caused an unforeseen shift in the structure of the blocks, stopping him completing his final journey in this world, with the structure shift, the glass cracked and weakened breaking away, while he kept travelling forward. Glass falling away, smashing to the ground halted the precise cut. He stopped suddenly, his spinal cord at the base of his neck pressed against the remaining cutting edge.

For a precious moment his body hung by a slither touching the far rear clamp. His neck mashed across it as if trying to fill the gap created by the glass, blood rays taking on their own life. The motorbike long gone from under him crashed in the distance against a wall. The sound, the impact reverberating, the aircraft hangar shuddered violently.

Hanging there in graceful bliss, Shyam's physical life ebbed gently away. His awakening in the afterlife told him, he had failed. Dewang Setna had been waiting to claim his soul through his shamanic practice, Shyam destined to be his servant for eternity. This time, there would be no escape through suicide. His future rebirth decided by a much higher being.

At first, Setna had gently guided him into simple tasks, but over the endless time, tasks began to take on a more sinister emphasis, Shyam was powerless to resist.

As a Shaman, Setna encountered the fear of others many times, but never once had he known his own until now. For the first time he had been controlling the will of another for his own bidding and it was working, but he felt a presence, many watching him, disapproving.

The speciality of the Shaman, conscious movement beyond the physical body taking the soul into higher levels of existence, to parallel physical worlds. Near death experience and out of the body termed astral travelling commonplace. Using spirit helpers the shaman is able to aid and control if he wishes, the direction of the souls of the dead as well as those, at the point of life and death.

Shamans view everything ever been known and can be known about at an individual, their history and use it for the care and interest of the person. They can also destroy a spirit by claiming the soul. Shamans bound by the ethics of the spirit world, they must strive to restore a person's link to their spiritual power at the point of their physical death. It is a defence mechanism for the individual, thus protecting the soul and spirit from harm in the inner world, by some abused.

Dewang Setna was abusing Shyam Rosha now by becoming the spiritual intrusion into his being. The role of the Shaman is to take the journey for the dead or sick and ask if they wish to end their spiritual existence or continue by showing them either path. All choose for themselves. Setna is holding Shyam, preventing the choice.

Although Shaman's have tremendous power, they need to be extremely careful, in terms of self-preservation, no matter how justified he can make it appear, control of the soul does damage not just to the individual, but also to the hidden universe, the inner world, where we all become accountable.

A Shaman can do harm for a short while, however, eventually everything they send out returns to them with such force, building on good or building on evil.

The wrong direction, results in their own physical death or extreme pain, their spirit growth diminished, the Shaman must heal not harm. Spirits know all. Setna knew and ignored this he would have to pay the price more likely with his life in the physical world.

Out jogging on a brisk early morning, Setna paused outside the Yufoa Temple, leant against the brightly coloured decorated walls for a brief moment in time. A stillness enveloped him, he realised he could not move. The familiar of the Goddess Kali Ma appeared directly in front, trying to look away, he became conscious of the pungent smell of stale blood. He dripped, soaked in his own pouring sweat, horrified. She began performing her deadly dance in front of him in his mind's eye, known as the antelope and lion. Unimaginable terror waved through him, the garland of skulls hanging around her neck came alive laughing at him. Her eight arms entwined themselves through and around him, pulling him toward her breasts.

He jolted, screaming the pitch of which, causing even the strongest to cower in fear. He tried to move again, began to run, he had to get away from the temple, he had to get out of Shanghai. Instinctively, he ran toward the railway station, terrified by the excruciating pain ripping across his chest like lightening striking at his very being.

He gripped his chest, pressure of pain in the centre, it spread to his shoulders and arms, intense tightness, burning. He felt, suddenly very heavy, he couldn't breathe, he had a feeling of impending doom as he began to fall, darkness hovering before him. At that precise moment, he knew he would no longer be of this physical world.

For Setna, his journey was just beginning, not for him the support of spirit helpers. He would exact revenge for his physical demise. Spiritually, he was strong, Shyam was still his zombie and would do his bidding in the physical world and he vowed somehow to find a way of controlling Kali Ma and destroy his enemies.

Dewang watched from above the stretcher being lifted into the Ambulance called to attend, he tracked the vehicle to Huadong Hospital in Pudong.

Once in the hospital he saw his body hooked up to various monitors. Only a few minutes, had passed before the Physicians and Nurses attending after several revival attempts agreed the time of his final closure. As they did so they failed to notice the

EEG scan was still recording brain activity. He, willing the connection from above took a window to the physical world, just.

Ignoring the scanner, they began to remove the electrodes previously placed from his scalp. When they were removing the final electrode, his head started to shake violently. The three Nurses and two attending Physicians froze and fear swept through their souls, they had never seen this before.

Quickly, they reattached the electrodes and the EEG monitor sprang into life, patterns of activity emerging. The team checked his heart he was clinically dead, bemused they needed help.

Dewang smiled to himself, he had caused this to happen he would fight to stay in the physical world as long as he could.

After what seemed an age with physical time having no meaning to him anymore, he realised an attempt to revive him was going on, someone shocking and pounding his chest. Oxygen pumping through his airways.

Although he had long departed, he recognised this would be his opportunity to hold himself in the physical world. In one surge, he would transfer his thought power from his withering carcass into this middle-aged crusader for life, sitting astride him fighting to give him life. As Jack Kefford shocked his body, Dewang Setna forced, through his will of shamanic psychic ability, his remaining brain activity to transfer to Jack Kefford's. Instantly the brain scanners died, recording no activity whatsoever.

Jack Kefford screamed clutching his head, falling from the patient's bed, slamming to the floor.

When Jack awoke he recalled the torment, he knew his life was exhausted, his patient dead. He felt an evil sat deep inside, he cried himself to sleep. He would also die the time would be decided by the presence resident inside him.

The first phase of Setna's plan was complete, now he could progress he had kept a foothold in the physical world and would grow gradually in strength. He watched his physical body taken to the hospital morgue. He did not care what happened to it, no one would weep for him.

Setna felt angry at not dying in his beloved India. In China's Shanghai, because of his designed software for a Chinese trade cartel, he had been betrayed when his software had been stolen and rewritten. A reverse engineering process-taking place, the term used for a rehash of his code.

His revenge began with a visit to the bedside of Jack Kefford from the young programmer, hired by the Shanghai Bell organization to alter his source code. Samuel Thornton had sought out Jack Kefford this was an opportunity for Setna. He watched closely reading the visitor. Setna soon realised this person held the key he needed. It would take two or three visits to learn enough and make the same leap. His container Jack Kefford in the physical world will die soon. Each leap would make his presence weaker, but he had to move on before the man died. Setna was becoming increasingly frustrated at fighting his container for control.

Jack Kefford had fought against his intruder with a passion that dictated his death. Alarming Setna, who had to find another carrier for his thoughts and had to find it fast. Sam had presented himself unwittingly.

Sam had spent several days with Jack discussing Ross. This suited Setna as he gleaned knowledge.

To Sam, Jack was a man with much regret, fearful he would never know Ross he gleaned as much information about him as he could. Despite this, the more Sam saw of him the more depressed he became.

The last two visits had strained their relationship, Jack told him of his mental anguish, of thoughts invading his mind. Sam became concerned for Ross's new found father, he feared he was losing his mind and tried to pacify him.

He felt drawn to the monitors, on one occasion Jack, was hooked to the EEG system with electrodes fixed to his scalp for reviewing his brain patterns, compelled Sam began to touch, feel, stroke the cabling. Strange sensations breezed through him gently like electricity without the shock, waves of warmth the feeling comfortable. He became conscious of Jack talking to him, warning him. It prompted the release of his grasp on the cable and loss of the sensation. He shuddered.

Jack looked at him intently searching his face.

"You felt that Sam?" asked Jack.

Sam nodded in disbelief.

"Avoid it, do not touch it again." Jack begged.

During Sam's next couple of visits, he became mesmerised by the monitor, the cable sensation becoming an addictive sensation, stronger and stronger with each visit.

The last visit followed the same pattern but this day, Sam noticed the almost complete demise of Jack. The last few visits were about them enjoying their sessions as something they shared together. Unwittingly, Sam had failed to notice Jack becoming progressively weaker and his own self, comfortable and open to accepting his thoughts.

As if by another's will they both hooked themselves to the machine placing electrodes to their foreheads. It was as though they were transferring each other's thoughts, sharing the history, moments in time for Sam to take to Ross.

The more thought processes there were, the more Sam wanted, gleaning information like a new electronic toy. As Jack lay in the hospital bed, he seemed to be wilting, gradually ebbing away.

"It's time, Sam." He grasped him by his hand. "Say goodbye to Ross and Ellen for me and get them to look after Lecia."

Waking in reality, Sam started and looked, really look at Jack and realised he had been literally sapping the life out of the man. Thoughts, the ones Jack had warned him of started in his mind.

Slowly, he had been killing Jack, he broke his hold on the cables and pulled the electrodes from his scalp.

Jack was sinking fast. Sam called for help it was too late. As the medics rushed to Jack, he ran out of the room, down the corridor and out of the hospital. Running he was chasing his demons, or were they chasing him.

Chapter 12

Penny was happy, deliriously comfortable with herself. During the past few weeks, her feelings had grown from sheer awe and wonder to utmost respect, leading to the deepest, most profound love she would ever know.

Since they first met, she knew these precious moments would happen, searching each other for reassurance of feelings.

Shy and inexperienced in relationships, instinctively David knew how to please her. A gentle man who made her feel the most prized treasure. Her fair complexion betrayed the golden glow of someone completely, unconditionally loved.

Penny knew he held feelings for her, but without her initial approach never would he have dared to follow his heart.

She loved him for his simplicity of consideration to her youth. Mature beyond her years and without care for unseen protocols. She embraced his years and his wisdom as her own merging in the splendour and wonder that he should feel the same way she did.

Watching his body rise and fall in his peaceful slumber by her side, realising this had been only the third night they had spent together in his apartment. She had already experienced what seemed a lifetime of joy.

As he stirred, David smiled at her beauty, their eyes shone at each other in their mutual greeting acknowledging their love for each other. He felt a depth of feeling he had never known before. She lay closer to him and they made love again.

Ellen, fragile in spirit loved her brother, getting to know him was special he seemed to understand her, laugh with her, feel the same.

Far from being jealous of the 'other woman' in Ross's life, she simply adored his Susan and felt lucky in gaining them both as family. He felt paternal to them both.

Her mother Lecia blessed him for taking care of her and accepted him as a son and Susan as a future daughter-in-law. Together their newfound family ties had grown gaining strength and happiness.

Ross was able to acquire a digital copy of the Indian newspaper print and get it enhanced and enlarged. David was particularly interested in the background figure of the picture positioned at the doorway of the building behind the three figures posing.

Even at its maximum enlargement, the figure and features were unclear. When he looked at the picture further through a magnifying glass, he immediately recognised Hudong Hua.

An almost sinister expression across his face suggesting he knew Matt was taking the photograph and he was watching, he had a hint of fear across his lips.

Ross needed to tell David, because he did not understand the significance of the picture.

Sam was troubled, within the group and with David to help, his confidence had grown tremendously, but when on his own he felt a presence inside. His mind full of unease, his sleep patterns during this last week had been broken so many times by differing, strange thoughts he knew were not his own.

Although Ross continued to check on his friend while with him, Sam kept himself upbeat. He desperately needed to talk to David as soon as the group get together again.

Ferral looked at the wall chart he and David had devised to try to keep a check on each individual. This included all members of the group and beyond.

This a way of reminding themselves of each person's positives and their difficulties, David thought needed highlighting.

Ferral already missed his new friend even though he had only moved back to his London apartment a week ago. Now used to him being around discussing all manner of subjects and watching him literally at work curing and saving the minds of their patients.

Although quite fond of Penny himself, he always knew there would be no contest as far as David was concerned. He genuinely felt happy for the pair of them. They have found each other at such a traumatic time. He hoped their relationship would be resilient enough to last.   Unfortunately, their nightly sessions of debate had stopped he was saddened by the loss.

Looking at the chart it served to jog the memory, although not understanding why David had insisted on some names being there but he knew there was a reason. With David, there was always a reason.

Ferral studied the chart in detail. The flip chart portrait style paper made up of four sections. The top section listed himself with David, Penny, Tisha and Ross. Susan would also have been listed with them in the top section unfortunately she had become caught up in the same issues as their patients.

Initially, he recalled, the problem began with Sam working in China. Ross had introduced him to Connectiqua who were the agency for his contract.

The agents, through Ross supported Sam's return home to the private clinic within Ditton Manor and owned by Connectiqua themselves.

This is the point where Ferral and Susan came in to treat Sam closely followed by Ellen and Matt.

Ross had enlisted the support of Tisha and Penny with the real bonus in Tisha persuading David to join them.

The second section of the chart showed Susan, Sam, Matt and Ellen, these were the victims and just as Susan should have been in the top section. Vijay too should have been there, but for the third section being the place for those perceived as causing or creating the problems.

Moving down the chart, Vijay written in the third section joined by Setna and Shyam. Both Ferral and

David felt these three were in collusion, despite Vijay still being a patient and the other two now dead.

The final section had just one name, which was Hudong Hua, relevant because Sam worked for his organization, which was the focus of most of the issues. David felt there was much, much more to learn, not convinced they would ever truly get to what the cartel's issues had been except it appeared to operate on a mafia type control or influence.

Around the edges of the chart on the left hand side were Ellen's mother and father, Jack husband of Lecia Kefford, and father of Ross and Ellen.

Sanjay Hammad believed to be Vijay Ahuja in spirit and Grace Tsai at the Pudong hospital also noted, but on the right hand side of the chart.

Below Jack and Lecia's names on the left, Bei Aolun's name is there. The young man Ross had met in China. An unknown to him had also been noted by David but not explained to Ferral, the name of Theresa.

Arrows across the chart linked the original friends, the family ties, Indian and Chinese connections and five of them listed as being dead. Those are Theresa, Aolun, Jack, Setna and Shyam, but who was Theresa? Ferral asked himself.

For David, it was time to go back to Ditton Manor, he had originally suggested his apartment but the group had now grown in numbers so the manor was ideal. Feeling self-indulgent with Penny, he did so love her. Not only must he check on Vijay whom he had neglected, it was time to bring the group back together.

Ferral had kept him informed of Vijay's progress. His food intake had been increasing, unfortunately his communication still non-existent. David knew Ferral believed Vijay to be faking his symptoms and he disagreed, feeling he had closed himself down for self-preservation against Setna. Agreed the symptoms were subtly different from the others, but in his mind, there is a grip by forces unseen, causing him absolute terror. The consequence led to a resigned Vijay, who withdrew totally inside himself. David wondered whether Vijay knew of Shyam as a zombie and feared a similar fate could befall him. He guessed he did.

Penny knew just by David's facial expressions she had monopolised him enough. He wanted to go back to the manor and gestured to him.

"The group?" She was reluctant to share him with anyone.

He nodded, feeling the same as her.

She would arrange for all of them to get together again and began to look forward to seeing their friends again.

The familiar growling sound of the Panhard against the gravel drive heralded the arrival of Ross. Tisha, once again his passenger. Ferral and Susan waited to greet them as the car paused at the entrance to the manor.

Susan beamed at Ross as he rose from the car. She hugged him as a long lost lover. It had been just an hour ago since they parted so Ross could pick up Tisha from the local rail station.

Ferral warmly embraced Tisha and ushered them all inside.

He watched them queuing for coffee and tea helping themselves to biscuits from the red clothed table behind the leather sofas of the drawing room. It could almost have been a teambuilding event, almost. He was glad they were back.

It was time for David to bring the group up to date and afford them no illusions on the challenges that lay ahead.

He believed the group needed a reality check they were all getting a little too comfortable.

His thoughts went to Vijay. When he and Penny first arrived he again, attempted to communicate with him.   The group needed to understand, once he started to force his will on Vijay the world would become a different place for all of them from that point. It would open up the scale of the issues they faced.

The buzz of chatter died down gradually as each looked toward David for the lead. One by one, they each became aware of the chart erected by Ferral on its easel at the fireside, casting their eyes without question over the sections.

"We haven't met for a while and there are some who are still fragile. Let us welcome Ellen and Matt to our exclusive group, I believe we are complete but for Vijay who is still classed as a patient," David looked at Ross positioned between Susan and Ellen his world full of contentment with his pal Sam sitting opposite. Too comfortable he noticed, as if confirming his earlier opinion of the group.

"Is Vijay to be part of this group when and if he gets well again?" Tisha asked.

"He will be yes, we need him, he knows fully what we are up against," David gauged their mood time to start moving forward. "He can help us fight the evil we face."

The mood amongst them changed. For Matt, Ellen, Sam and even Susan they knew in their minds what David meant, their feelings were with them. Ferral, Tisha, Ross and Penny paid attention listening carefully noting the rigidity of the other members at David's words.

"I believe we are ready to begin," David's serious tone chilled them.

All furtively looked from David to the chart and back again trying to assess the significance. Tisha broke the silence.

"David, are we in danger?"

"Yes Tisha, before I do explain, lets update ourselves in what's been happening since we last got together," he suggested.

"Let' go around the group," Ferral suggested. "Ross, will you start us off?"

Ross spoke of the newspaper print informing the group of the names of the four figures pictured as he handed copies around the group. The names coincided with section three and four of the chart.

"Talk to us about Hua and the Chinese cartel Matt," instructed David forcefully.

Surprised Matt's complexion coloured, uneasily he spoke not used to the group and not really understanding what they were facing.

Looking around the group, he bowed indicating what he was about to divulge should be treated as confidential.

"I intend to go back to Shanghai and to Alcatel," informing them of his decision, Matt decided to tell the group all.

"Matt became involved with Hudong Hua and Shanghai Bell Company following his approach to them via their parent company Alcatel and its hotel's venture. While each subsidiary operated independently, he was operating through the main management board, which allowed him entry into their 'secrets'." The groups gaze fixed on him.

"There were a group of ten companies in the cartel essentially designed for trading, but through Hua," he pointed to the newspaper print in front of them. "There is a 'seedier' side. Control, likened to the Italian or Sicilian mafia of old. Rules have to be followed, standards to be maintained."

"Are you saying they're gangsters Matt?" Penny enquired.

"They are not quite Triads, Gangs or Tongs who operate in the drugs arena but more bullying, thug type activities for protection and control," Matt considered. "It was forcing smaller companies to use their products or services."

"We're never going to solve that one are we?" Ferral prompted.

Matt shook his head and David confirmed. "There is only so much we can tackle right now you're right Ferral; we've different problems to solve."

"What do you know of Setna?" asked Ferral impatiently, feeling they had strayed from the main issue.

Matt breathed in deeply.

"I engaged Dewang Setna because he was the best. A major player in the software industry of India, I'd heard great things of him." Internally he now questioned his wisdom.

"Why go to India for the resource Matt?" interrupted Tisha.

"He and his organization were, are, the best software house in the world the cartel wanted the best, India has the world's most talented information technology IT people." Matt continued with his story.

"Setna begun working for the cartel extremely well and was very popular. He took on everyone's ideas, had many of his own and produced some amazing software programs to allow the cartel to access every customer who were sold goods and much more extending to their particular demographic origin."

"I remember it was the best piece of written software code I've ever seen," confirmed Sam.

"Problem, he locked into the banks for the credit checking of individuals. The cartel, were able to obtain almost any information on individuals who traded with them at the press of a button," Matt discussed. "He obtained this information by illegally hacking into the banks data vaults without them ever knowing."

"Did you ever question this Matt?" Tisha asked.

He shook his head. "This was between Setna and the Cartel, I only found out because Setna had begun boasting about how he could use it against them to gain control despite him having written the code for them," Matt recalled. "He played a dangerous game."

"The result being, when people couldn't pay they were 'helped'. The more they were helped, the more the individual had to do something in return for the cartel."

"Like what? Ross questioned. "Favour's?"

"It could take the form of making sure the cartel was used all the time for business or if not, willingly forcing someone to do their bidding so others would comply," Matt paused for effect. "Problem came when individual heads of the cartel went alone to 'solve' their own issues through those that 'owed' them.

"Greed, blackmail, extortion, beatings and many times death happened," Matt went on. "The cartel is untouchable."

Matt continued to explain to the group.

"Setna started to get involved big time, he'd gained so much knowledge and started to suggest ways of gaining more information, more money and controlling the beginning of a thug culture. An army doing favours under the will of the cartel. At the beginning, the cartel were quite willing to gain more control because they were making huge amounts of money. Setna wanted more of the action, a bigger say in what went on. In short, he too, wanted control. The cartel put up with him for a while, there were enough riches to go around and they were getting unimaginable results. Setna's demands grew he had information on all the members in the cartel enough to ruin each one of them.

"What were you doing Matt?" Susan asked. "How involved were you?

"I'm guilty of knowing it was happening and guilty of suggesting solutions and enjoyed the protection of being included in the decision making," he admitted.

"Why do you wish to return? Are you not part of the corruption?" Ferral suggested getting disgusted and losing respect for Matt.

"I have thought about this and feel I have a great deal of information and an insight of the cartel's workings," collecting his thoughts, Matt continued noting Ferral's growing disgust. "They trust me and if anyone is to stop them I can."

"It's a different fight you will have in the future and I am sure at some level this group could help," David supported. "For now please help us with our own fight."

Matt bowed to him.

"Yes, Yes of course and thank you for the support," he said gratefully. "Unfortunately for Setna, he made one vital error he attempted to blackmail Hudong Hua, The chief executive of the Shanghai Bell," he looked on the group. "Hua created a plan for his removal with the rest of the consortium's agreement and as he'd used Connectiqua in the past he decided to contact them."

Matt nodded to Sam in the group. "This is how Sam became involved and his brief was to unpick the software, change a few things. The cartel wanted to establish whether they needed Setna of not."

Sam spoke. "They did, his written software code was brilliant and securely tied down as to be almost unbreakable."

"Almost?" mused Ross he knew of Sam's reputation in the computer industry. Sam was among the elite in 'hacker' terms.

Sam began to describe his approach to the problem and stopped short, looking around the group and their glazed eyes, he even noticed Tisha stifle a yawn.

"Anyhow," he said changing tack. "My brief was to rewrite the code so it could no longer be recognised as written by Setna and we did it."

"We, was someone helping you Sam?" Queried Susan.

"Yes, I gained a friend in Bei Aolun."

"He died, didn't he?" pressed Susan. She looked toward Matt. "Could this be suspicious?"

"Without doubt it's suspicious Susan," Matt acknowledged. "This is exactly what the cartel did."

"Setna was no fool he realised what was happening but instead of trying to do a deal. He tried to force the cartel into making him a partner member." His gesture to the group suggested this had been a mistake.

"I gather Setna died from a heart attack running from the Yufoa temple," Penny stated, leaving the thought open.

Matt shrugged he didn't know the details surrounding his Setna's death.

"Physically, I understood him to be very strong and extremely fit," Matt considered looking toward Penny. "It has to be another suspicious death."

"Do you think it was cartel related, he did die of a heart attack?" asked Tisha.

"I don't know maybe it is a coincidence." A wry smile spread across his face, he shrugged his shoulders.

"So what happened to you, Matt?" quietly spoken Ellen asked, feeling a kinship towards him having spent window time alongside him and Sam.

"Although commissioned by Alcatel who is the parent company of the Shanghai Bell, I actually work for a group of North American businesses who were looking for a foothold in China," Matt told them more.

"My brief was to get completely involved in how they do business in China. They were looking for long-term commitments operating from the sidelines 'looking for opportunities' was the phrasing. They were in it for the long haul the building of relationships.

"Setna had delved into my own background and attempted to caste suspicion on me personally and my motives for being there. He saw me as a threat and said so to me openly."

"You met him?" David's interest heightening.

Matt nodded. "The man had an aura like he was used to being served. A holy man type except, I knew otherwise. Setna thought wrongly I had been employed directly by the Shanghai Bell Corporation and the cartel, so set about ruining my credibility," he remembered discussions with Hua about this.

"By the time Setna had found out about his North American chums and their backing it was too late for him. Hua and the rest of the cartel sided with Matt believing they could make more money from Alcatel's operations bringing in the Americans and it's hotel venture, with him specifically working for their major shareholder. It became self-preservation by the cartel. Setna was never a part of this. Ever vengeful, Setna vowed he would destroy me as his control gradually loosened over the cartel," Matt discussed.

"Hua arranged for the local newspaper to take some photographs. He thought this would be good to have them down in front of the Shanghai Bell's building. The photographer lined all three of them together with Hua insisting I supervise the shoot," Matt said bemused. "I'm not clear why it was necessary, but Dewang Setna centred the picture with Shyam Rosha and Vijay Ahuja either side."

"If Setna was looking for revenge, how was he toward you?" Ross pressed him.

"Strange, I would say. Kind, friendly, not what I was expecting." David saw the agitation creep into Matt's manner and facial expression.

Calmly David spoke to him. "Keep going Matt, it will help you and we will understand."

"As the photographer flashed, the picture changed. I was aware what was happening, but it was compartmentalised. When I recall, I had four pictures in my mind."

"The picture being taken, the business being done on the hotel venture, my favourite place, the stables in Ireland with the final part lost in a maze of deep thought and particularly fear. I knew this other part was there but I was afraid."

"What was that part Matt," queried Tisha. "Why were you so afraid?"

"I felt, no believed I would die," he groaned at the memory. "Strange dark forces beckoning me toward them."

David pushed him knowing Matt was starting to drop into a dangerous mind-set where he would start to regress again.

"This has been happening within his own mind," David explained to the group.

"Suddenly the business window closed," Matt started to sweat he went on to explain. "I could no longer see them or the Shanghai Bell in the background and remember I started to become dizzy." Letting the words hang and prompted by David again.

"I found myself retreating into the photo shoot window and became conscious of the camera's lens shutter and described how he was aware of his screaming as the snapshot was taken a second time with the shutter coming down and closing that window in his view.

"Keep explaining Matt," encouraged David.

He now had only two windows left and recalled he immediately retreated into his stables in Ireland. A grey mist began to cloud the scene, the window becoming smaller and smaller, he ran to hide in one of the small barns attached to the stable block, darkness looming. Matt closed his eyes to sleep.

"Wake, Wake!" David shouted at him, it shocked the group. "You are free, quickly move and wake!"

Matt opened his eyes, surprised, perspiring profusely he stood up. How quick and easy it would be to return to his entrapment. It shook his normally steely resolve.

"My God, I was so near to being lost again. This time forever," he muttered.

The group rose immediately to support Matt realising they had witnessed some of what he, Sam and Ellen had been through.

David finished the story for him.

"Matt became trapped in his mind and understood it to be real and therefore would not fight against it. The reality is he's not free nor are any of us," David suggested. "When Matt's comfort window closed he became locked in a world he accepted as real, we all would."

"Sam," pointedly David turned to him. "You are troubled, talk to us."

"David, how on earth do you know?" Sam never waited for the answer the group had stopped being surprised by David's insight.

"I wake for what are just brief moments each night. In my head there are sounds, voices, I feel I am going mad," he thought carefully before continuing. "As I become used to the voiced sounds I realise they're not mine. Listening to Matt compartmentalising, was very similar."

He described a part of his mind where he was an onlooker, like viewing a screen. He had seen some of the group's homes where they lived, past present and future.

"Can you give us some examples," Tisha suggested to him.

He looked directly at David. "You had a visitor, Shyam, who left you a present of a rat and I know Theresa."

Ferral raised his eyebrows without comment.

He went on to describe what he had seen in each person's home, briefly walking through the wall colours, ornaments, some friends seen and even where photographs of loved ones were kept he related to each one of them in turn.

The group were shocked they looked smaller as a frightened group. The invasion into their own privacy meant so much to them. They stopped feeling comfortable they were at risk themselves. David looked straight at Ferral's chart to confirm the name written there.

"Who is looking at us Sam?" interrogated David. "Who is watching?"

"I don't know." Sam was scared he had lived with this fear for a while now.

"Think Sam, think hard!" pressed David it is important.

Sam reached into the deep corners of his mind searching for an answer. He explained for others his view had been fleeting. The doorway, a porch, a face, an impression, the concentration had been on David and his apartment.

The channel for this had to be through Shyam Rosha thought David as Sam had never been to his London apartment so how would he know the layout unless he was being shown to make him feel as if he was giving information.

Sam was struggling with his knowledge, Tisha and Susan sat beside him supporting holding his arms and hands.

"Look at the picture I passed around Sam," Ross said to him. "Look closely."

Sam drew in his breath sharply and pointed to a figure in the picture.

"Good God," Ferral exclaimed. "You're pointing to Vijay and he's here, are you sure?"

Sam nodded shaking realising his danger was only a corridor away.

"Calm down Sam," pacified David. "He cannot harm you here at the manor."

More of concern to David is the obvious open spiritual channel of communication between the three men in the newsprint picture. Suspecting Shyam of passing information, the link was evident with Vijay as well.

Gripping onto both Tisha and Susan, he pointed to his forehead. "He's still in here David. In here!" he broke down holding Tisha tightly for safety.

"By the way, the meetings I was checking on to see where Vijay was, coincided with the dates you cannot account for him!" Penny injected.

"I don't understand how Vijay could have been in so many places at once," Ross looked in wonder at his new found sister as she spoke out for the second time within the group."

"He too is being controlled Ellen, he's been operating spiritually," responded David gently. "Tell us what happened to you."

Tears welled in her eyes as she recalled the love she still held for her father Jack. When Ellen learnt of her father's death, her first instinct was to get him back home. The second was to find out how he died.

She did not believe he had just died from a heart attack. In hindsight she realised she should not have gone into the Huadong Hospital demanding all and alienating everyone.

From her father's paper's she knew she had a brother. She thought this was Sam.
Sam acknowledged her somewhat wistfully. 'How lucky is Ross,' he thought.

She had learnt during a consultation with a patient of the hospital Jack had become ill, she also realised Sam had been to see him just an hour or so before his death.

"What happened to you Ellen?" it was Sam he wished they were related in some way a fair-haired strong-minded beauty. A little frail right now he considered.

"I had asked, no demanded to see where my father had actually died and after a while been shown into a hospital room with the requisite monitors for protecting or supporting the patients, I realised this could have been anywhere and it wasn't helping." She began shaking. "It was while standing by the monitors that a strangeness, a musty atmosphere began to develop, pervading the room, heavy, I was struggling for breath. The door had opened and what I assumed was a doctor entered."

"Let me guess Sanjay Hammad," offered David. "You wrote in your diary CD-SH the Clinical Director."

Ellen nodded. "I wrote it when I met him as a record to remind me, I'd made notes ever since arriving at the hospital."

"Will you look at the photograph?" pleaded Ross.

She too pointed to a figure only this time it was Shyam Rosha.

"Now I really don't understand," Ross said frustratingly.

"There is a definite spiritual link between all three Ross," David explained.

"Isn't he supposed to be dead?" queried Ellen.

"Difficult to say, clearly he was alive when the picture was taken, but at the points of you seeing him, Susan and Ross going to China together with him visiting my London apartment, he had to be dead," David suggested.

"Do we know how he died?" asked Ellen.

"Yes a suicide. So the family informed me," Tisha offered. He decapitated himself by riding a motorbike into glass that's all I get at the moment."

"I can think of better ways to go," offered Ross. "Too many coincidences."

Ellen continued with her story at the prompting of David. She could not get over the rotting smell, old dead flesh.

"Sanjay," her breathing increased as she remembered. "Spoke gently to me soothing, mesmerising."

Without effort she followed him down a corridor through a tunnel, deeper and deeper unable to keep up she ended running she recalled.

"The smell was getting worse like gas, pulling me down. I could not breathe and likened it to drowning. As this thought entered my head my brain seemed to disappear," she emphasized. "Nothing, not a thought, impression or view, darkness, abyss until David woke me."

"What do you think of Ellen's experience David?" Ferral asked out of his depth.

"She has been lucky, I believe she was being groomed, prepared to follow the same path as Shyam," David expressed. "He now lives between two worlds as a zombie controlled by powerful entities. A supposed suicide could have been arranged for Ellen too."

"I have you to thank for my life and my sanity," Ellen spoke sincerely to David.

David bowed to her. "You may yet have more to face, you will have to be strong and remember my advice."

Ellen smiled as she recalled the place for Ross, Sam and Susan, in her creation their future to be enjoyed together.

Chapter 13

As the lunchtime buffet arrived, there was an audible sigh across the group. Tensions and nerves heightened to extreme.

Ferral explained the meaning of the chart to them, mostly in turn as they arrived back to take their seats on the sofas with plateful of bites to eat, ready to listen.

Penny looked at her troubled David from across the room, he had given them all so much and especially her, a joy, she had never experienced before. How much did they really know him, it would be interesting to learn more of this wise man in their midst. What are his passions, did he have secrets did he have a life outside of her and the group.

Their eyes met showing he understood what she was thinking.

"Will you tell us of you David?" She looked deep into those probing eyes from across the room both were smiling. Beaming, brimming full of togetherness their eyes held for the loved. She hoped he knew she meant well for him.

"My dear Penny, you're so wise and yes the group, my, our dear friends, should know more of me!" David acknowledged meeting her eyes with pure love and fondness for all to see.

"We have much to face together, most of you have been through such trauma while others have been so supportive," he paused looking at the sea of faces wondering where to begin. His voice trailed off in thought, deciding on the point which to start their journey of getting to know and understand him.

The stillness and quiet respect they held for David showed in the group's attentiveness as he began to speak. Most held him in awe, others appreciated first hand, what he had brought to them, what he was capable of and others loved him dearly.

David began by painting a picture of his known evolvement spanning many centuries. He was on a journey that would one day make him the 'perfect' being whatever it should deem to be.

He had studied many, many religions and cultures, truly believing in a higher being for all.

"During the last twenty year's I have been exploring my past and have successfully traced his evolution back to France in the early eighteen hundreds. Although a Frenchman, he travelled to China as an ordained priest. Sadly, dying as a martyr during the persecution of the church at the age of forty two in eighteen fifty. Why the earlier part of this life had drawn me into also being a priest."

David raised a hand to the group. He knew this surprised them they wanted to know why he left the church and how he could know he was, had been a Frenchman.

Describing how life had become regimented he'd began to question not only his belief but the way of life. The daily practice, despite the church being about communication and spiritual attainment. He found more interest given to numbers through the doors. Profits from baptism, weddings, funerals and property development in the selling of church land including parish churches themselves for high priced homes, not helping the communities they served at all. Unfortunately, this is the reality of today's world. For him he didn't have to like it, he had reached a point where he decided to join the real world.

Throughout his life, he always knew he had a special skill, but in the teachings of the church it was frowned upon. He had suppressed it for many years. As a positive, he believed it served to strengthen his psychic abilities.

About twenty years ago, he was travelling in a friend's car and while the details are sketchy, his friends, a couple, lost their lives and although injured, he became conscious of helping them travel spiritually to their better life. This had the effect of awakening in him something precious, where he could give benefit to many lost souls.

"Sorry David but I have so many questions," it was Ross ever the sceptic. "Where did you take them? How did you travel? What abilities?"

"Hold on Ross, give him a chance to answer," Tisha came to David's rescue. "Perhaps I can answer these questions for him." She offered gesturing to David. "I do have first-hand knowledge of his abilities."

"David understands how you think and feel about things, you know beliefs and stuff. Throughout time, there have been psychic's helping those people who have died. Mostly showing them how to find loved ones or places in the hereafter and where they belong. There are guides of the spirit world for those who die or have already departed, their waiting to help you and some like David, who are of sufficient development spiritually, in the physical world help when called upon." She paused waiting for Ross's question.

"How are, how is David called upon, if it is spiritual? Asking looking at both Tisha and David. "How do you know that someone has died? The world is vast."

"There is a sense that advises you, I cannot honestly explain. It is like having an antenna alerting you to a crisis. A plane crash, a war battle, multiple deaths needing support," offered David. "The reality is, people have died."

"David never changes the reality for the living or dead, whatever has happened, it's not possible," offered Tisha.

"What possible stress could the dead have?" Ross posed. "Surely they would be at peace."

"Ross, you know better than that," scolded Tisha. "Souls of the departed need guidance, which is the reality, people react differently. What is stress to one may be an adrenaline rush to another, excitement versus stress and all those feelings in between. It is the perception of events making the difference to an individual," Tisha explained. "Some are excited crossing to the other side, some terrified."

"So the perception of the reality in the persons mind is altered to free them of their stress." Ross understood.

"It's giving back a person's sanity previously driven insane because of those real events." Tisha continued. "He turns a fear into a friend, a myth proved incorrect, a belief worked through, comfort and security where none existed in thoughts before," Tisha concluded. "Those are David's abilities, Ross."

David fielded questions about his family. A father disappointed with his choice of career. A mother, reluctantly, accepting the lack of a grandchild. Being the only child, He was the end of the line. Both died naturally when their time had been reached, he recalled sadly he missed them both physically. He spoke to them on a mental plane frequently. He decided not to mention this to the group they were not that ready to understand yet.

He described himself as a psychic medium, but even the group recognised he was much, much more.

Matt ventured. "I know you've helped me David and to all of you, this man has saved my life," the group acknowledged his comments. "As a businessman, how on earth do you eat David, How can your lifestyle pay? Please don't give me the crap that God will provide."

David laughed loudly at his bluntness. "That's easy, fortunately my parents were quite wealthy and the accident I spoke of provided some compensation too. The priesthood does not provide pensions, but I supplement my income with spiritual readings, workshops, private life mapping and general spiritual blessings," he became conscious he had been talking of himself too much.

"Enough of me, he said. "There are years ahead for us to be friends and for all of you to know me better," he was thankful for lightening the mood among the group but he needed to stress the seriousness of their situation. "We need to work through our current problems. Rest now for tomorrow we begin our journey into the unknown."

Overnight, the group had gone their various ways, some staying in the manor itself, others at the Marriot Hotel nearby.

David and Ferral preferred to doze in the study armchairs, neither paying much attention to their need for sleep.

By now, the two men had become used to each other's company and had spent many such nights in discussion, which both found immensely relaxing. Coffee percolating throughout the night, caffeine keeping their brains alert.

David was already missing Penny who was staying at the Marriot.

"Troubled?"

"Very."

"Come on David we have to work this through, all night if we have to."

Ferral had transferred the chart from the drawing room to the study and pointed to it.

"Let us look at each individual including us. We need to understand the strengths and weaknesses of the group," David suggested. "You and Penny need to stay out of this. We will use Ross with the others. You must stay away from the danger." David noted his disappointment.

"It will be the difference between us surviving, I assure you."

"There is a real threat?" Ferral stated the obvious. "And why not Penny?"

"As protection, it is likely she will be used against me."

David went on. "Apart from me the stronger ones are Tisha, Matt with Sam borderline. The weaker being Susan and Ellen."

"Where's Vijay in all this?"

"There is a barrier stopping me connecting with him but I do need to force him into the circle." A worried David confirmed.

"Circle?"

"Like a séance each person sits around a table and joins hands."

"You're not serious," mocked Ferral horrified. "You surely don't mean like 'is anybody there' do you?"

"Well yes pretty much," David said coyly. "It's without the words. The object is for all in the circle to keep their own thoughts and gradually with help their minds will merge into one."

"You're help?"

David nodded.

"Do we know the risks, what's going to happen?" Ferral demanded, more out of frustration at his lack of involvement.

"Honestly, I don't know, there will be a series of obstacles and traps we will face," David responded as best as he could. "Each person has differing levels of stress and different demons to fight. The risks I'm afraid are all too clear the members of the circle could die."

"Tell me the worst why don't you." Ferral mused calming down.

"Whatever happens live or die, it will leave a marked impression on all of them in the group," he volunteered. "Mentally some may never recover."

"Vijay, does he hold the key?"

"No. For a different reason I believe Sam is a key part," David replied. "Vijay without question is an important part."

"Why would you believe Sam is the key David?"

"I feel he will have someone by his side to help us."

As the night unfolded Ferral posed many questions for which, mostly David didn't have answers, he told him to be ready to wake them either individually or as a group but to watch them carefully, it might just save their lives, if they are in trouble.

The following morning the group reformed and David looked forward to seeing Penny again. Realising he had missed her. He was glad she would not be involved in the circle.

She knew he needed his space, his time to work out the problem. She would try not to expect too much of his time and just be there whenever he is ready. Penny loved the time they had together and it fulfilled her knowing his eyes were for her alone.

David wanted to share his thoughts with the group and at the same time needed to explain what they could be facing.

Most psychic travel occurred in the dead of night. Not by coincidence did the phrase originate. Mind travel, astral plane discovery is not something to undertake lightly. Many hardly realise they travel nightly within dreams, their worries expanded or solved. It is possible they are regressing to past lives. The journeys are endless and rewarding in the long term, each has a purpose and meaning.

At different levels, whether mentally sorting out the days or weeks events in a dream or considering a wish, dependant on how far up the scale an individual's development is, would determine the level on the astral planes they could reach.

He needed to prepare them, practice the unknown, assessing how each will react. The complication is Vijay.

He decided to approach the group as if he were teaching a class or holding a workshop on the subject.

The group agreed they would need his guidance and were ready to listen intently.

Using Ferral's flipchart he began outlining what he felt they needed to understand.

"We all have dreams, which are normally about day to day issues. Either worries, wished for events, our comfort zones or most likely general rubbish acting mainly as an encryption of all of these thoughts."

"I never remember mine, David," Matt confessed.

"Not many people do. If you read any of the textbooks on the subject, as soon as you wake up you should have a pen and pad ready for recall. It's a great idea except most forget the pen and pad are even there." He smiled.

The group collectively laughed.

"For some their abilities either knowingly or not, are more developed. These will also fall into several categories, whether they remember or not. On the astral planes, some people can have a heightened awareness where he or she helps and supports lost souls, but has no recall on awakening that they ever do such a thing. Others use their recall to do research into their past lives checking on places they have travelled to, certainly I do. All confirms whether the life they live while asleep is more than just in the single mind thought and dream or whether it is by way of spiritual being."

"This worries me David," a troubled Ross posed the scenario. "A person could believe all they dreamed and none of it would be true as you said, could be rubbish."

"Agreed, you need to have an open mind and believe. If you recall us having a conversation and we both remember, you will believe. If you were the only one who remembers, would you still believe? It is a matter of faith in yourself," David posed.

"Let us assume for this purpose, what I'm saying is true and there is a structured life beyond the physical being. Just as on this earthly plane, our perceptions of surroundings or events are all different. Nothing changes on the mental and spiritual planes."

"I just don't get it," Matt interrupted. "In everything there has got to be a beginning and an end."

"Why does there have to be?" David asked opening up the discussion further. "There is a development path for each person. Free will dictates how they progress. Reincarnation, where rebirth occurs along the way, some believe, some do not. Most do not recall past lives but enough do to make you realise or at least, appreciate it may be true."

"Why is it not more recognised worldwide, David?" Susan asked.

"But it is, when you start to investigate you will find the knowledge is quite widespread. It's just most people are afraid of speaking out for fear of people suggesting they are mad. Stigma, a powerful tool keeping the masses down, how often do you hear people say what they do for a living? An Accountant, Lawyer, Bus driver, Checkout Operator, Computer nerd or Psychic medium?" David offered. "Which one starts to make people feel uncomfortable?" he posed, not expecting a response.

"They believe Psychics can see into their very being. What food, what thoughts and who they are sleeping with. As a practicing Psychic I know we are unfortunately avoided, the image portrayed is one of ghosts, magic, death, above all it creates fear," he paused for thought. "People like to keep their own thoughts of mind and not believe it could be opened or shared with others. Television helps but even then it's about getting messages from the 'other side' or finding 'ghosts' and never teaching about spiritual development which is unfortunate. If you just go to psychic fairs as we do," David deferred to Tisha. "You would gauge there is a huge interest in the country as a whole."

"And are you able to see this far into minds, seeing what we are thinking all the time?" Ross became nervous at the suggestion.

"No, it's more relative to your actions, feelings and intended outcomes. It is the spiritual being which is read not the physical, I can assure you," David noted the relief on more than one person in the group.

"Remember always you're a spirit. You all have been and will go through many lifetimes. Some you will recall, almost all, you will forget. Your spirit requires many lives to learn all of the real lessons of life, to enable you as an individual to become perfect, this is why people suggest they have done things or been to the places before, but know in their current physical existence, they never have. It is likely they have lived a past life been reincarnated and as plausible they would have travelled in the spirit world or dreamed of it based on their readings or conversations. We as individuals have to decide which is it and what we believe. Many religions have variety of ways to work through this. All merge in the belief eventually, of the spirit world."

David offered a list of reading material to help their knowledge.

As the session continued, he explained to them the seven levels or areas of the astral world.

The group just listened in awe of the man.

He explained the differences of the planes with its energies and vibration frequencies. The physical earth above the 'astral' is a thought and emotional plane mirroring the physical. A further step is the 'mental' plane, where our own guide's guardians and those who work for us, as goodness for humanity, exist. Moving onto the 'buddhic' plane where we, as beings, are more spiritual and recall of the physical existence becomes less and less." He realised there was a risk he was overloading them, but if they retained any information it would serve to help them.

"Next is the 'Nirvana' plane, a place of peace and tranquillity, anything resembling earth, has long gone from any recall. The spirit is becoming ready where the teachings suggest our spirit separates as spin offs. Each with something to learn, humility, patience, consideration and so on. When the physical dies all these parts merge back with all the perfected learnings. This takes place on the 'Para Nirvana' plane."

"I'm not I'll remember all of this David," suggested Matt.

"Not to worry, it takes years, but being told does register somewhere in the subconscious I assure you."

"Thanks Tisha, "he appreciated her support and continued.

"After many reincarnations, many spin offs the evolution is complete and is at the very centre of all the planes, the spirit comes together at the 'Godhead' or 'seventh' plane. At this point a being is at its ultimate and is again at a beginning of more learning, more perfection and starts a further journey again."

By now, the group were mesmerized and eyes glazed over in confusion.

"It is enough I talk to you about the structure and as we develop our lives together, friends you will understand more." David suggested. "We can talk about what is described as Heaven or Hell which is deemed Earth versus Astral but this is too simple."

"How do we ever get to the top state or plane if we cannot even remember a dream?" Ross queried.

"Through Chakra training," he responded.

"What the hell is that?" Ross apologized to laughter around the group, lightening the mood.

"This is the structure for meditation." Tisha volunteered. "Spinning like a wheel, the chakra distributes life force energies through each point of our bodies. Yoga and Buddhist teachings in particular touch on this for promoting well-being."

"It is a preparation tool to allow calm and expected spiritual travel," David offered. "I am sure Tisha will only be too happy to teach you."

"Let us consider the actual travel, I am afraid you haven't got the many years luxury of learning the art it takes to both understand and travel the astral, However, I will help you. You need to understand the different aspects."

David discussed out of body experiences which most had heard of, projecting through visualizing the experience, he briefly went through around thirty differing techniques, desire, raising arms, meditation, flying and self-induced trances. It led him to consider those with self-doubt, or being too excited, fear of possession, of meeting demons and fear of death. He hoped he was showing death as a likely consequence of astral travel going wrong, but with the right help and training it need not be.

After his talk and lunchtime passed David and Ferral stood by the fireplace in the drawing room, watching the group reassemble from their after meal fresh air break, wondering whether they would be up for the challenge.

Tisha as ever, aware today was significant. She clucked around her Samuel like a mother hen.

David could see Ellen trying to become part of Sam's life the only barrier he is not aware of it.

Ross and Susan merged now as one completely inseparable. David hoped they would fulfil all their potential together.

Matt bounced through the doorway cheerful and upbeat. He arrived with Penny sharing a joke with both laughing at the varying asides each making.

David recognised the pang of jealousy rise within, a new experience. Subtly making him question himself and his worth in her eyes.

Penny caught his look of anguish and understood smiling at him in reassurance her beauty enhanced by being loved so much, in their brief moment of connection, any doubts left him, their love absolute.

Most of the group helped themselves to the coffee on offer as they looked toward David and Ferral for a lead following the morning's session.

David asked for Sam, Tisha, Matt, Ellen and Susan to join him at the new round table set up behind the sofas in place of where the breakfast and lunchtime buffet had been. A green baize cloth now draped over the table surrounded by eight chairs.

David removed two of the chairs as the five noisily arranged themselves to fill the place gaps left by him.

He asked for Ross and Penny to join Ferral on the sofas and advised them to keep quiet no matter what they hear or see.

"Ferral will act when he senses danger," David assured them. "Ross she will be OK," he referred to Susan.

David began by shuffling the group around the table placing Tisha at the first point he positioned Sam to her right and Matt to her left. To Matt's right became Tisha and to his left he positioned Ellen. This meant Sam had Tisha to his left so he placed Susan to his right.

This allowed him to establish his intended Pentagram. The table acted as the outer circle with five points of reference. His placing meaning if lines were drawn, it would almost represent two reversed triangles within each other. With each person heading their own triangle, Tisha heads Susan and Ellen. Matt heads Susan and Sam. Ellen heads Sam and Tisha. Susan heads Tisha and Matt and Sam heads Matt and Ellen.

He explained the five-pointed star is one of the most powerful symbols in human history in particular recognised by both Indian and Chinese cultures. The pentagram represents the ancient civilisations as well as symbolising Christianity. Each point represents fire, water, air, earth and psyche or energy, fluid, breath, matter and mind. He gave many interpretations helping them understand.

David's voice consciously deepened becoming quieter, almost whispering, where it was barely audible to those around the table.

"Just like a séance, please touch or hold hands. Do not be afraid," he emphasised. "You will gradually become tired. Remember you will become conscious of a thread as you leave your bodies. This can be white, grey or silver as you travel on the astral plane. Spiritually this links you to your physical self. Protect this at all costs, it is very strong but do not forget this, otherwise you will die," he said forcefully.

A tear ebbed as a sound from Ellen.

"Don't concern yourself my dear. David will protect us," Tisha comforted. "At the moment we are just practicing aren't we?" She looked to him for agreement.

"Absolutely this is a test run. A little later, I will also include Vijay and Ross into the group. Beware there are four of you that have entities attached to your threads. These are like barnacles on a ship, acting like hooks for elements, evil, to take hold."

His quiet tone had progressively become mesmerizing to them and whilst hearing and understanding what he was saying, they began to fall under the spell he was creating. As sleep beckoned, darkness fell on each.

Like a breeze, gathering pace into a wind or a train rushing by at speed, the tornado circling ever faster swirling around them.

Ferral, Ross and Penny noticed those in the group, gripping each other's hands, eyes tightly closed, rocking to and fro, back and forth, without sound.

One by one, David touched each soul briefly as he passed through the ring of the circle, their astral awakening saw him disappear into a grey abyss. The mist fog, threatening to clear, fear checked and touched their being.

Tisha, the first to be aware of David as he passed by, a light touch as he pulled them from their physical alignment and placed them within the astral level where each could be comfortable. She had been here before many times. To her with the abilities she had this was quite normal and expected. In the distance, she saw Matt still asleep. Surprisingly Samuel to her right was awakening. She wondered what he was going to make of it. Arising from their sleep Susan and Ellen's mist began to break up and clear.

Suddenly, everything shut down each pulled, dragged back to their physicals. Sam had broken the circle frightened on awakening. He fought against the wind not understanding. He had shocked himself awake.

Gradually as each woke and released their grip, Sam realised what he had done and by the time they all became awake he was apologizing profusely to all.

Placated by David as a normal occurrence for the first time experience, he asked them what they could remember.

Matt quite disappointed the only one not waking. He could not remember anything. Ellen and Susan had become aware of David touching them gently on passing faster and faster in a circle. Tisha had woken at the beginning to see others and their shapes, mentally picturing the triangles set out before her. She recalled David's touch and become conscious of her heightened senses.

David was pleased with them all and said so. He appreciated the level Tisha had attained already in her psychic development.

Sam had been shocked he had noticed the thread and saw himself at the other end convinced he was dead. He tried to pull himself toward his body and as he did so this took him out of the alignment, David was trying to build.

"Now you all know what to expect let us see how long we stay the next time," David suggested.

Ross fascinated asked. "Any chance I could get involved David, I would like the experience."

"Be assured I am keeping you in reserve, but don't expect fun Ross," he smiled at him.

He turned back to the circle and in the same mesmerising tone. "Come let us try again and calmly this time. Remember you will feel the same and see strange things, be put off balance, at odds, different. It will become normal for some of you and unusual for others. Approach all you see rationally, we will all be as one mind."

This time each in turn awakened to the sound and touch of David going through and around them rapidly. Matt told himself to rationalise totally in awe of his surroundings the group within a much larger circle than he had imagined. It appeared to him to span for miles, the triangle lines mentioned by Tisha lit up like air terminal runways, to the path of each other comforting.

He became aware of thoughts not his own and knew he was listening in to the thought patterns of the person he faced. Turning to his right Tisha straight ahead, Sam had the same wonder as he began to consider what was outside the circle. Immediately by thought David told him to concentrate on the now and get used to seeing the thoughts of others and being on their level.

By his will, David instructed them all to return and wake up in their physical bodies.

To Penny, Ross and Ferral each described the experiences as David applauded them for remembering. This is very difficult when considering how easy it is to forget a dream.

"What comes next?" Ferral asked.

"Thought training, I can get you on the level but your will and how you impose it is important. It is the only protection you have." David suggested. "This is a mental not physical process."

"Why do we need protecting?" Ellen enquired.

"As I mentioned earlier because four of you already have entities or elements attached to your cord or threads feeding off your minds." David answered.

"I never saw anything."

"Matt you never really looked they're grey or black patches in your cord, a thinning here, a frayed edge there. You have to look for them," David implored.

"How can they harm us?" Sam asked, not wishing to think about it.

"One, most importantly they can stop you returning to your body by severing the cord or certainly block your entry back," David discussed. "Secondly and more importantly, they are hooks placed there by a higher intelligence and psychically more developed to control you and your thought patterns, trap you if you like."

"Can we stop it happening?" It was Susan's turn to show concern. "How do we repair our cords?"

"If the circle does not break and if the elements are not too strong each cord is renewable dependant on the last travel," he paused for effect. "The danger is very real you must all fight with a clear mind."

"Can we beat whatever it is?"

"Maybe, Sam maybe. It depends on its level of attainment skill and will."

Relishing the fight Tisha asked. "When do we go to work David?"

"Tonight Tisha, so get some rest all of you," he suggested looking at the group.

David sat on one of the leather sofas with Penny, Ross and Ferral sat opposite.

"What are our chances?" asked Ferral. "Can we help?"

"Of course, you are helping by supporting us, Ross come over by the round table," requested David.

Ross and David sat quietly facing one another.

"Ross I am going to take you on the same journey as the others and show you what they see. I will expect you to take over from your sister Ellen if she falters; she is the weakest so is likely to break ranks. We cannot tell if this will happen but whatever, if the circle is broken you must, must," he emphasized. "Join in and keep the circle whole."

"What if two of us break away and I have already joined."

"Then I also will join it and if necessary Vijay will also come into the equation. My intention is to put another triangular layer above where you will be able to easily drop into the pentagram."

"Where will you be?"

"Around you, I am not part of the protection you have but within the upper layer of the circle." He reassured. "Your next question Ross is easily answered. Ferral will attempt to wake us all."

"Oh, that fill's me with great comfort I always wanted to know what death was like!"

As Ross's journey began, he could feel David's pull. He felt outside of himself watching. He could see himself at the table eyes closed at peace and looked for his thread noting it was clear of the entities talked of by David.

He looked down on Penny and Ferral he heard them talking. Penny discussing the pressures David being under. He felt cold and instantly believed this was a state of mind, his hearing crystal clear he felt light, tremendously fit and agile, he became self-conscious of what he might look like.

He felt another tug David was pulling him towards a light high above him. He travelled at an amazing speed. The higher he went the brighter the colours.

Rising high above the manor, above the country yet saw every part of the detail. People were all around him walking through and past him chattering like hollow shadows aware and not aware brimming with their own purpose. Still David pulled, he could hardly catch his breath he thought about his breathing how was he alive. Was he alive? Another tug, he had started to panic conscious of another level.

Different people, normal they were moving out of his way excusing themselves, they noticed him, were talking to him, as they passed by. He checked his thread, thin but still visible and intact. Where was he? He was keeping up with everyone's pace but it was fast. A further tug he recognised where he is outside the Shanghai Bell building in Pudong. He watched the comings and goings of people fascinated. He felt weighed down as if this level gave him some gravity.

He became conscious of a pulling on his thread dragging, he tried to resist he liked where he was. Travelling fast he stopped his resistance. Images of country, manor and the drawing room racing past, he woke up.

David, Penny and Ferral all sitting at the table were watching his reaction.

Ross mouthed "Wow."

David smiled. The others laughed.

"Remember what you saw and your experience it will help your expectation next time," David suggested.

As evening approached, they each tried to gain rest. David strolled in the quiet of the manor grounds with Penny. She worried at the burden he carried.

"I'm afraid for you my love, I feel you're in such danger, you're protecting others but who is protecting you?"

"Meeting you because of this situation has for me been the ultimate joy," he said complimenting and pacifying her. "I've experienced feelings I didn't realise existed.

"If what we have has to be brief then I'm a better man for knowing you," he portrayed genuine emotion towards her.

She cradled her head against his shoulder praying their love would go on. They strolled in silence enjoying their precious moments together.

The group reformed following a light evening meal arranged by Ferral only Tisha sat at the table ready for the challenge ahead.

"Please," David ushered. "Be seated at the table as Ferral brings in our guest."

Once each had taken up their previous positions, David informed them if for whatever reason the circle breaks Ross will replace them.

"Sam please take these, I've been meaning to give you them they are rightfully yours," Ross handed him carved as arrows, two brightly coloured orange pieces of wood joined together crossed with reed given to him by Aolun's family as good luck symbols.

The drawing room door opened with Ferral leading the tall-wizened old man, a flicker of light, a glimmer of sanity in his eyes.

The clinic had to force feed him at times to keep him alive and his struggle with life showed. Unless he came through his trauma, he would undoubtedly die.

"Vijay will join us and will sit as I will alongside the five of you we both will be there as you travel.

"David, it means you are not with us at the table." Tisha's confidence visibly ebbing away. "Will this strain the five pronged pentagram circle? Where will you be?"

"I will be around all of you guiding, helping and supporting. Vijay himself has an important part to play if he is to survive," David let his voice trail off as Vijay blinked he acknowledged his words.

"The pentagram is still intact five is the right number and not all of us will stay the distance," he went on. "You will be protected, that is its importance."

"Good luck to you all, this is the moment in your life you may always remember, trust each other completely," His tone lowered into a quiet deep nasal twang.

With the ground work already laid it became much easier getting the group to the same level.

David sped around the circle, tried, but hit the wall represented by Vijay. To move around the circle clockwise, he joined a triangle this one the line which runs from Ellen and getting to Susan then moving around the circle again on to Sam and so on. This had the effect of making them stronger. The more times he made the run, the stronger each became.

It was time.

Instructing each in turn, he asked them all to focus their will on Vijay with the view to opening his mind. Vijay knew this was going to happen because he had been reading their minds. He was weak and could not challenge them himself.

One, two, three times they tried all five merged their minds fully. On the fourth time a breakthrough, they went for the fifth time and what they saw stopped them in their tracks. Fear immediately replaced confidence, doubt replaced certainty, their focus fragmented. Their fear like fire running through their veins bristling, as one mind each experiencing a chilling panic. Suddenly they were literally living their collective worst nightmares.

Susan, ever since she had been to medical school realised her worst had been the extraction of her organs on the operating table for donation, still alive knowing and feeling every cut without anaesthetic.

Matt cremated alive clawing at the inside of the oak rectangular box screaming, realizing the heat of the furnace rising as his flesh slowly burned, cooked inch by inch.

All fully centred on their ways of death, Sam, a common burial alive, six feet down and tons of earth gradually forcing, breaking its way through the wooden casket testing the quality of its maker. Ellen felt the teeth of a tenon-saw moving back and forth across her flesh, scraping on the bone of her leg, every tear of flesh pulling like lumps of hair dropping to the floor, butchers meat for a dog. She watched her joints rise as a pile, until only her torso remained.

Tisha, with her psychic awareness, offered to Satan, tied down with rats crawling through every orifice each following the path of a serpent slithering before them.

Living their fears as one mind the group locked together in their own abyss.

Vijay, separated as the zombie he had always dreaded, controlled forever as a puppet for others bidding.

After what seemed an eternity their very lives, souls and wills claimed to almost extinction. They are being beaten ground down without hope.

Gradually each became conscious, a faint brief flicker of light. A voice, a gentle touch a feeling of warmth, began to grow.

The light became stronger, the touch firmer, the voice louder and recognisable.

David urged them to wake up asking for their trust to follow him.

Each one opening their eyes simultaneously afraid of what the view would hold. Aware of their surroundings, sighs of relief audible to Ross, Penny and Ferral.

"You've only had your eyes closed for ten minutes," pointed out Ferral to a group who felt they had just experienced a lifetime of anguish. All were surprised immediately searching for timepieces to confirm the statement.

"There's no concept of time, we drift through past, present and future without barriers. It is but a brief moment of our earthly time," David confirmed.

"Welcome to the group Vijay, welcome," Tisha sitting opposite him realised they had, as a group assumed his fear too and he nodded, smiling weakly.

He knew what just happened and spoke for the first time since he had arrived at the manor.

"Thank you, thank you, very much," Vijay displaying the typical Indian graciousness of side-to-side head bowing to those that have helped and deserved his respect, his accent thick and rich in his native Indian dialect.

"I've been waiting to die."

"Vijay you made the group whole, will you take up the fight with us against Setna?" David held out his hand to him, shaking his in friendship, an action the rest followed in their own way.

David watched Vijay his inner strength struggling with his abject fear.

"Please, please help me and I will try for you," he stammered wanting so much to belong, at last his life opening up to a freedom previously unknown to him nor dreamed.

"That's all we can ask," it was Sam still relieved at coming out from his own nightmare.

They each explained their view of what had happened, the nightmares each held and how David had pulled them out.

David pointed out to them they must look for light and solutions in every corner. Recognise their fears and rationalize them. Assess what is real and what is not. They were all getting stronger but hadn't faced any real challenge.

As the group broke up for the day, Ferral moved toward David for his summing up.

"How were they?" He asked.

"Fledglings only, but Tisha has the insight. What concerns me most are the elements, entities attached to their cords," Ferral's facial expression betrayed his lack of understanding.

"They're not necessarily evil in all cases, but these are spiritual beings that do bidding for a higher master or intelligence psychically." David explained. "Like limpets they cling on to weaker souls, chewing, gnawing away at the persons thread, gathering information and feeding off the energy which helps themselves to survive."

"A type of spiritual leach," Ferral's understanding increasing. "How many have these?"

"Sam has a couple, quite sizable and noticeable. Ellen, Susan and Matt have smaller ones attached.

"Tisha is free entirely having now seen Vijay's thread he is covered. He needs help before we reform the circle," David showed concern.

David collected Vijay from one of the drawing room windows Vijay was seeing life here for the very first time.

"Vijay my friend come with me into the courtyard. Please bring your much needed food," David noticed how hungry Vijay is, by the way he grabbed the bites from the running buffet supplying them all whenever needing to replenish themselves, Ferral had suggested this as a likely comfort support to match the possible traumas.

Vijay diligently went through his plate of food as they strolled in the fresh air. He had decided to put his faith in this wise man beside him. He had not felt this safe in a long, long time.

David realised the greyish hue gradually began to fade in favour of his normal tanned complexion. Even his previously dark lank hair had started to assume the sheen of health.

Quietly Vijay spoke. "My thanks to you, I was dead and shouldn't have returned my life is yours. Know I'm very, very afraid."

"Yes we have much to repair in you," David suggested.

He held Vijay's hands speaking to him softly gradually imposing his will upon him taking Vijay on his own journey looking into his background and home life.

As David watched, the journey took him to China and events leading up to the photograph. He saw the friendship Vijay had built with Shyam. The sadness of seeing the zombie like creature his friend had become.

He spent time removing the elements attached to Vijay by touching them and releasing their hold. He watched as they scuttled away from Vijay, like shoals of fish. He became stronger for it.

David searched through Vijay's mind for his special place. It was a mud hut, where his grandparents played with him as a child, outside of Nepal.

Poor families sticking together as a community supporting each other unconditionally, cricket the favourite past time of the children. Wooded branches makeshifts for stumps. Lumps of old cut timber for the bats, reeds tied together pressed hard to make the ball.

He watched Vijay field for his team. He allowed time for him to cement the images of better times. David had a feeling of 'being watched' from a distance. Despite this, he had to push on into the mind of Vijay for information about Setna.

Dewang Setna, he learnt was a renegade Shaman. Steeped in a religious upbringing he originally brought well-being to his followers. Sadly, a person corrupted by the power he used to help individuals and died because of it.

He is now testing his strength on the spiritual astral planes and succeeding by controlling Shyam Rosha, Vijay and planting the seeds in the minds of the patients David has had to treat at the manor, hoping he had managed to wrestle Vijay away from him.

David woke Vijay and suggested he joined the others in the drawing room. It was time to begin the fight.

Chapter 14

David and Vijay both entered the drawing room where the circle formed and then extended to include Vijay who joined the group.

David spoke to all of them. "You are all aware of the dangers and what's in store. Believe you will be OK at all times. Remember, rationalize and stay calm. Believe some, not all, its common sense so you make judgements. Some of you have elements or entities still attached to your cords, pull them off and I will help, scare them, anything, get rid of them or they will weigh you down," he continued.

"Embrace your fears don't let them control you. Stay as one mind, if the circle breaks close ranks, I will take care of the fallen ones and Ross will probably enter," He looked around the group for acknowledgement. He noted the decided lack of confidence among them and tried to motivate them. "Expect the unexpected, stay as one mind, you will succeed. Good luck to you. We will win together."

David went across to Penny and openly kissed her gently on her lips without word.

"Ross, I expect to come for you so please stay relaxed."

Ross moved toward Susan at the table and touched her hand.

"Ferral you know what to do."

He nodded.

David's tone deepened as he spoke again to the group reassuring with the same mesmerizing tone as before. Gradually sleep washed over them. David believed they were ready as they could be. He felt the same shiver of unease run through him he had first encountered and experienced several times since his first meeting with Shyam at his London apartment.

The circle passed through their worst fears and nightmares shrugging them off easily as David intended, his words hauntingly telling them to rationalise. Through these first moments out of their bodies, each became aware of their elements. Black and grey figures, entities attached to their threads, trying to break the contact with their physical bodies and hold on to their spiritual self. Drawn to the weaker members each entity moved from one to another getting stronger. Both Tisha and David worked hard together to pull them away, touching them moving through and around them at speed attempting to disorientate the beings. David and Tisha's goodness burning through them as shafts of light breaking through their black and grey embodiments.

Vijay joined them both as David had freed him earlier.

With a suddenness, catching the group by surprise, the freed elements attacked Vijay with such venom guided to him by a superior force. He yelped like a dog, bitten ferociously and started to sink into the lowest division of the astral known as Avichi, the hellish place, where souls are tortured, tormented. Losing his will, he was fast succumbing to a depth of despair unable to develop his own spiritual life, trapped literally by the elements.

With so many entities claiming their victim, their opened up below the group, a vast chasm enabling more entities to rise up to join the attack on him. As one mind, the group dropped towards Avichi in free fall in an attempt to save Vijay. Dragged down by entities, the group were holding onto Vijay gripping him fighting hard to save him, but they were fast losing ground, themselves steadily pulled downward toward a sea of souls.

The heat making steams of sweat fire upwards like serpent tongues. Glue like saliva wrapping around their limbs and torso subtly pulling, forcing each one of them downwards.

Hell or purgatory beckoned, dragging them to their certain death. Vijay screaming to the rest of the group to release their grip on him to let him go and save themselves before they die too.

The group took up the fight their will of mind trying to drive the elements from Vijay. Rapid speeds of light darting in and out of the dark grey clouds formed as smog almost blocking Vijay's very existence. The group fought relentlessly against the threat following David's lead, sounds of laughter eerily touching each of their souls. At David's insistence, they maintained their battle for Vijay but continued dropping fast gathering speed towards the abyss.

To the surprise of Ferral, Ross and Penny, David woke up.

"What has happened?" concern voiced by Ferral.

"Help me please wake the group, quietly and quickly as you can. I must get back, leave Vijay alone, do not wake or touch him," he insisted.

Moving toward an armchair positioned at the edge of the middle window of the drawing room he checked the slumped body of Vijay on a chair by the round table.

David sat positioning himself he ordered.

"Wake them, wake them now!"

The scene he returned to, a desperate a tug of war against the elements, death the inevitable outcome for the group holding on despairingly to Vijay all dropping like stones towards Avichi, not knowing what to do, believing holding on to him the right thing to do.

He waited watching for his moment. Each one in the group struggling. A split second passed, they were gone.

Vijay disappeared overwhelmed by the claiming entities his screams noting his distress.

David willed himself to Vijay's side and although the elements tried to attach themselves to him, his spiritual attainment meant they would never be able to take hold. In the moment, they released their grip on Vijay to attack him, David pulled Vijay from them travelling higher and higher, faster and faster until Avichi closed beneath them and Vijay was free of all attachments.

David pulled him upwards to the Nirvana plane higher than Vijay had ever attained. It cleansed his spirit breathing life into his whole being. His soul alive and strong Vijay felt goodness at the level.

David mentally communicating to him suggested it was time to return to the manor.

Tisha woke first with her first word of concern being for Vijay. In turn, they gradually came to with Ferral asking for quiet pointing to Vijay and David still asleep.

Away from the window and the table the five related to the others what had happened. They were sorry to have to let Vijay go and feared David battling alone without them would not save him.

"Do you realise David came back?" Ross opened the question to the group.

They shook their heads in disbelief.

"He asked us to wake you but leave Vijay alone." Penny informed.

Ferral made them aware of the stirring of David and Vijay.

A sigh of audible relief rang out amongst them.

David smiled at them and checked on Vijay. He looked well.

"I'm OK David, very good, I'm well never better, thank you, thank you my dear friend." Vijay just short of tears, so grateful to him.

A general buzz filled the room, excited at the battle won, congratulating each another.

The tone of Penny's voice spread an eerie silence within the drawing room.

"David you're not celebrating, it's not over is it?" her words catching all in the room.

He shook his head. "I'm afraid not people, It has only just begun."

"Has it all been for nothing?" Tisha asked despair creeping into her voice.

"No, No Tisha we have won a battle, that is all it was a test of the strength we have no more," he conceded. "Next time we will face the true test."

He hesitated. "We have yet to fight the war."

"What do we do now David? I thought that was it?" reasoned Sam.

"The good thing, Vijay has been freed, cleansed; he is now stronger and able to join us in the fight," David acknowledged Vijay's agreement.

"The pentagram group needs to travel again," he volunteered eliminating Vijay from this round. "We need to free and cleanse those of you who still have entities or elements attached."

He suggested they sit at the table again, Ellen and Susan were afraid to go again so soon. Sam and Tisha were ready Matt was OK but did not wish to go again.

Within seconds they were travelling never realising David had put them to sleep, fluorescent green surrounding them.

David reassured them no harm would befall them the colour will highlight the elements. He suggested they get to work.

Matt cleared by Tisha, which left Sam, Susan and Ellen.

The three David, Matt and Tisha freed Susan. She appeared weaker for it because of the fight for Vijay, but she joined the fight for Sam. By now Ellen was sinking fast, she too had become exhausted following the fight for Vijay. Several elements circling and squeezing the life from her the thread visibly frayed. With Sam freed all five fought hard for Ellen. Hurting and weakened, but surviving. David formed a circle around her and told her to wake up.

The group watched as she disappeared like a mirage from sight. Then the group became conscious of David enveloping them keeping them safe impressing on them to continue to rationalise and stay calm. Expect the unexpected.

"Wake, Wake up group now!" David ordered them mentally.

"That was quick." It was Ferral's voice causing a nervous laugh as a reaction from them all.

"I believe this is enough for the day." David applauded them openly. "Well done to you all, I feel tomorrow we will be ready, I suggest you get some rest."

Late into the evening, he sat in the courtyard, listening to the rustling of the wind gently breezing through the trees. Water dripped somewhere creating a hollow tin sound. Animal sounds in the distance bringing a slight chill with the night air, high above the stars, pointing the way to outer galaxies.

David and Penny silently sat together, bodies close, arms entwined, letting the courtyard envelope them. Pure heaven David thought. Hell is for tomorrow!

The early morning held the chill of the previous night's air.

Ferral had given David a name and directions of how to get to a nearby primary school he wished to acquire a blackboard and white chalk.

While David did have a purpose for the chalk the real reason was for time to talk to Ross on his own, by asking him for a lift to take him to the school ensured it will happen.

The Panhard purred comfortably as they travelled along the winding country roads of Berkshire. It was the first time David had been in Ross's car appreciating the love and care he lavished on it.

"It seems a lifetime ago since all this began," Ross considered. "Is Sam alright now David?"

"Pretty much, like us he's still at risk," he offered. "I believe he will have enough protection for what is to come."

"This ride is not about chalk is it David?"

"No Ross, I need to prepare you so you understand what is in store for us all," David said solemnly.

"Yesterday didn't finish it then?"

"No today is the showdown. Tisha is ready and aware of the unusual and can rationalise what she sees. You are also stronger than the others, it will be important for you to make judgements for others should Tisha and I be busy."

"What's going to happen David, do we even know our enemy?"

"Oh yes Ross, it is Dewang Setna."

"But he's dead, Penny told us he died in China," Ross was confused.

"Exactly, he is dead," David emphasised. "Therefore we are in his world, we have our feet firmly in the physical, and Setna is in the spiritual making him the stronger."

"How, why is he doing this, surely he can't harm us?" Ross believed.

"Let me take you on Setna's journey as it relates to our group. Setna once, would have been described as a holy man, a Shaman in India, there for the good of the community he served in his native land except, he was also quite a genius in terms of writing computer software code and he'd seen an opportunity to help and support his beloved country. Bear in mind there are several aspects to Setna. Good business sense, love of his native land and the ability to transcend the physical and spiritual worlds as a Shaman," David paused.

"What's a Shaman?"

"A way of life running through certain prominent families steeped in mystery, where the teachings are passed down through the age's father to son apparently dating back to prehistoric times," David recalled from his readings. "Setna is a result of a long line of powerful occultists."

"What are they able to do?" Ross's interest awakened.

"Some say they are able to change the weather," David smiled. "Seriously, they're noted for their control of spirits, interpreting dreams through astral projection. They can diagnose and cure human suffering."

"Isn't that a good thing?" reasoned Ross.

"Absolutely, but they can also cause harm."

"How has Setna affected us as a group?" Ross asked, understanding better.

"Tisha's mental journey to her childhood, memories by a cottage stream playing by her father who was fishing. Two boys coasting down the stream in a punt, Setna was there on the punt and tipped Shyam into the water. Shyam himself came to my London apartment. In India, both Shyam and Vijay were Setna's partners, Vijay more in business and Shyam more in childhood." David looked to Ross, checking if he appreciated the connections building.

"Did Setna kill Shyam?" Ross asked.

"It's likely, yes, or his control of him led him to commit suicide," David considered. "He tried to wrestle his own soul away from Setna."

"Did it work?"

"I'm afraid not, let's move to the Chinese angle. Matt introduced Setna to the famed cartel. The cartel tried to swindle Setna out of his software by bringing in Sam to work with Aolun. We know Matt and Sam have mentally suffered and Aolun has died."

Ross shook his head the connections amazing him.

David continued. "Let us move to the hospital in Pudong. I believe the cartel somehow, caused Setna to have a heart attack Chinese spirits at work no doubt, probably because he was getting too close to their operation I cannot be sure. From what we gather there was at least a confrontation. Enter Jack Kefford, who ended up dying himself trying to save that spark left in Setna, but fortunately not before Sam had spent some time with him. Ellen followed, looking for answers and herself found mental anguish."

They pulled up outside the small Community Primary School found from Ferral's directions. Little people in blue uniforms, running through the gates to the sound of the playground bell calling them in to assembly.

Ross waited in the Panhard as David went in search of the head teacher.

Chalk in hand, blackboard in the boot David settled back in the car to begin their drive back to the manor.

"So there has to be more connections David?" Ross continuing their previous conversation.

"Matt, Ellen and Sam ended up at Ditton Manor and touched on Susan who went with you to Shanghai. Susan encountered Vijay or Shyam. Vijay came to us too,"

"It has become complicated."

"Yes with the common theme being Setna, he appears to have controlled those close to him and set off a chain reaction in others."

"Why would he do this and what harm can he cause us now?" Ross was shocked at link after link.

"Revenge, his stolen software and his pride insulted," he suggested.

"What convinced you it was him?"

"I viewed Vijay's mind, and I saw the newsprint picture of Shyam, Setna and Vijay recreated in Vijay's mind. Setna himself was laughing at me."

"Bloody hell!"

"The harm he can cause now he is free to operate in the spirit world is immense. He probably still controls Shyam. He would've made some sort of deal with a higher being to continually be able to attack us from the spirit world," David thought about this carefully. "What worries me Ross is, who is it he's done the deal with?"

They were getting close to the manor as Ross asked. "You said earlier you needed to prepare me how?"

"Simply you must rationalise, be strong for others, you will see mind blowing stuff. It could be anything, gory limbs, heads severed, even your own. You have to remember your thread. You will be in spirit form, you must look to protect the others at all costs," David urged him.

"Are we all going out together at the same time on the astral?"

"Yes this time we must!" David thanked him for the lift to the school and shook his hand holding his wrist in complete friendship Ross felt his respect.

The others, separated around the building, were either sitting reading in the drawing room or walking around the grounds, sitting outside in the courtyard or like Ferral and Susan attending to the business of the clinic itself.

David decided to let the morning go towards relaxing the afternoon would be soon enough for all to come together.

He went in search of Penny, and caught up with her walking around the manor walls with Tisha.

"Hi both," He greeted and naturally kissed Penny on the cheek. Tisha and Penny linked arms with his either side and continued their walk together, chatting as if he never joined them.

Back inside, David went to the drawing room and the circular table where he straightened the green baize cloth covering. Taking the chalk from his pocket, he carefully drew line by line the pentagram.

As he finished he looked up and realised he had an audience and to no-one in particular suggested they each study the drawing and memorise the flow of the lines.

"If any of you get into trouble you must picture yourselves holding on to a line and being within the circle. This will give you protection," he assured them.

By late afternoon, David felt they had rested enough.

Ferral and Penny once again were not involved they had their own instructions, both needed to look after those who returned and Ferral needed to look carefully at each ready to pull them back and wake them if necessary.

David worried, this will be a new experience for him never had he used his psychic abilities in anger. He felt concern and wondered how his actions, might be viewed in the spirit world. He dismissed the thought.

The rest of them were chattering nervously, each dealing with their own nightmares. David avoided comforting them at this stage believing, their fears would provide them with a degree of protection an edge to keep them looking over their shoulders.

They silently sat at the table, five of them at the points of the pentagram understanding the clear lines to follow. Ferral had placed three additional chairs for the others.

Tisha, Sam, Ellen, Matt and Susan each at their original points were joined by David who sat opposite Tisha between Ellen and Susan he directed Vijay to sit between Susan and Sam opposite Matt and asked Ross to sit opposite Susan in between

Matt and Tisha. This had the effect of overlaying a triangle over the pentagram and not breaking into it. David suggested this quietly keeping his tone of voice even as he spoke.

Watching, Ferral and Penny noticed one by one in the group they fell to sleep, their chins resting on their chests. Hands crossed on top of the table positioned touching a chalked line of the pentagram. Unlike a séance, Ferral noted their hands and bodies did not touch. The lines of the pentagram joined them instead.

On the astral plane, David believed they were expected elementals ready for them. The hooks Setna had amongst them very real.

All eight, found themselves sitting on a fairground carousel a blaze of colour set before them, riding the magically painted horses, spinning around faster and faster to tunes dating back, centuries gone by. Designed for their enjoyment to create a false sense of confidence.

David left them immediately disappearing from view.

Childlike, they remembered with excitement the feelings of joy riding on these magnificent machines giving them a special kind of pleasure.

Rows of four horses, swinging back and forth they travelled at high speed, side by side. They were not alone. In front and behind the group, others were enjoying the ride. The group members began to wonder who they were. Children yet not children, people yet not people. As they spun ever faster, the figures started to disappear forming shadows black and grey replacing them. Waiting, waiting to pounce.

The carousel slowed, instead of seated in rows of four and three with David gone, they were seated not on painted horses anymore but in cinema rows, stall style seats with the show about to begin.

Confronted with blinding, screaming noise shocking them almost awake, almost. Fear rising to the surface within each, they held one another tightly waiting as the darkness enveloped them.

Black space, silence hung in the air ominously.

Locked in their seats in a visual wilderness, they were powerless to break free.

Brightness growing rapidly upon them the carousel still moving now as a stage, it slowed almost to a stop. They were watching pantomimes. A stage full of differing acts performing for them. They were being drawn into being part of the performances juggling, dancing, acting, playing instruments. They became aware of the stage turning they could not move, dare not, where would they go? Puppets without strings forced to watch.

The stage stopped turning and the acts disappeared one by one as quickly as they had appeared. Black again, silence, the curtain had fallen.

The group watched unsure what to do searching through the darkness mesmerised by the being literally growing in front of them getting larger and larger before their eyes. They looked on in wonder. Fascinated by the sharpness of the colours, blue, gold and red, hands drawn out toward them beckoning, each dwarfed by the sheer size and scale of the figure. She sat higher than the highest skyscraper and as wide as an airliner. A magnificent sight, a beautiful creature of myth beckoning them toward her, inviting them to her bosom, she was though, a spiritual creature to be wary of.

Slowly like a magnet all seven, Ross, Susan, Sam, Tisha, Matt, Vijay and Ellen were being shunted, drawn, pulled, by their seated row towards this gigantic woman of beauty sitting legs folded in the yoga lotus pose, padmasana. Twenty severed arms protruding from her waistband a garland of skulls, their decapitation recent, decorating her neck and breast. She proud of the conquests gained and thirsty for more tapping into the fears of their souls.

Ellen screamed recognising the face of her father amongst them.

"Rationalise my sister." Ross shouted at her. Jack Kefford's face immediately disappeared from view, her nightmare.

Eight huge arms each the size of airliner wings swaying from side to side in front of them, tuned to a perceived rhythmic chant, a hundred serpents writhing around her limbs enjoying her. They mere infants by comparison.

The group drew closer fixed on their path knowing she was reeling them in towards her.

Drawn mesmerised by the hypnotic chants the group almost reluctantly giving up themselves as a sacrifice as the loss of will to fight swept through their very beings.

They became conscious of a flesh rotting pungent smell, watching as she pulled from behind her a blood dripping live head severed at the base of a neck once joined to a male torso.

"Setna!" cried Vijay in disbelief, all his fears hit him at once terrified at what he saw. The man used to be his friend and mentor before…, he left the thought hanging in his mind.

The group felt David's presence touching them deliberately and talking to them gently.

"This is Setna's own astral nightmare, we are living it with him and he is using it for revenge to trap us."

"Join me, join me Vijay, your friends too," shouted the blood dripping head of Setna.

Vijay immediately became zombie like, the seeds planted by Setna, enacted designed for him to make him his slave.

Susan had been shouting and pulling hard trying to free Vijay from the mental hold Setna had over him. She was desperately weak but was determined not to let Vijay go. She cried out for David.

David moved toward Vijay's slamming into his side with the effect of shocking him out of his state. David passed through him fast like a speeding train,

Vijay realised quickly what had happened, Setna's hold on him released, his head swaying, held firmly by Kundalini he was laughing and shouting loudly to him. "I will come again for you, remember me my friend."

Setna's face disappeared replaced by Shyam. Vijay gasped reeling and started to drift downwards away from the group in terror.

Suddenly, the group separated their stall seats disappearing from under them. Each one individually, being dragged with sheer will by the being in front of them, each arm assigned mentally, forcing them to her.

Tisha began shouting at Sam to stop pulling Ellen towards what they would later realise was the woman Kali Ma the destroyer or Kundalini, the Indian mythical goddess.

Ellen screamed at Sam for help but he too was locked with the same mental seed sown by Setna, Sam realised this was the feeling he could not shake off, if he became trapped it was likely others would automatically follow. Forced to drag Ellen as well as himself into capture. He was sacrificing Ellen for the freedom of his Mother and Father, Jennifer and Charles who he saw were part of Kali Ma's garland of skulls.

He was touched on his hand and held the cross symbol of Aolun which Ross had given him.

It gave him strength mentally, looking again in search of his Mother and Father both images had thankfully disappeared.

Mentally David told Tisha what to do. Tisha feigned helplessness and began falling she yelled at Sam crying for help. It drew his attention stopping him it was enough for David to pull Ellen away.

"Wake up Ellen you must return now." David ordered.

Sam realised he had been tricked and portrayed anger towards Tisha. He immediately felt the pull of his cord. He rationalised, Tisha had been saving him and Ellen, calming and went to her side. He watched as Ellen disappeared in the surrounding mist.

Locked in a mission, Matt and Susan searching for a way to fend off the mental anguish, drumming louder and louder, terrifying images of raw flesh being eaten as live screaming bodies were the feast. Attacked by their own seeds of fear, planted by Setna not as strong as Vijay's or Sam's, but his laughter cut through them as a knife. Susan was collapsing from sheer exhaustion because of the fight for Vijay earlier.

Kali Ma grabbed Vijay and Setna began to bite ferociously into his neck he needed to sever Vijay's head so she could attach it to her garland of skulls, by doing so Vijay would fulfil his promise to her, instead of his own he would give up to her another's soul, then he would be set free.

With Vijay caught by the goddess's arms and Ellen breaking from the group, she disappearing to return to the manor, the others immediately broke up drawn toward the danger.

Blood spurted from Setna's hold on Vijay and covered Susan like sticky glue pulling her toward the garland of skulls. Kali Ma's arms reaching out for her, attempting to grab a new trophy.

Ross went to Susan's aid, caught by her waistband arms. She began ripping his flesh tearing pieces of him and feeding them to the live skulls around her neck, his ripped skin revealing open bloody flesh and juice for the serpents. He was being progressively destroyed each slither sliced for cannibalistic pleasure, the dripping blood drank by the serpents adorning her body like bracelets.

He heard David gently talking to him. "It is an illusion Ross rationalise. You are spirit you are not bleeding you cannot be harmed in this way."

Immediately the gnawing sounds of the skulls stopped, laughter chilling through his being. They still had Susan and Vijay.

Both Tisha and Matt trying to fight for Vijay aware of Susan's and Ross's plight both getting trapped themselves being dragged ever closer to her. Doubt crept through the group they knew they were losing the fight.

The sounds of David continually reminding them to rationalise and remember the pentagram, while being drowned out by Setna shouting for joy, his offerings to Kali Ma meant he would soon be free to roam in the spirit world, a whole being again to exact revenge on others who had crossed him. He was enjoying the fight he and his goddess were winning.

David realised this was the deal the freedom of Setna soul. He doubted it was Kali Ma's to give up or that she would, willingly let him go.

As Sam struggled, a voice said to him. "Be strong, I will help you, I will protect you. I am your guardian now," Sam gasped, his good friend Bei Aolun was by his side. He felt the boost of confidence beat through his soul.

Ellen had woken to Penny on her left and Ferral to her right with both comforting her and pointing to the others still deep in sleep. She told them what had happened so far. She felt she wanted to sleep but through fear chose not to. David had left instructions with Ferral to keep those that woke from sleeping until they all returned.

The table, continually checked by Ferral as his brief, David had asked him to watch them all carefully. Vijay appeared troubled. Hands still resting on the table they had slipped to the left side of a pentagram line, Ferral gently as possible moved them back on. He noticed his head was leaning awkwardly to one side. He looked closer to see if he could position his head better. He put his hand under Vijay's ear to cradle his head and put his other hand on his neck in an attempt to move it. His hand touched the baize of the tablecloth and he realised it was moist. His hand instinctively, drew back covered in blood, Vijay's neck bleeding freely.

Ferral started shaking and talking to Vijay pushing and pulling him back and forth to David's suggestion.

"What's wrong with Vijay?" Ellen questioning Ferral's action then saw the pool of red growing on the table.

"Help me with Vijay, quickly!" his voice urgent.

Ferral had the choice either he forced him awake or treated the wound. He decided on waking.

Gradually as if in a drunken stupor, Vijay began to arouse. Very shaken and for a short while could not believe where he was.

Ferral dressed Vijay's neck wound as Penny and Ellen listened to his update. Within seconds of Vijay finishing, Ferral shot up.

"I have to wake Susan, Ross and Matt now, Help me, help me." He urged them. "David is in my thoughts telling me to do so, quickly."

Ferral showed Penny, Vijay and Ellen what to do.

As they each in turn stirred, the explanations came.

Ross had been trying to get to Susan. Blinded, she was hooked on the garland of skulls. Matt himself had been fighting a long battle with a serpent held by one of the left arms of Kali Ma.

"How did you know her name?" Vijay asked.

"I don't know we all did, you too, yes?

Vijay nodded.

At the side of Sam there to protect his friend, Aolun whispered. "Let us try to destroy her and Setna together." He, at last, determined to pay back Setna for his pain and anguish of bleeding to death in the hospital bed in Pudong in front of a scared screaming beautiful woman. He was unaware Setna had controlled his spirit from the moment of his car crash and used him. Setna had decided to make Susan and Ellen believe they were seeing a loved one and used his body as the patient in the hospital bed with the image of either Vijay or Shyam for effect.

Setna had not appreciated Bei Aolun had broken free of his hold and had now become a spirit guide for Samuel Thornton.

Sam had become fearful, Tisha was fighting with the waistband of hands trying to force release their grip on her, he had seen Vijay fade away and he assumed him dead. The group had disintegrated and Setna seemed determined to get him now. He looked for Matt, Ross and Susan they were nowhere. Fear arose within him his turn coming. He welcomed his friend but doubted his strength to fight against Setna and Kali Ma. Mentally, he tormented by sounds shapes, images of sheer horror placed in his mind.

Aolun, unfortunately young of spirit had the brash of youth and although quite dead, he and Sam were both, easily deflected from causing harm.

Sam screamed entities directed at him swarming all over. Setna set them to feed off him. He created another fear that his group including Ross, Susan, Tisha and Ellen subconsciously were part of Kali Ma's skull set. Sam began to wilt from the battery he was taking from the elements. He began to give up.

David and Tisha joined forces pushing their will on Setna and Kali Ma.

Not enough, Kali many times in will stronger than they both were and used to challenge.

David took stock there were now only three of them and even with Aolun's help, they were being pulled towards the destroyer, once caught they would be trapped and put around her neck, Setna would then go free to attack those released back to the physical.

David tried to boost Sam's morale. "You can do it, you know it. You will win."

Mentally Sam grew as he fought, losing his attackers but he was still slowly being drawn into Kali.

David's own Chinese helper Liu Ying appeared at his side a welcome addition.

They all were becoming weary, losing their strength and the fight. An age had passed since they started, but during the fight, Kali and Setna were calling on every possible evil element or entity for strength seemingly a thousand fold more than they had in an attempt to claim their free wills.

David knew they would have to retreat to fight again they were all locked into the inevitable path where their very souls would be claimed for eternity. If this were his time, he would try to make it count in his personal fight against evil.

They were all in her grip she dripped with the blood of previous battles the stench even in this spirit world unbearable. It suffocated them as Setna's and her breath alone began to soak through them, invading, claiming them.

Setna laughing aloud awaiting his release by Kali he was enjoying the moment of triumph soon to come. He too knew they were faltering. His excitement getting the better of him knowing the price they would pay, it pushed his strength higher waiting for the kills.

As they became closer David noted Shyam was part of the garland of skulls no longer a zombie, sadly, some kind of peace.

"I cannot free myself," panicked Tisha. "She is pulling me, she is too strong."

David realised that he also had started to accept the fate of death. Her shouting pulled him out of his melancholy. He was wilting evil was winning.

He called on Tisha, Sam, Aolun and his own helper to provide one last push and fight to release themselves.

"Everyone start praying to whatever God is for you, but start praying now," shouted David, his tone causing shock amongst them.

For a brief moment Kali Ma's grip of will loosened. David noted fear in her three eyes for the first time since they had begun.

A brightness appeared from behind them small at first then developing strong full of warmth, shooting rays of light, fanning out across the misty darkness, the carousel a distant memory, decay lifting, smell diminishing.

Kali Ma, Kundalini the goddess destroyer looked smaller. Setna began to shrivel in the hands of Kali Ma. His triumphant grin replaced by horror and the realisation his soul was about to be lost forever. His blooded expression took on surprise as his head visibly exploded out from her hand. Dark rays shooting from his skull. Justice at last, was served his soul no longer capable of growth.

Setna, a mere pawn had now been merged as a garland trophy the facial silent scream visibly merging with Shyam as another trophy, his soul claimed, lost forever in evil. Kali Ma was never going to give him up.

David bowed and acknowledged the bright figure before him, turning once again to face the force of

Kali Ma. She continued to shrivel in size before his eyes blinded by the blaze of light behind him.

Kali Ma the destroyer, fading into oblivion literally being blown away into the distance, Tisha, Sam, Aolun and Liu Ying, David' Chinese spirit guide froze in awe at the goodness radiating in front and all around them strengthening and recharging their very souls with spiritual enlightenment, goodness, destroying the darkness beyond.

Sam embraced Aolun. David and Tisha thanked Ying. David would see him again soon.

Gradually the process of conscious, awakening in the drawing room of the manor began as the remaining part of the group came back from their journey.

David viewed the sea of faces looking towards him relief at their own safety.

"Is it over David?" Ferral posed. "Really over?"

"Yes," David confirmed. "It's over my friend."

Chapter 15

After a restful and peaceful night, one by one the group reformed in the manor's drawing room. Joyous at their success and safety.

Sunlight somehow shone brighter today, through the three majestic windows, drawing their rays inwards warming their souls.

Thoughts centred on the time spent by them all and especially by the initial three patients, Sam, Ellen and Matt, positioned looking out, how far each had come together within the group. A bond of special friendships created, likely to last forever.

David and Ferral had suggested before they went their separate ways that some debriefing should take place to help the patients.

The familiar coffee smell and biscuits laid out were a comforting sight of normality, ten souls replenishing themselves following weeks of trauma. At last, mentally comfortable.

David watching them helping themselves knowing they would have questions and some, maybe not straight away would have nightmares in the future because of their mental battles, which would undoubtedly leave scars.

Glad it was all over, he was saddened because his life had changed with friendships, he had never ever known before. He would go back to his old life knowing they were around, supporting him as his friends. He hoped Penny would stay with him a little while longer, trauma, tragedy and adversity can bring together unlikely pairings. He hoped what they have, lasts a little longer. Not for the first time, he found himself looking properly at her and their relationship and feeling an old fool, not expecting her to want the same kind of special relationship he needed and wanted.

"How did this begin?" Ellen looked toward David.

"It was all about power, building an organization, then the control of people, expanding all the time," he suggested.

"It certainly seems true of Setna," agreed Ferral. "And to be fair the Chinese cartel."

"Dewang was a shaman from quite a young age, he controlled his village at will." confirmed Vijay. "When we grew up he truly was a good person. Building his business he changed, especially once he went to China. He lost sight of the people he used to care for."

"What went so wrong for him?" asked Susan. "A controller of people, a good businessman, it should have been ideal."

"From what we know, he wanted control of the cartel in Shanghai, but the culture difference meant he was never going to be able to do that or bend them to his will like he could in his homeland. This was something he had never known, so the more he became frustrated, the more he looked for different ways of control. He resorted to blackmailing the cartel," Matt told the group.

"This isn't what you do to the Chinese, they realised he knew too much about them because of the data housed through his supplied software. Therefore, at first they looked to gain control of the software code, indirectly, as it turns out through Sam," Penny had learnt.

"Setna wanted to be part of the cartel, trading within, he could extend it to India and by blackmailing them he believed he could do it," David went on. "We have no way of knowing, though I suspect through a Chinese medium, they tapped into Setna's greatest love and fear in Kali Ma.

"Not by coincidence did he die, running from the Yufoa Temple." Penny offered. "Some type of apparition must have happened to have made him run in such terror."

"You believe the Chinese could've had him killed?" Ross asked recalling the conversation with David only yesterday.

"I would say it is more than likely, the cartel did operate like the Italian mafia," Matt agreed. "Although I doubt without proof anything could be done."

"Forgive me folk's!" Tisha interrupted. "We're not seriously after some accountability for Setna's death, are we? In the scheme of things I would say good luck to whoever did it and well done. He has caused enough grief for us all," she noted David wince at her words. "There's no need for you David to look at me like that, if you were not such a good person you would feel exactly the same."

Everyone laughed and agreed with her sentiments.

"I still don't understand why Kali Ma didn't succeed for Setna against us, he obviously summoned her," suggested Sam more seriously.

"You're quite right," David agreed. "But she was also his greatest fear, his not yours, I suspect the deal was for him to secure more souls and thus he would be released from her grasp or she claimed his soul forever, which happened."

"You're saying we all still have our own fears to face," Tisha suggested. "Including, those about Setna."

He nodded.

"Why did you make sure we faced our fears together first?" asked Ellen.

"Nothing that he or anyone could have thrown at you, could have been worse than your own fears," he suggested. "He brought his worst to you, without realising you had already faced your demons, but he needed them as hooks into your souls. We were just lucky he faced his first. You'll remember he died running away from them at the Yufoa temple."

"Why were some of us easier to treat than others?" Susan posed ever the psychiatrist and standing close to Ross.

"Setna had spread himself too thinly. He could control the physical when alive and the zombie in Shyam. Dead is about forcing people through strength of will and trapping their minds through fear, he just tried to control too many at any one time," David discussed. "In Shyam the first and Vijay his hold was total. Beyond this point each was, to a lesser degree."

"Did you feel like a zombie Vijay?" Ross questioned.

"Not at all, I always knew Shyam was controlled and realised he was literally suicidal because Setna wouldn't release him, I believe that's why he took his own life. As for me it is like operating as a robot someone instructs, you do, it is simple. How or why it happens is beyond me."

"Shyam decapitated himself almost." Tisha told them. "Why would he do that why not take pills or drive off a cliff?" she looked to Vijay for the answer.

"It is in the culture you come from, if you remove the head from the body, evil cannot claim both and therefore the whole is free, Vijay considered sadly. "This had to be the thought of my dear friend."

"Up until that point the group had not appreciated Shyam Rosha as a person, only the terror he had been a part of," a belated sadness for a person they knew hung in the air among them.

"Sadly Ellen's and Ross's father also died," it was Sam continuing the reflections.

"Setna followed his mental grip on Vijay, Shyam and with Sam through Jack Kefford," David continued with the thoughts of control. "This closely followed with Ellen, Matt and later Susan. By this time his hold was getting weaker and weaker," he went on. "A significant point would've been when he died. The exact time could have released them if we'd known and acted precisely."

"I was being attacked by elements David, how did you know what to say to me, you gave me such an immediate lift so I could fight them," Sam queried thanking him.

"It was something Tisha mentioned to me a while back. How it was natural for you to win. You never ever lost. I used that thought," David accepted his thanks.

"I thank you David for my life," Vijay shook his hand it was time to depart.

"I am sorry we couldn't save Shyam," responded David sadly.

"He was gone before you ever knew of him, hopefully his soul will return to normal one day," Vijay suggested wisely.

David agreed.

"What will you do now?" queried Ross.

"Setna, Shyam and I still have a thriving computer software business in India, I will pick up the reins now my two partners have gone," Vijay suggested. "My friend Sam will join me and has accepted a partnership."

"Oh Samuel I shall miss you," cried Tisha to a beaming Sam. "I know you will be happy."

"Come on David, look into your crystal ball and tell us what we are going to be doing in the future," an amused Ross posed teasing, he a true converted believer.

"You and I will be together on yet more journeys Ross and of course I will be at your wedding to

Susan," David replied mockingly. "And the day will come when we will all come together again."

"In better times I hope." Tisha showing her fondness for him.

Susan's jaw visibly dropped. Her eyes met with Ross's and told her what she needed to know, her heart skipping a beat.

"Ellen will be your bridesmaid," David went on.

Susan blushed and kissed David on his cheek. "You are a lovely, lovely man, you must give me away."

David bowed to her. "With pleasure my dear, it will be an honour."

David held Tisha's hands in his and lightly kissed her lips sadness enveloping him. "My thanks for your unswerving support, you will of course, return to your normal life and we too will see each other again soon."

"I take that as a promise David," a matronly Tisha said expectantly.

He turned to Ellen. "Support Lecia and make her part of your life with Ross and Susan. She needs your new family as much as you do," She hugged him tightly she missed her father Jack terribly, she vowed to get closer to the man in front of her, she owed so much to and held with such fondness.

Noting her sorrow, he offered. "When your sadness is gone, we will find him together, so you may say goodbye properly," she cried.

It was Matt's turn, he told the group of his intention to return to Shanghai and finish the hotel project with Alcatel.

"If I ever find out whether the cartel had a hand in Setna's heart attack I'll come back to the group for advice before I do anything," he turned to David. "I owe you my soul my friend, if there is anything you ever need, anything at all, let me know David."

"Your friendship is enough Matt," two friends shook each other's hand warmly.

They all expressed their concern for him.

The group tinged with sadness with their break up, all spoke of their promises to keep in touch and to call on each if in need. It was Ferral asking the final question stopping stopped them all in their tracks.

"David on the chart," this caused the entire group to turn and look at the fireplace, where the easel stood.

"There's a name you haven't spoken to us about, who is Theresa?"

The group waited expectantly.

"Ferral my dear friend, you're right I didn't discuss her and sadly for most you haven't had the opportunity to meet her."

David told them of a charming old, gracious woman, dear to his heart whom in life, he used to give readings to and who in turn treated him as her son.

For many years they had spent hours enjoying each other's company, she was, is, an absolute joy to know. He told of his sadness at knowing the last time they met would be their last in this world.

The group had been listening intently.

"But why is she on the chart David?" Ferral asked as the rest of the group felt the same. "What has she to do with what we have all been through?"

David looked around the group probably together as one for the last time.

"Only those who know what she has done for them can answer that," he looked to Tisha and Sam.

The realisation spread amongst them all.

It was Sam, who spoke, as Tisha was unable to being in shock, the realisation hitting home.

"It was her wasn't it? Theresa, she was the light, she destroyed Kali Ma."

A gasp went throughout the group in disbelief.

David nodded smiling proudly at his recall of her. "A truly, truly remarkable lady."

-o-

Books by the same Author
Alan Baulch

Finding Bridie

As a young teenager in the 1960's Bridie London develops the life
Threatening Meningeal Tuberculosis.
On Medical advice and because of risk to her siblings and his greengrocery business, her father Desmond London delivers her to a mental asylum offering the isolation she needs.
Unwittingly he gives up his parental rights consigning her to a life in an institution. At last there is an opportunity to release her from the mental torture after fifty years, with siblings unwilling to help, Desmond finds someone who can.
The corruption found by Haydon Robbins would shock the nation, with the real Bridie missing he must find her before it is too late.

Love, Life, Fantasies & Poetry

A thought provoking first volume of 30 Short Stories, Tales and Ramblings with 20 Poems spread across different genre's.
From Love in New York, A Scare in the Dark to Something Crazy, Asylum Seeking, The Pain of Redundancy, Spine Chiller and a Spirit of Hope.
With Poems on Time, Friends, Work, Teenage Angst and Human Values.
A Collection to Enjoy.

Mind Trap

Samuel Thornton arrived as a patient at the Berkshire clinic direct from Shanghai. The grip on his mind total. More patients arrive the grip on their minds the same pure evil.

Without out the help of David Bareham an ex-priest they will all die and be used as tools for the pleasure of Kali Ma herself.

Friends rally and a group with David is formed. They have to tackle the spiritual evil attacking them.

The group are taken on a journey following past lives, death and business corruption. Their experiences cause them to fear for their very souls.

Death beckons, they become trapped in a fight they couldn't possibly win alone.

The Tracer

A gas canister explosion in a scrap metal yard leaves Michael battered, an Amnesiac without a past.

By a 'quirk of fate', he is left with a unique gift his mission is to trace the missing.

Struggling with his identity, he enters a world where kidnapping, murder, rape, robbery, hate and great sorrow are normal.

Single-handedly he offers the solution for driving terrorism into extinction while providing the answers for solving crimes across the globe.

He has to be stopped, the only question who will get to him first?

-o-